IN LOVE WITH A LAS VEGAS OUTLAW 3

By: *Londyn Lenz*

IN LOVE WITH A LAS VEGAS OUTLAW 3

Londyn Lenz Catalog

(in order)

Quest

"Sir, are you sure this woman didn't take anything—"

"What the fuck did I tell you earlier?! Not a damn thing is in her system and if you refer to her as *this woman* again, you will have a big fucking problem on your hands!" We were in the back of the ambulance and these muthafuckas were trying my patience. The police had just called me and told me my mother was poisoned.

I had a choice to head on down to the police station and have them tell me more information, or ride with Christian to the hospital. The choice took no time at all to make. Christian fainted in the middle of us arguing. I never in my life seen nothing like it before; she was shaking, bleeding from the mouth and now she's unconscious. No way could I leave her; I was staying until she was back home with me, recovering.

"I can't get a vein to insert an I.V." The responder said to his partner.

Looking at Christian's pale and drained face, then looking at the responders' expressions, I snapped. I pulled my Bolo machete out and had the sharp end pressing against the responder's Adam's apple. I spoke to his whack ass through gritted teeth and made sure I had a stare down with him.

"Listen to me, you carpet riding lookin' muthafucka. You betta stop talking and start fixing my woman right fucking now. I swear to you on my mama, I will kill everybody in this fucking truck if she dies." I roughly let him go. "Now get fucking to it!" I shouted, and he got to work quickly this time.

His partner was scared as hell writing on some

chart shit, but he hid it well. I answered what I knew about Christian, which was a lot except her last menstrual cycle and her blood type. Once we got to the hospital, an I.V. was inserted and the paleness in her beautiful chocolate skin was going away, but she still didn't wake up. I was rushing behind the nurses that took over and rolled Christian to the back. A male nurse blocked me and I pushed his arms off, looking at him like he was crazy.

He held his hands up when he saw my face. "I apologize sir, but I need to know if you are next of kin?"

"Man, that's my fuckin' wife, watch out!!" I mugged him and walked through the double doors. I don't care if I had to lie my ass all the way through this bitch, I wasn't leaving Christian's side.

**

I was standing up, looking out the window on the

top floor of the hospital. The windows opened in the suite room, so I had it cracked a little. So much was going through my mind and the first thing was Ma. Poisoned. Poisoned. Poisoned. I kept saying it over and over because it was a puzzle to me.

Was this an accident? On purpose? I had our guys watched that facility like a hawk ever since Ma got those flowers delivered. I knew we didn't slip; no new employees were hired and all the new patients were legit. After things calmed down with my woman, I was about to get to the bottom of this. Blood was about to spill and I didn't care whose it was I had to drain.

"Quest?"

I turned around so fast when I heard my name being called.

Christian was sitting up, looking confused with her eyes darting all around the room. "What happened? Why am I in the hospital?" Her confusion turned to fear and tears started falling down her face.

"Hey, hey. You're good, bae. I got'chu." I tried to wrap my arms around her, but she slapped my hands before I could even comfort her. I looked at her like she was crazy.

"I-I had a seizure, didn't I?" As she asked me that question, she tried to take the I.V. out of her arm.

"Yo' what the hell are you doing? Stop!" I grabbed both of her hands and was about to shake her ass.

"You don't need to be here, Quest. Call my family and they'll come. You can go."

"Christian, you on some other shit right now. Why the fuck would I dip? I waited a little bit to call your family because the doctor said you needed some rest. But I hit them up about fifteen minutes ago, they are on their way."

Her eyes were looking everywhere but at me. "Aye, calm down and talk to me because something is up. Why didn't you tell me you had this going on?"

Christian just shook her head slowly and tears kept falling. "It doesn't matter. You're him, all over again," she said in a whispered tone.

"Come again; who is him?"

Instead of her trying to answer me, she was trying to pry her hands free from my grip.

"You betta chill the fuck out and talk; you ain't got no choice, because I'm not leaving." I looked at her, serious as hell tightening my grip.

"I didn't tell you about this because our intentions weren't to be anything more than having sex. Now that you know, I don't expect you to do anything but leave. You'll think this is nothing, but we both know that will be a lie. I'll start to get in the way of you living your life, you'll pull further and further away and eventually, you'll walk away. So, let's cut all the bullshit out and get to the real." Finally, she looked at me and in her eyes I could tell she didn't mean what she said. They were searching mine, looking for anything that could tell her she was wrong. I swear I felt like her eyes were calling my name, begging me to prove she wasn't right.

I ain't gon' lie; that shit had me about to cry and that's not even me. I had already showed my weak side to her on her porch last night about Ma dying. I couldn't afford to turn into no sensitive punk. I swallowed my tears and just kissed her. I didn't even care that I could taste the saltiness from her tears. I wasn't surprised that she kissed me back; she wanted this just like I did. After kissing for a while, I pulled away slowly and put my hand on the side of her face.

"I'm not him, you hear me? I said I'm not-fucking-him, Christian. I wanna know everything about you, now that I know this. The only thing that will change is me being on yo' head more, that's all. I still want you and I still love you, girl. I'm done playing and you need to believe me, that I have broken up with Kamila. I been did it before that shit at my crib went down. I'll put an end to her contacting me, but you gotta do two things for me." I interlocked our fingers.

She looked at our hands holding and then up at me. "What's that?"

"You gotta be my woman and not leave me. I'm out here alone as fuck at the end of the day. All the shit that happened was already designed before it took place, and that includes us meeting. Let's rock for real and for each other."

She ran her fingers through my long ass beard, then she looked up at me and gave me a sexy smile. Her chocolate face was breathtaking and I just loved all shit about Christian. She could be putty in a nigga's hands but still go toe to toe with me and my sly mouth. This was the one for me, without a doubt.

"Ok Quest, let's rock."

Wasn't shit left to do but seal what we just agreed to with a kiss. After I had my fill for right now, I let the nurse know Christian was awake. While she checked her out, the doctor came in and went over all the information. Christian was used to this shit because she was telling him how everything works. I got mad as hell when she admitted that she didn't take her medicine. While the doctor wrapped things up and told Christian he wanted her to stay until tomorrow, her Mama walked in. I knew it was her because Christian and Symba have family pictures all over their fireplace at their house.

"I'm ok Mama, I promise." Christian was laughing because her Mama was hugging her tight as hell.

"You were doing good for seven months, what happened?" Her Mama asked her.

Before Christian spoke, I knew she was about to lie,

so I killed that. "She didn't take her medicine, but I can promise you now that I'm up on game, that won't be happening again and she will be getting her rest every day," I assured her.

She looked at me, then at her daughter, then back at me again. "I'm sorry, who are you?"

"Mama—"

I cut Christian off and introduced myself. "I apologize, my name is Quest. I'm your daughter's boyfriend."

Her eyes looked me up and down and the biggest smile came on her face. She then glanced back and forth between me and Christian. "Are you really her boyfriend? Don't lie to me now, young man, I'm a saved woman and I don't wanna have to beat your ass."

I couldn't help but laugh because she was so serious. "I swear to you I'm not laughing, I love that girl very much. I'm a little pissed at her because I knew nothing about her having any limitations. I would have been on her a—butt and this wouldn't have happened, at least not intentionally." I corrected myself because I didn't know much about seizures but believe me, after today, that was about to change.

"Oh my goodness! Can I hug you?!" She asked me with excitement.

"Absolutely," I responded, smiling.

She gave me a warm hug that only a mother could give. Christian was laughing and shaking her head.

"Whew, chile!" She looked at her daughter still cheesing. "He's so handsome and strong, got all his teeth and a good grade of hair like we do! He's tall so if y'all have boys, I smell NBA!"

Yo', I was dying laughing and so was Christian.

"I'm sorry, I'm just so happy Christian actually has a man. For so long, I assumed my daughter was gay and just didn't want to tell me."

"Mama, please!" Christian yelled out of embarrassment.

"I'm just being honest, but oh my goodness, you did good chile." Then she whispered to Christian like I couldn't hear her. "He's a stallion."

Her Mama was funny as hell. "Well, I'm glad you were here. I should pop her ass for not taking her medicine. Christian always feels like if she doesn't have an episode for a certain amount of time, that she can just stop taking her medicine and going to appointments. I tell her all the time to stop doing that. One time she was in a car and had a seizure. Thank God she pulled over when she felt funny.

"Mama, he really doesn't need to know all of that."

"Yeah I do, I need to know it all. I also want you to know that she's in good hands. This ain't no game for me and I don't sell dreams. Me and her the real deal, ain't that right?" I glanced at Christian who was trying not to blush.

I gave her an earnest expression.

"Yes, it is."

My phone chimed and I saw it was the detective texting me about Ma. I needed to go holla at him before he left his office. Now that Christian was out the woods, I didn't think anything was wrong with me dipping out for about an hour or two.

"Bae, I gotta go take care of some business. Give me about two hours and I promise, I'll be back, I'll have Lori bring you some things up here so you can be more comfortable. When you get discharged, you will be at my place for a few days so I can watch yo' a—butt." I had to keep catching myself from cussing.

Her mama was seemingly shocked at how I was handling her daughter. Thing is, Christian had a handle on me too, but this thing about her health, I wasn't about to play with.

"It was really nice to meet you, Quest." Her Mama stood up smiling. She hugged me again.

"Nice to meet you, too. You'll be seeing a lot more of me," I assured her.

"I was just at lunch with Nina. She wants to have a barbeque cook-out at my house, so I hope you'll be there."

I nodded my head. "No doubt, I'll be there," I responded while putting my phone in my pocket and looking at Christian while I opened the door.

"I'll be back, I love you." I wasn't waiting on her to say it back, she will when she's ready. Closing the door I walked towards the elevator and my phone rang.

"Yo'," I answered because I didn't know the number.

"I love you too, bae."

I bit my lip when I heard Christian's sexy voice chime in my ear. I forgot her phone was at home; we were rushing out the house to get her to the hospital and I wasn't thinking shit about her phone.

**

"Thank you for meeting me again, Mr. Foster." The detective in charge of Ma's case greeted me.

The fact that I just said those words still baffles me; my mother was dead... after I had just spoke to her the other day and she was in good spirits. Now, I was planning to cremate her like she always said she wanted. I might keep some of her ashes. I'll probably keep them inside an iced-out butterfly vase since she loved some butterflies. I don't know. Right now, I just knew this was fucking with me, especially being here now and getting some truth told to me.

"Thanks for staying late. My girlfriend had an accident so I was at the hospital with her." I sat down in front of his desk.

"I'm sorry to hear tha,t I hope everything is ok." He sat down behind his desk and took out a file from his drawer.

"Yea, she's good. So, let's get to it," I told him, ready to aim my anger towards the right person or people who did this. "First let me ask, is there any way that she could have done this herself?" I needed to ask the obvious first because let's not act like Ma had all her screws in place.

"I highly doubt it, as a matter of fact, I'm so confident with saying *absolutely not*. Ricin is a poison found in castor bean. It can be chewed, swallowed or injected."

"So, someone injected it in her?" I asked, making sure to remember the word *ricin*.

"No, someone injected the chocolates she ate with a great amount of it. That person wanted to make sure your mother didn't survive."

Damn, hearing she was targeted fucked me up. I

imagined her being confused, scared and probably looking for me to come and rescue her. I never wanted my mother to think she was a burden to me or anyone. That's why I picked the facility I picked, because there still was a lot of independence they gave their patients.

I wanted her to always feel like a person, a person who had some short comings she had to get through. My point is, I didn't want her feeling like she had any worries, fears or concerns. Hearing that she was poisoned and I couldn't help her was fucking me up. I didn't realize I was in a daze until the detective got up and closed his door.

"Mr. Foster, if I may be frank?" He asked me and I nodded my head.

"I've been with this department for forty years, longer than you've been alive. I've seen it all and I also know this entire city, hell state criminals. I also know when us cops look the other way, whether we are paid to or whether we have three local Robin Hoods who make our jobs easier. Although it's not right, let's be honest. This system isn't kind to the poor or minorities, so here comes three individuals who takes matters into their own hands.

They go a step further, purchase a property in a rough neighborhood. They eliminate criminals who have been on our radar for years, some on the FBI radar. But like I stated earlier, money will slow down the process of them coming to justice. All of a sudden, they're disappearing without a trace. No questions are ever asked because of who they were. The news doesn't cover the story because we make sure they don't.

The streets calm down and residents move in less fear. The discreteness of these three individuals is what we honor the most; they leave nothing for us to clean up. My point of all this is, this system has been working and we have no intentions on changing it. So, what I'm about to tell you, I expect you to remember what I said." He had a vital expression on his face as he leaned forward in his chair behind his desk.

I knew what he was talking about, I understood it. "You have my word," I told him and he handed me the file. Opening it, I read the first page. It was more information about the poison and then it said how much was in Ma's system. I flipped to the next page and there were pictures of the garbage in her room. It was an empty box of Godiva chocolates; those were Ma's favorite. No matter what was in the inside, she would smile and fuck'em up. I went to the next page and I saw the surveillance pictures. I had to breathe in and out, close my eyes and try not to pop off. I just gave the detective my word. I had to think of Christian's face so I could come back.

"The good thing is, your mother just went to sleep. No pain or suffering. You can keep the file," he said and gave me a sympathetic look.

I closed the file and stood up. "I appreciate this. You got my word. Nice and discrete, have a good evening." I walked out of his office and knew where I was going first, but my phone rang and I had to put my plans on the back burner.

"Bro, I gotta hit you—"

"Yo', Lori just called me. The complex is on fire and I think Angel was in there!" Dominick said in a panic over the phone.

"Fuck! Aight, I'm headed there now." I got in my ride and rushed to the complex. Man, I swear on my own damn life, I didn't know what I was going to do if I have to turn around and bury my brother.

Nina

Once I was done inside of Walmart, I put my three bags in the car and finally drove home. Walking inside the nice lobby of my apartment, I was grateful that I was on the first floor down the hall. My phone rang and I saw it was Symba. I answered as soon as I turned the key in my door and opened it.

"Hey auntie Sym-Sym what are you—"

"Nina." Her voice was in a panic and I could tell she was crying. "Christian had a seizure and it's not looking too good. Dominick and I were going to the hospital, but he had to drop me off instead of staying with me."

"Oh my goodness Symba—"

"Nina, Dominick couldn't stay because while we were

driving here, he got a call that the complex was up in flames."

My grocery bags slid out my hand and onto the floor. My sister and my boyfriend could be dead. My heart dropped and my hands became soaking wet. I turned around to head back out but instead, my door was slammed shut before I could leave.

"You ain't going no fucking where." Marlo had his hand pressed on my door and was looking at me like I was a target. "What's up, boss bae?"

Eww, he said that name and my stomach turned and did flips. I stepped back slowly; Symba was yelling in my ear.

"Nina, is that Marlo!?"

I couldn't believe he was this close to me, in my apartment as if he lived here. A quick replay went through my mind. Not even our entire relationship, but two months ago exactly, I caught him fucking a man, unprotected at that. I had never taken a STD test before, which is fucked up because I knew Marlo was a hoe, but the feeling I had sitting in that clinic had me thinking the worst. I hated Marlo, but I also knew he wasn't going to bow out gracefully.

"Got damn you look good, can a nigga get a hug?" He walked to me with his arms out.

I backed up and shook my head. Symba was in my Bluetooth yelling so loud that I knew Marlo heard it.

"I gotta go," I said to her and hung up. "What are you doing here, Marlo? I'm not about to ask how you found out where I live. I know you've been following me. The feel of decay, heartbreak and embarrassment would creep up on me from time to time." I needed to get the hell out of here; my sister and man were in trouble, but Marlo had my attention for a second. I knew I would eventually see him again, and now that it's here, I was ready.

He looked the same: still chocolate, waves, and a

gold grill in his mouth. He had a durag on with some black jeans, a royal blue shirt and some blue and black Jordans. Marlo never lacked in the physical category, it was everything else he lacked in. I think I always knew it, but I was so blinded by love and being loyal because he was my first. It took me getting with Angel to recognize everything I was missing in having a real man.

"Wow," he said, standing in front of my door squinting his eyes at me. "I got'chu feeling all of that? I remember once upon a time all you could feel from me was love, like I was the only one in your corner. And of course this dick. This dick had you feeling all kinds of shit." He licked his lips, looking at me.

My stomach turned. "I don't have time for this shit, Marlo. My sister is—"

"In the hospital, I already know. That bitch Symba has always had a loud ass voice, like someone stuck a megaphone down her throat. I honestly don't give a fuck what's going on, you owe me this shit. We had ten-years together and you think you can just throw that away and move on with someone else!? Like we didn't create a life and lose a life together, us! Me *and* you, not you by yourself!" Marlo always does this; if he felt he was about to lose a battle or he was wrong, he starts yelling so loudly. He did it when I told him I was pregnant and asked if he wanted me to get an abortion. The difference now is, none of his old tricks was going to work on me.

"Marlo, I do not love you, I am no longer in love with you. I haven't been since Nicholas died. You haven't had me all that time. You had a hollow me... a shell, a person who was living in an obelisk. It's been over between me and you; it was cemented when I caught you—"

His face tightened up along with his mouth. I saw his fist scrunch up and his eyes fill with rage. No lie, he even started shaking. If this was a cartoon, I believe steam would have come out his ears.

"You don't know what the fuck you're talking about," he said calmly, but yet with so much viciousness behind every word.

"I know exactly what I'm—"

He cut me off like I knew he would and started that yelling shit. "YOU DON'T KNOW WHAT YOU'RE—"

"I KNOW EXACTLY WHAT I'M TALKING ABOUT, YOU PUNK ASS BUTT PIRATE!" I've been around Symba too much because I called him what she had called him once I told her what happened. I had never yelled at Marlo before, not in a defensive way. I've cussed him out but there was no firmness in my words. I never meant anything I threatened him with. Now, however, I meant every word that came out my mouth. It must have made him infuriated because he charged at me. Slammed me hard against the wall with his hand around my neck.

"I had you first. I broke your uptight ass in with this

dick. You think you can stand here and disrespect me? I will kill you right where you stand. Now if you just hear me out and let me explain... I'm not like that Nina, I love you and only you."

The sound of my gun cocking was loud, and I raised it to the side of his head.

"Get your hands off me before I splatter your brains all over the walls." I kept strict eye contact with him as I continued, and he stepped back slowly.

"I am not the same Nina you once knew; she is dead and never coming back. You have nothing to explain to me because me sitting in a fucking clinic waiting for STD results was enough. Whatever you decide to stick that boy dick in now is no longer my concern."

I was stepping slowly to the door, making sure not to take my eyes off him and keeping my finger near the trigger like Angel taught me. I never liked guns, but he told me everyone should know how to use them for protection. That man taught me about guns as if I was in class learning a subject.

Dominick owns a gun range and we have been there plenty of times practicing. When I moved into this new apartment, Angel hid three guns. One was in the living room under the table next to the wall Marlo pushed me against. I had no problem killing him right now if he came at me one more time.

Opening my door, I continued walking backwards in the same stance.

"You're dead to me, you hear me bitch? I will kill yo' ass."

I chuckled and said, "You should have did that when you had the chance." Now completely out the door, I closed it and made hurried down the hall. I could hear him yelling and breaking shit in my apartment. I didn't give a damn, I kept walking, and fast. Not out of fear, but I needed to get to my family. First thing's first, I needed to call my auntie Symba back so I could know what was going on and where I was needed first.

"Oh my God." I said to myself as I pulled up on the corner where the complex was.

I called Symba and was able to speak to Christian. She was awake and doing good. Knowing that, I knew where I needed to be. Symba didn't know anything more. I called Angel over and over, but got no response. You couldn't even get close to the complex because of the firefighters, police and yellow tape. There was a helicopter flying, a news van, cars stopping and people on their phones recording.

I felt like I was in the middle of a circus. The black smoke was all I could see as I ran up closer, pushing people out the way. Once I finally got close, my knees got weak. The complex was up in flames. I mean every inch of it was on fire, it was unrecognizable. Sirens went off and an ambulance truck sped off. I rushed towards where it was and saw Dominick and Quest.

"What's going on, where is Angel?" I asked frantically, trying to hold back tears.

"He was in the back of that ambulance, baby sis. Ride with us, we're headed up there now. You can't drive in all this chaos."

I followed them and they got through the crowd easier than I did, probably because of how big they were. It was like having two brick walls on the sides of me. Dominick opened the back door for me to get in and he drove, so I knew we were in his truck. While they talked, I stared out the window.

They didn't know if Angel was alive or not because by the time they made it to him, he was inside the truck. They arrived a little before me, so all I could do was pray and hope he was ok. Seeing Angel's face in my mind wasn't helping. His laugh, touch, those puppy doe eyes I have fallen madly in love with...I couldn't lose him, not this quickly. Hell, not at all.

"Baby sis." I heard Quest call me.

Turning and looking in his direction, he continued.

"That nigga a fucking fighter, he ain't going nowhere, you hear me?"

I gave him a closed mouth smile and nodded my head.

We got to the hospital and rushed through the door. Dominick's crazy ass parked out front and told the security if his truck wasn't there when he got back, then that was his ass. All three of them were like that: threatening, a force, and not to be challenged. As we got to the front desk, the double doors swung open and we all saw Angel lying on the gurney. His shirt was ripped open and his beautiful caramel skin was covered in dirt and dust from the fire.

"Hey, wait, you all can't go back there!" The nurse yelled, but we didn't listen. As soon as we got back, there was chaos so crazy that Quest and Dominick pulled me back out.

"No! No! I need to be with him!" I cried out.

"Come on Nina, it's wild as hell back there and we'll be in the way. We need to give them a few minutes, then we can get some answers." Dominick said, calming me down.

"I'm about to call his Pops." Quest took his phone out.

"Be strong for my brother, he needs that shit bad as hell right now." Dominick said to me, patting my back.

I took a deep breath and wiped my tears. He got up to get me some tissues and a bottle of water. It took all of thirty minutes for the doctor to come out and talk to us. Basically, it was the smoke inhalation that had Angel in a fight for his life. He was able to get Lori and three of the doctors who works for the guys out. That's how so much smoke got into his lungs and air waves. When the doctor walked up to us, Angel's dad came through the entrance at the same time. He looked just like him, only older and a little taller.

"Can we see him?" I asked the doctor.

He looked at us nervously, "Well, not all of you but—"

"Fuck all of that, get'cho ass out the way," Quest cut him off, and the doctor hurried and moved so we could head on back.

Angel was in a regular room by himself and he wasn't awake yet.

"You can go ahead." I looked at his father with a kind smile and told him.

"Oh no, young lady, you go first. My son has told me a great deal about you, including how much he loves you.

If he hears your voice first, maybe he'll wake up." He ushered me to go, and I didn't hesitate.

Even dirty, Angel was still so sexy. That perfect jaw line, lips and those full black eyebrows... I touched the side of his face and kissed his lips.

"Wake up My Angel, please. I need you and so does everyone else." I whispered in his ear. Sitting up, I kissed his lips again and then just looked at him. I held his hand a few times and let it go eventually so his dad could have a turn. As soon as I did, his machine started making a loud beeping sound. Now I'm no expert in the medical field, but I knew the beeping wasn't good. The doctor and nurse came rushing in and Quest pulled me back.

"What the fuck is going on?!" Dominick asked with his eyes wide and pissed.

"His heart rate is dropping and there is blockage in his air waves again from the smoke. We are about to put a tube down his throat to help him breathe."

"Get my son right!" Angel's father said sounding just like his son, that I thought it was actually Angel.

Tears fell when I saw them stretch the hospital bed all the way back and pry his mouth open, then shove this tube down his throat.

"Hurry nurse, his rate is dropping lower." When the doctor said that and the machine got louder, I panicked.

"I can't get it in, it's too blocked." The nurse told him.

Everything was happening so fast. The beeping, Quest, Dominick and Angel's dad cussing, the doctor yelling at the nurse, and did I mention that loud ass machine? Angel was dying. I was about to lose someone else who I had fallen deeply in love with. No! Not this time, I wasn't about to have this happen. My tears were pouring down my face so fast that my vision was becoming blurry. The machine got even louder and I watched as the doctor pulled down Angel's hospital gown and the nurse rolled this machine in to shock him. I snapped. Before I knew it, I pushed the nurse out the way.

"WAKE UP!!!" I hit Angel so hard, dead smack on his chest. I didn't even know I had that much strength in my little fist. I just replayed my life for the past ten years, then the past two and I saw me being without him. I would go deeper into depression and once again have happiness snatched from me if he died.

As soon as I hit him, Angel's eyes popped open and he jerked up, then fell back on his back even harder. He was coughing and blinking his eyes fast. They were looking around frantically. Everyone's mouth and eyes were wide open, including mine, and I'm the one who hit him. Even the damn doctor was looking like he had never seen anything like it.

"Yooo', you muthafuckas should put her ass on the payroll!" Quest said laughing and Dominick agreed.

I looked at my hand and then wiped my tears. My smile came because as the doctor checked Angel out, he was still wide awake.

"This is definitely my daughter in-law! Holy shit!" Angel's dad expressed, making us laugh.

"He's ok?" I asked the doctor, looking from him then back at my sexy man.

"U-Um yes, he is fine. His voice might be a little scratchy, but it's nothing some warm tea and Theraflu won't fix. I do want to keep him for at least two days. I'll have the nurse bring him a spirometer. It'll help him with his breathing." He gave the nurse instructions and told her to get transportation ready so Angel could go to another single room.

Knowing these guys, he was probably going to be in a suite. I stepped back so Angel and his dad could see him. I needed to breathe for a second; let's not act like my undercover fag of an ex didn't break in my place, choke me up, then I pulled a gun out on him. Oh, and my sister had a seizure… and Angel was in a fire. That's a lot within the course of a few hours.

The nurse walked back in the room with tea, water and the breathing device the doctor told her to bring. I took my phone out and called Symba back so I could tell her what happened with Marlo because I didn't need her bringing her loud ass up here tripping. I was going to tell Angel, just not right now. She answered on the third ring and I was so glad it was just her and Christian in the room. Symba told me Mama and Grandma just left and they were waiting for me to update them.

"Baby sister, get'cho ass back in here before this fool act up." Dominick stuck his head out to me and said.

I took my hair out my tight ponytail because it was giving me a headache. I got back in the room and went to Angel's side. "Hey, My Angel, how are you feeling?" I asked him smiling and kissing his lips. I didn't care that his face was dirty from the fire.

"I'm good, better, now. Where'd you go?" He asked me while interlocking our fingers.

"I'm sorry, I stepped in the hall so I could call Symba and tell her everything was fine. And I needed to check on Christian; she's in the hospital too from having a seizure." We were talking low and close to each other's face. His dad, Quest and Dominick were talking and laughing.

"Quest told me, I'm glad she's ok." He moved some of my hair behind my ear. Angel always did that because he says I did it when we first met. It was nothing I paid attention to, but clearly he did.

"I apologize for scaring you. I can't say I'm surprised this happened."

I gave him a puzzled expression. "What do you mean?"

"Nothing, chicken nugget, don't even worry about it." He kissed my lips again and then told me to give him his tea.

"Ok son, I'm about to go check in my hotel. Figured I'd stay close this way until you're discharged," his dad said.

"Pops, you know you can stay at my place," Angel told him after they hugged, and his dad kissed the top of his head. The gesture of affection was so sweet.

"No thanks, I wanna gamble and probably get me something young and tight to lay under."

I, along with Quest and Dominick, laughed. Angel scrunched his face up.

"Nobody wanna hear that shit, Pops."

His dad looked at me and said, "It was nice to meet you, Nina. I hope to be seeing more of you." I smiled and shook his hand back. "It was nice meeting you too, Mr. Mckay. My mom is having a barbecue this weekend. I would love for you to come; it's a family thing."

"I will for sure be there, thank you for inviting me. Take care of him for me." He said, referring to Angel.

"I promise, I will." I reassured him.

He left out and the nurse came in and said they were going to move Angel to the top floor in fifteen minutes. I knew they were going to upgrade him; everything these guys did had to be the best.

"So is it true what they said, baby? You blew a nigga chest in because I wouldn't wake up?" Angel asked me with that sexy grin I love.

"Hell yea that shit was true! Tell him baby sis. Tell his ass how you punched that nigga in the chest like he owe you money!" Quest hyped it up even more.

I was laughing and covering my mouth. Dominick demonstrated jokingly on Quest's chest.

"It wasn't that bad." I finally got out after laughing

so hard.

"You weren't having that shit, huh?" Angel's sexy, deep voice asked.

I shook my head and we kissed again as my phone rang. It was a Facetime from Symba. When I answered it, Christian was on the phone which made me grin. Anytime she had a seizure, I always loved to see her face so that I knew for sure she was ok. Sometimes, Christian would lie and say she was fine, just so we wouldn't all worry or Mama wouldn't be overprotective. But I always knew; one look at her and I could tell if she wasn't ok.

"Hi sissy. I know you want to see my face and my phone is at home." Her smile was pure and her eyes were bright, all good signs.

"You know it, I love you Christian and I'm so glad you're ok." I blinked fast to stop my tears.

"Girl, her fine ass nurse just left. Imagine me getting a cold and then, boom! His fine ass is my nurse!" Symba and Christian were cracking up.

I started coughing really loud and shaking my head, but it was too late. Dominick stood on the side of me and signaled for my phone. Angel's door opened and Quest headed out so fast it felt like he left smoke behind.

"Imagine me beating the fuck outta you and him, and then boom! You muthafuckas is in critical condition."

Angel and I laughed so hard, Angel had to take a sip of water so he wouldn't choke.

"Hang up and call my phone, now." Dominick told her and his expression said he wasn't playing no games.

It was so crazy to see Symba do what a man told her to do. My auntie never played that shit. She watched Grandma, Mama, Christian and myself strike out on love, so her heart was very guarded. I don't know how, but Dominick seemed to have broken down all her walls.

"Let me go handle this fucking girl," he said then he

hugged me and gave Angel a fist pound.

"Glad you good, bro. Me and Quest will be back up here tomorrow." I caught the look Dominick gave him and then he walked out, answering his phone.

"Angel tell me the truth. Are you in some kind of trouble? Was that fire set on purpose to harm you?" I asked him after I cleaned his face off with soap and water. The nurse brought me a hygiene kit and some hospital sweats for him to put on until he could shower when he gets in his room.

"Nina, I don't need you focusing on any of that. I was honest with you and told you my lifestyle. With that comes enemies, but believe me, I got it under control."

As he talked, I used my hairband from around my wrist and put my hair back in a ponytail.

"Yo' what the fuck happened to your neck?" When he asked, I wanted to pause and rewind.

Marlo must have left a mark on me from when he

choked me. I didn't want to tell Angel right now. He already had enough on his—

"Nina!"

He made me jump a little when he called my name so hard and forceful.

"I asked you a question and you betta...you know what, come here."

I didn't move because his face looked screwed. I think because I've never seen him look angry before. I mean I knew he wouldn't hurt me but he still didn't look like my sweet Angel at the moment.

"Get the fuck over here!" He closed his eyes for a second like he was trying to get his emotions under control. "Could you please get the fuck over here before I come to you? I promise, you don't want that." He asked calmly and I started walking.

"It's nothing, Angel. You're acting out over nothing."

I said, and he forced my hand down so he could see.

"Yeah, aight. I'll be the judge of that." He moved my face over gently like he didn't want to break me, but he still was looking mad. Then when he was done, he kept his eyes locked on mine, clearly infuriated.

"Don't lie to me, Nina. That ain't how our shit is built. Right?"

"Yes, you're right." I answered. I knew I couldn't lie if I tried.

"Who did that to your neck?"

I breathed in and just told him. "After lunch with my Mama, I went home and my ex-boyfriend was in my apartment. I don't know how he got in there or even how he knew where I lived. I've blocked him completely out my life; that's why Burt and Mary have been letting me drive one of their cars. We got in a heated argument but... Angel!" I yelled at him because he snatched his I.V. out his arm and got out of bed.

"What are you doing?!" I asked, watching as he put his feet in these grey hospital shoes they gave him.

"I'm getting the fuck outta here so I can go kill that muthafucka." He grabbed my hand roughly while calling somebody named Cyrus, and to pick us up from the hospital.

"Angel no, you can't do this!"

Turning to look at me with his eyes squinted, he spoke. "You taking up for this nigga? He put his hands on you and you're standing here pleading for me not to kill him?"

"I don't give a fuck what happens to Marlo, I care about you and your health. You were just in a fire. Your heart slowed down, and you almost died! You need rest and—"

I stopped because he grabbed my hand again in the middle of me talking. He kissed it and then we were out the door. The nurses were calling his name and asking where he was going. They advised him not to leave, but Angel wouldn't hear it. We got outside and a grey 2020 Yukon pulled up. Angel opened the back door for me to get in and then he got in next.

"Where to?" The guy, I'm assuming was Cyrus, asked.

Angel told him my address and then we took off. The whole ride, he didn't say anything to me. He didn't look at me but he still held my hand in a secure way. All he did was stare out the window, looking furious. We got to my apartment and Angel told his friend not to pull off. When we made it to my door, we realized that Marlo left it wide open.

"I swear, I hate him." I said very low to myself. Like I knew, he had broken shit, snatched the cushions off my couch and I could smell pee strong as hell on my floor, like the black bitch never drank water. But that was all he did;

he didn't touch anything else in my place.

Angel didn't say anything when he came from the back, he just grabbed my hand again and we left out.

"That's the last time you'll step foot in that place," He spoke with finality as we got back in the truck. Cyrus took us to Angel's house after he asked me for Marlo's full name. Cyrus put it in his phone, and I knew he was probably going to look Marlo up.

**

"So, he didn't say anything to you?" Christian asked me.

"No, He kissed me on my cheek when he left this morning. On my damn cheek like I'm an old ass granny." I said annoyed. I folded my legs Indian style on her queen size bed.

She was still in the hospital and scheduled to go

home later today after the doctor went over her MRI results. Quest was up here, but he left when me and Symba came because he wanted to give us some privacy.

"Well at least you know he's not that mad at you that he couldn't tell you bye," Christian said while putting some Twizzlers in her mouth.

We stopped at the gift shop before we came to her room. "Yeah, but he's not treating me like he normally does."

"He's having a tantrum. You should have popped your titty in his mouth like the way a baby puts a pacifier in its mouth to sooth itself." Symba's crazy ass said, laughing and putting Cheetos in her mouth.

Me and Christian were laughing too and shaking our heads at her.

"I'm for real. Dominick called himself having a tantrum because of Christian's fine ass nurse. I popped one of these double-D's in his mouth and he shut the hell up."

We were all laughing even harder.

"You're so aggy auntie, but no, I didn't try to have sex with him because I didn't want to be rejected."

Christian and Symba fell out laughing and this time, I was left out.

"Girlllll, ain't no man turning down sex, especially if it's from the three of us. Get him right tonight and apologize." She shrugged her shoulders and put some chips in her mouth.

"You're right. I missed Angel holding me last night so much, I might fall asleep with his dick in me." They laughed at me, but I was for real. I was so used to Angel, thinking of being without him didn't work for me. We developed a routine so quickly and I adapted to it.

"So change of subject, I got some shit to spill." Christian said while she put her candy down and adjusted herself in her bed.

"Quest's ex is Kamila." She told us.

"Kamila? The bitch at your job that don't like you?" Symba asked her.

We knew all about her; Christian used to talk our ear off about how they didn't get along. One day her and Symba were on the strip and ran into Kamila and her friends. I guess some drama broke out and they were about to fight, but security broke it up. I would have been there but that's when I was deep in my dark place. But I don't play about these two, so if I was there, believe me, I would have got down with them.

"Yup. Anyway, she popped up at his house, came in, snuck me and we fought. Y'all know I only let a hoe get one hit on me and I snap. I tore her ass up, that's why me and Quest were done. Apparently, he broke up with her and she was having a hard time letting go."

"Damn, so the bitch was on her Elsa bullshit, not

letting go." Symba always said something to make us laugh.

"Well whatever she's on, don't hesitate to call us if she tries something." I said, looking at Christian.

"I wish Kamila would try anything. I will drag her all through Kelin's Realty. I love my job, y'all know the connections I want when I build my own brand. But I'm not about to let her come at me again."

Since we were admitting stuff, I decided to tell them what I thought about Angel and the fire. "I think that fire at the complex was set on purpose."

"Why do you think that?" Symba asked me.

"Because Dominick gave him this look before he left yesterday, and Angel told me the lifestyle they have comes with enemies." I looked at both of them.

"Quest thought I was sleeping this morning when he was on the phone. His mom died and it wasn't an accident or suicide. That's all I heard, and then he went into the bathroom. I didn't want to say anything to him because of how sensitive the subject is."

"Damn, I'm sorry to hear that." Symba said and I agreed. "I don't think they're related though but I'll ask—"

"No, he hasn't told anyone and neither will y'all." Christian said and we agreed.

"Well look, Mama wants a barbeque at her house, so Grandma can introduce her new boyfriend."

"Wait, what?" Symba got serious and asked.

"I invited Angel's dad. See if Quest wants to invite some of his family," I told Christian,

"Quest doesn't have any family. Both his parents are dead and he is an only child. Oh, but he does have an aunt that he told me about. I'll see if he wants to invite her."

"Um, excuse me!?" Symba shouted. "My mama has a man and no one told me?"

"Your sister just told me at lunch the other day," I said.

"I knew already." Christian retorted, smiling.

"And you didn't tell me? Wow, Christian." Symba shook her head.

"Grandma didn't want me to tell either of you. Nina, you talk too much and would have told auntie, and auntie, you run all Grandma's men off. You're like the step-child from hell." Christian was cracking up, but mine and Symba's mouths were open.

"I don't talk too much. Why would Grandma say I talk too much like I can't hold water?" I spoke first.

"Nina, did Mama ask you to tell Symba that Grandma had a boyfriend?"

Oh shit. When she said that, I couldn't even say anything.

"Exactly, sis." She laughed some more.

"I do not run all my Mama's boyfriends off. I'm not a child, I just can tell when she has a nigga that ain't right. Like, remember Jerry? He had a perm and a comb-over. Then Simon, he always smelled like old ass gym socks and he talked rude to her. I see shit that y'all don't and I call it out."

"Well Grandma loves this guy and they're serious, so we need you to be nice, *SYMBA*!" She said her name loud and hard.

"Yeah we'll see about that, he bet not be ugly or stank." She said and we all cracked up.

**

I've given up on love
But I gave up on the chance
That I'd ever fall
Head over heels (Yeaaah)
And all the stars
I wished upon
I never thought

That one would fall
Down on me

Amerie's-Just Like Me was playing on repeat while I set the dining room table for me and Angel. I decided to get cute for him tonight and cook his favorite meal, steak with a garlic and butter sauce to keep it juicy, baby red mashed potatoes, asparagus and sautéed peppers and onions. I had two candles lit at the dining room table and the lights dimmed. The cherry wood and gold décor in the dining room gave it an elegant, romantic feel. I opened a bottle of red wine on ice and I had cherry cheesecake from the bakery cooling in the refrigerator.

Now here we are
And I want to
Make the most of it

Want to hold you
And get close to it
Baby, let me love you
Don't let go

I heard him come through the door and I got nervous. I hoped he liked it and wasn't so mad at me that he wouldn't appreciate what I did. I then had to think of the man Angel was. It wasn't in his character to treat me like that. Just like how he said goodbye to me and kissed me on the cheek this morning. Even though it wasn't how we usually said goodbye, he still looked me in my eyes and showed affection.

I was not used to that. Marlo and I would just not talk until I said something if he were upset at me. I think he knew I would come to him and like a fool, I used to every time, even if I knew he was wrong. I looked myself over in the mirror that was in the dining room. I had on green silk with black lace two-piece pajama set.

The shorts were cheeky and the top was spaghetti strap. The lace was see through, so you could see my breasts and caramel nipples good. I had my bundles wavy with a part in the middle and it touched the middle of my back. I put my feet in these black, 4-inch heel slippers with fur on top of them. I looked sexy, and it was all for him.

"Hey baby." I greeted him with a warm smile when he walked in the room.

Angel was the sexiest man I had ever laid eyes on, no matter what he wore or what he was doing, he just looked good. Today, he had on some grey jeans that hung off of him perfectly, a black and grey shirt that had the word PRADA across it; his five o'clock was perfectly lined up around his face and lips. The waves in his hair were on point like always and his watch and diamond studs shined, telling you that he had money. He looked at the spread on the table and then his eyes danced around my frame.

"All of this for me?" He asked with a sexy, confident grin.

I nodded my head, biting the corner of my lip. "Yes, it is, how was your day?" I asked him while I pulled his chair out.

He walked over towards me and I thought he was about to sit down, but instead, he took my hand and brought me in for a big hug. He smelled so good and felt even better.

"My day was terrible, and I couldn't wait to get home to you. I hate being mad at you. That shit fucks with me, even though this is the first time." He said while still hugging me.

"I know, that's why I did this for you. I apologize for not telling you about Marlo, I just wanted you to focus on getting well," I admitted to him.

"I know and I love you for that, but Nina you can't keep shit like that from me. You don't make nothing better by withholding something like that in. I'll rip any-fucking-body apart if they hurt you. Seeing his handprint on your neck tipped me over. But knowing you didn't tell me is what hurt; I apologize for that silent treatment shit. That ain't even how I roll, I just didn't wanna explode on you." He was looking at me now with those puppy doe eyes I love.

"I won't keep anything from you again, I promise." I kissed his brown, soft lips and our tongues wrapped around each other.

"This food looks good as hell, you cooked it?" He asked and then he winked when I smacked my lips.

We sat down, said grace and dug in. Our conversation was light. We joked, laughed and just had a good flow like always.

"You look so damn good. That's a new set?" He asked me when we finished dessert.

"Yup, I stopped at Nordstrom and picked it out. I

was hoping you'd like it," I said, standing up to take our plates in the kitchen.

He sat back in his chair, licking his lips while examining my legs. "You was wrong, chicken nugget. I don't like it; I loves that shit. It fits you just right."

I blushed and walked in the kitchen, singing along with *Amerie*. Putting the dishes in the dishwasher, I was glad tonight went amazing. I felt some arms wrap around my waist and some lips on my neck.

"I love you so much Nina; you are my whole damn world." His deep voice tickled my ear while he went back to kissing my neck. Then, he turned me around and picked me up, walking us back to the dining room. He sat down in his chair while we still kissed passionately. I wanted to take him upstairs and put it on him but once he touched me, it was a wrap. I'll save that for round two.

"Uhh, I love you too Angel, so much." I said after he pulled my top off and started licking on my nipples. I took his shirt off too and sucked all on his neck. I was in love with getting Angel's scent all over me. It was hypnotic and turned me on to smell like him. I undid his jeans and was about to pull them down, but he stopped me.

"Hold on baby." He said, reaching in his pocket.

I just knew it was a condom because we have been careless as hell lately. But when he let his pants drop down with me still in his lap, he put a red velvet box in my face. I looked at it with wide eyes and then I hurried and looked at him. His face was serious and he was looking me so intensely in my eyes, I thought he was staring through me.

"Open it." He said to me.

The hesitation, nerves, butterflies and anxiousness inside of me was insane. I gasped so loudly when I revealed the eight-carat round cut engagement ring. I'd never seen a diamond that big in my face; it had small diamonds all around the band. My hands were shaking and my heart was beating so fast.

"Angel." I whispered his name, still in shock.

"When the fire broke out at the complex, I only had you on my mind. When I had to go back in them high ass flames to make sure no one was in there, I just kept saying I gotta make it home to her. I saw your face when I was unconscious, I heard every voice around me and I waited to hear yours. Once I did and I felt you grab my hand, I swear to God I knew I was good. But, when you let my hand go I lost it.

It felt like I fell right back in a dark tunnel. That's when I knew I wanted you forever, Nina Simone Curwin. I want us to adapt to each other so tough that it's like breathing. I want to build with you, have experiences with you and have you carry my kids. I want it all and I want it with you by my side." He put the ring on my finger, which fit perfectly, and then he looked back up at me. "I want you to be the neck that supports me and hold's me up baby. All while I be the foundation for you, will you marry me?"

I couldn't control my tears; they were falling like crazy. I was blown away as my eyes looked at the ring and then to him. I placed both my hands on the side of his face gently and I looked in his eyes. It was like I couldn't believe this was all happening, but I knew one thing. I loved Angel. I loved every flaw, and I didn't want life without him.

"Yes, yes I will marry you, Angel Dylan Mckay." We both had a big grin and then we kissed. I was wet, and his dick was still hard like earlier. I lifted up so he could pull my shorts down and he went back to sucking and licking on my nipples.

Every time I look

Into your eyes

(When I look in your eyes I)

I just think of

How you changed my life

When he was inside of me, we both let a moan out and I held still for a minute. My arms were wrapped around his neck and he was kissing my shoulder. I started moving slowly, letting my right arm fall to my side and my left one staying wrapped around him. Angel squeezed my waist and then my ass while I was grinding so good in his lap.

"Fuck, Nina." He grumbled and kissed my chin, then my lips. "Naw, see you cheating me, Nina. You not going all the way down on that dick," he said, then he grabbed me from under my legs. He wasn't lying; I wasn't going all the way down because I would cum over and over with him hitting my spot.

"You think I'on know how to make that pussy pop back to back?" Angel said, and he pushed me all the way down.

"Uhhh, uhh, ahhhh." I cried out as he held a big grin

plastered on his face.

"Yeahhh, chicken nugget, there goes those cries. See, you can't cheat me Nina. I know my pussy too good." He grunted out while making me go up and down.

"I love you, My Angel, I can't wait to be your wife," I moaned out while cumming.

"Say that shit, again," he said, while making me wind in slow circles.

"I love you My Angel, I can't wait to be your wife." We had some good ass sex in that chair; I thought my orgasm was going to last a lifetime.

Angel

I know it seems soon, but guess what, I couldn't give a shit. I know Nina is the one for me, I don't need years to waste time deciding. Any man who has a woman waiting around that long is full of shit. I knew she was it for me when I started wanting to be different, better and putting an effort into making her happy. It's the same instinct a woman has when she becomes a mother; it's natural and just develops. It's not hard and it ain't rocket science, you just have to have a man and not a man in diapers.

So, a nigga was engaged and I couldn't be more concrete about my choice. After me and Nina let loose in my dining room chair, we came upstairs to shower and get it in two more times in our bed. Shit feels good as hell to say 'our'. Everything I had from this moment on was hers.

Not just the money and material stuff, my entire being was Nina's and I wouldn't have it any other way. Lying on my chest naked, I enjoyed her skin against mine.

I had to soak this up because after tonight she wasn't going to have me to herself all day. That fire that happened at the complex had Philly written all over it. They moved exactly how I knew they would, loud and with a bang. Power moves are easily predicted so I already had our shit set. The Law is always steps ahead of our enemies, that's why we survive the way we did.

The only thing we did in the complex was bring bodies there for our doctors to work on. Once we met with Gunna again and his boyfriend Tucker, I knew I had to insure us. We moved all our records, safes and organs to another location I bought under my Mom's name. It was bigger than the complex, hidden and guarded. I figured a raid, shoot out or fire would take place at the complex because muthafuckas who don't get what they want turn into pouting crybabies. Me, Quest and Dominick agreed to move like usual and let Philly strike first; now, it was all out war.

"Do you think your mother would like me as your wife? We both know your dad likes me." She looked up at me with that beautiful face and asked. Nina had a classic beauty: clean skin, low cut eyes and her lips were downward shaped and soft.

"Hell yea, Moms would have loved you as my wife. I told you that when you first called out that I was bossy."

"Do you have pictures of her, if you don't mind?" Her sweet voice was always considerate of my feelings.

I sat up in bed and opened my nightstand drawer. Nina wrapped the sheet around her and sat up too.

"I have so many pictures of her; my pops stayed taking pictures," I chuckled at the memory and I grabbed two photo albums out my nightstand.

"Awww, Angel you were adorable as a baby." She smiled wide looking at me laid out on a baby blanket.

"Your mother was stunning, always smiling so big when she's looking at you," Nina pointed out.

"Moms loved her three boys," I told her, referring to my Pops and me as one of them.

"Who is this?"

I looked at the picture she had in her hand and I got a quick knot in my stomach. "That's my brother, Axel."

"Wow, you, him and your dad have those same puppy doe eyes. I can tell you loved him very much," she said, looking at more pictures.

"Yeah that was my best guy. He got on my nerves, but he was bro." I turned the page of the album.

"My Pops finally got him that leather SpongeBob jacket he had been wanting." I smiled at Axel in the picture, hugging the coat.

Nina was smiling too until I gave her the picture and her smile faded. "H-how did he die?" She asked.

"He was shot, police said it wasn't meant for him because some other gang members were killed in front of the store he was at. But me and my family knew the deal; Axel was gunned down and they took his jacket. My bro was only ten years old when he was killed, senseless—

I stopped because Nina had tears coming down her face and she covered her mouth.

"Chicken nugget, you ain't gotta cry." I was about to wipe her tears, but she started shaking her head.

"I have this jacket...I mean I don't have my own, it's his exact jacket from this picture. I know where it is."

"Huh?" I asked her confused as hell. I waited for her to talk, she was shaking and trying to get herself together.

"Nina." I said her name and she looked at me. "We don't have secrets, now talk."

"Marlo and his friends were sitting around our

living room table. They had guns and I knew they were up to no good. I was studying, but I went in the room when they started talking. Later that night, he came home with blood on his hands." She pointed to Axel's jacket.

"He threw that jacket on the couch, he said it was for someone." Her eyes looked at me, full of tears.

"Angel, I swear I didn't know that was your brother. I never even asked questions because I didn't want to know the truth—" She stopped talking when I jumped out of the bed and headed to my walk-in closet.

"Angel?" I heard her calling me, but I didn't answer.

My mind was racing and the anxiety was building. I don't know how I got dressed so fast but I had on socks, sweatpants, a t-shirt and some black NIKE gym-shoes. Grabbing my keys, phone and wallet, I flew down my stairs, into the garage and hopped in the blackout van we used to do jobs. Taking my phone out my pocket, I called Cyrus.

"Yo', I need that information, now. Just text me his address and his family's spot." I hung up the phone and hit the freeway to head to the hood. I didn't know where I was going, but I knew it would eventually lead me there. I would finally have the name of my brother's killer. My fiancée's ex was that person... I don't believe this shit.

This whole time, she was a link to me avenging Axel's death. I don't know how to feel. I would be lying if I said I didn't have any feelings towards her involvement. Nina is loyal and it pisses me off to know she was loyal to someone who wasn't shit. He gave her a fucking kid's coat with blood on his hands. Who the hell wouldn't ask questions?

But then again, I thought about her neck. Maybe he used to hit her. The thought had me tightening my grip on the steering wheel. I think Nina was so in love that she didn't want to see what was there. Meanwhile, her nigga got to continue living his scum of a life, not realizing he took a boy from his Moms, his Pops and his big brother. He destroyed lives over a fucking jacket. I was going to make him beg me to kill him.

BAM!

I kicked open the side door of Marlo's house. Like I said earlier, he lived in the hood and I knew the area. I was being careless which wasn't like me, but my mind wasn't thinking the way it normally does when I break in a house. First, I'm never alone. My boys are usually with me. I didn't scope out the place and see who or how many were inside, I didn't even care. All I had was myself, my Mack-10 gun and my rage.

I knew this was the house he shared with Nina because I could see a woman's touch and I saw a few pictures. Clearly, she met him in high school and he was older than her. After I went through the living room, I made my way to the back. There was no upstairs or basement, so

I knew off rip he wasn't home. Either that or he was waiting for me to open one of these doors, because I wasn't quiet at all.

The first room was clearly his bedroom. I looked under the bed and checked the closet. Nothing but clothes, shoes and a mixture of his and Nina's stuff. He hadn't let go, he still had this place the same as if she was returning. Fat-fucking-chance, my nigga. I'll kill every muthafucka on this block before I let him have her again. Not just because of Axel, but because no one but me was having that woman.

Yeah, I'm in my feelings right now, but I haven't changed my mind about Nina. Opening the second room, I looked at it a bit confused. It was jet black, nothing was in there at all. Closing the door, I went to the bathroom and then the closet in the living room. I snatched down the coats and jackets all the way until I got to the end of the closet.

"I'll be damned," I said to myself when I grabbed

Axel's SpongeBob jacket. It still looked as good as new; same size and the inside had his name written on it by Moms. I leaned my head back quickly to stop the tear that tried to fall.

"They will pay Axel, swear on my life." I kept the jacket close to me and was about to head on out, but I looked on his dining room table and a few things caught my eye. One was the glass tray; it was one in the bedroom and bathroom, so that told me the nigga was a junkie. I wonder if Nina knew that or if that was why she left. I never asked details because I don't focus on yesterday's trash.

If a man lost Nina, then he wasn't shit to begin with and that was that. The second thing I noticed was a purse. It looked like an old lady's purse, so I flipped it upside down and stuff fell out of it. Some hard candy, a brush, tissues, pepper spray, some lipstick and a wallet. I opened the wallet and the cards were taken out.

You could tell because it left prints where they all were but the driver's license was there, and it was Mrs. Newman. So, he is the one who broke in her house and beat her up. She told me it was three guys, so I take it they were Marlo's crew. This nigga was aching to be killed and I was about to make his wish come true. I had seen enough. I headed out to my next destination.

"Who the hell is banging on my got damn door like that?" The woman yelled and I knocked harder on purpose.

As soon as I heard her unlock it, I pushed it open so hard it hit her in the face, causing her to yell. Some nigga jumped off the couch, but I hit him hard in the face with my Mack and grabbed the gun on the coffee table.

"Who else is in here?" I asked the woman, looking at her like the low key crazy muthafucka I was.

Holding her nose that was dripping blood on her shit she said, "No one, my sister is spending the night over her boyfriend's house."

"What the fuck you want? The Law don't do shit like this." Dude on the couch with a fucked up eye from my gun, spoke.

I leaned against the front door looking at both of them. She was in some panties and a tank top and he had on boxers.

"You don't know half about the way The Law handles business because if you did, then you would know everything we do is for a reason." I then looked at the woman.

"Are you Marlo's Moms?" I asked her and before she could answer, dude started laughing.

"Man, you doing all of this over that bitch Ni—"

TAT! TAT!

"Ahhhhh!"

"Shut the fuck up." I said calmly to the woman. "I

hope the nigga didn't mean anything to you because I enjoyed that," I said laughing and she turned her nose up. I pointed my Mack at her. "Aht Aht. Don't look at me like that, because then I'll think you're being disrespectful like your boyfriend...what's his name?"

Wiping her tears and fixing her face she said, "Abe, his name is Abe. It's my son's best friend."

I looked at the guy's dead body and then looked at her, still laughing. "So, Marlo is your son then. And you were spreading that Mama pussy to his boy." Nodding my head, I continued. "I get it, you got a fat ass and needed some young dick to knock the cobwebs off that cooch. I don't give a fuck about that, what I want you to do is deliver a message for me. Tell your son Marlo that he got the worst of the worst hunting for him. You think you can do that for me?" I asked as a knock on her door came. I knew who it was, so I opened it as she answered.

"Ye-Yes, I can do that for you."

My clean-up crew came inside.

"I thought you said it was two bodies?" One of them asked me.

I looked at Marlo's mama and smiled. "It is."

TAT! TAT!

I gave her one to the head and one to the heart, just like I did her boyfriend. I took satisfaction in her thinking I wasn't going to kill her. Knowing I killed one of Marlo's boys was a cherry on top.

I went to the other address Cyrus sent me, some nigga named Reese. This had to be one of his other boys. Either way, Marlo wasn't home on purpose. When his disrespectful ass friend brought up Nina, that led me to know that Marlo knew we were together. He knew I'd be coming for him.

I could hear kids at the door running around all loud. I don't kill kids and y'all know why I killed Marlo's

Moms. Anyway, I went to the back of the house because the door was open, and the screen door was see-through. There were two garbage cans on the side, so I knocked one of them over, causing it to hit the house.

"Reese, the damn cats knocked the trash can over again!" I heard some bitch yell to him.

"I'll get at it in the morning!" He yelled back.

That didn't work for me, so I knocked over the other one a little harder spilling out the trash. The loud chick yelled again for him to go out back. There were no lights in their backyard, so you couldn't see me at all.

"You gettin' on my damn nerves, Roxanne. I swear!" He talked shit while making his way to the back door.

I brought out my pistol with the silencer on it for this.

PEW!

One shot to the head as soon as he stepped all the way out. I caught his body before it hit the ground and drug it to the back alley where my van was parked. Putting it in the back seat, I made sure to keep my head lights off and drove down the alley til' I hit the street. I know I should have taken his body to our new complex and went home, but I need to clear my head.

**

"Let me get this shit straight, Nina's ex and his boys killed Axel, he took his jacket home and has had it for all these years. These also the same niggas who robbed Mrs. Newman and fucked her up. You been sleeping here for two days because you're on a hunt and didn't tell us? The three bodies upstairs is Marlo's Mama and two boys?" Dominick repeated everything I told him like he was slow at comprehending, but it was more like he couldn't believe it.

"Yeah nigga, you heard me the first time," I said,

coming out of the bathroom in my office. We had shop set up here like the complex, only better and in secret. For all the streets knew, we were closed except to our buyers on The Black Market. We didn't need word getting to them Philly niggas that we were back in business.

"You know, because of Denise I get it, but if you're dead, then what? You on a hunt means we all on a hunt." Dominick was right, I was looking high and low and couldn't find Marlo. It was because I was making it known that I was looking. I already killed three of his people.

"You right, my bad. I was just on one for a minute but I'm good now," I admitted to them. Quest was looking like his mind was full.

"You good, bro?" I asked, snapping him out his trance.

"Last Friday when I said shit was cool with my Ma, I lied." He was standing up leaning against the back of my couch. "She died and a few days later, I met with the detective who was in charge of her case. He told me she was poisoned by her food laced with Ricin. Come to find out, Edith did it. I've been on a hunt for her ass and she practically vanished; the shit has been fucking with me. I don't even know why the hell that dirty bitch would do that, but believe me, I'm finding out."

Me and Dominick looked at each other and then at Quest. It was quiet for a minute as we just processed what he told us. I knew my boy was feeling fucked up, alone and like he had no blood fam. Yeah, he has his aunt, but they are not that close. He had us, but nothing was like blood sometimes. I think me and Dominick were thinking alike because we made our way over to him. Dominick was closest, so he hugged Quest first then gave him a pound. I went next and showed the same love.

"I'm sorry man, that shit is fucked up beyond words. You know we got'chu, whatever you need. We'll find that bitch and she will tell you the reason. It's a reason behind every action. She'll fuck up and we will be right there," I assured him.

Dominick nodded his head and agreed. "Y'all sitting on some heavy ass shit, got damn. We done withholding shit, right?" He asked, looking from me to Quest.

"No doubt." I told him and Quest nodded his head.

"Those Philly fucks think they won, they still got them hoes tricking tuff. Cyrus told me his old ass be paying for pussy from time to time. Anyway, we need to send another message." I told both of them while zipping up my duffle bag of dirty clothes. I had been sleeping here on my couch to just get my thoughts together with everything.

"Fuck yeah, I need to slice some people up right about now." Quest commented with a solemn expression.

"We need to still keep shit normal the best way we

can for the girls. I don't need Symba down my back or stressing. You should talk to Nina too, she knows something is up with the fire. My woman down my neck asking questions every day, tryna make sure I'm out here being safe," Dominick informed us.

I miss my chicken nugget. As soon as I leave from here, I was going to her job to talk to her. I haven't seen her in two days and that was too damn long. We texted but I was being dry. I know she's in her feels right now and I gotta go fix it.

"I'm on it when I leave here," I told him.

"Me too, I need Christian healthy and not worrying. She told me about her Mama's barbeque and we got your birthday bash coming up," Quest said pointing to Dominick. "That will take our minds off everything for a while."

"Facts. My dad and his friends got that wild ass

beer bash party at the trailer park coming up too. Symba's loud crazy ass will love it," Dominick laughed and said.

We'd been to those a few times and it gets crazy, but I know he ain't bout to let shit happen to his girl.

"Aight, let's chill for a few days unless it's work," Quest suggested and we all agreed then left the new complex.

I pulled up to Eternal Peace Funeral home and got out my car. Burt and Mary, the owners always looked out for her even before I came in the picture. Burt did business with us, he always had some wisdom and advise which we soaked up.

"Now you know I should make you leave, right?" Mary was doing some paperwork at her desk when I walked inside. They had a top-notch luxury business; it was expensive to have a funeral here. They offered specialties that a lot of funeral homes didn't, number one in the Northwest.

I dropped my head in a shameful way then looked back up at her with a smile. "I'm here to fix it, I know I fucked up," I told her truthfully.

Putting her papers down, she sat back in her chair and said, "Mmhm, Angel she's special to us, more than you know. Please don't go down there if you're going to break her heart."

"I swear I'm not here for that at all. I just want to fix this. I got her, Mary, on my life I got her." I told her with sincerity in my voice.

"I believe him, sweetheart." Burt walked in the room looking at me with the same disappointment she had on her face. "You can go down there." He told me and it was like my Pops was shaking his head at me.

I nodded and made my way to the elevator so I could go get my woman back. When I got of it, the cream and peach hall led to the enormous room where Nina worked. When I got down there, I heard her R&B music playing on low and she was doing makeup on a body. When she saw me, her whole mood changed and not in the way that I had grown used to. When we would see each other, her eyes would light up and that smile that I am so in love with would appear. Now, she looked hurt, confused and a little disappointed.

I was about to say something, but she spoke first. "I know why you're here." She said, walking towards me looking delicious as hell. I noticed she took her long weave out and wore her real hair in its shoulder length curly state. I didn't care how she wore it, Nina was always breathtaking to me. Even in dress slacks and a V-Neck button up blouse, she still looked radiant.

"Here." She held up the engagement ring I gave her. "I was going to leave it at your house the first day, but I couldn't bring myself to do it. On the second day I pretty much got the hint."

My nostrils were flaring and I had to swallow hard to prevent from snapping.

"You need to stop talking right now, Nina Curwin, and put that ring back on your fucking finger. I know you're pissed at me, but I needed to clear my head. I apologize for having thought the worse, but you need to understand, Nina. I been wanting to get the fucks who killed my baby brother for years. I never thought it would come down so hard and my fiancée's ex was part of it."

"I understand that Angel, but I need you to know I had no idea. I mean, I could look at the jacket and tell it belonged to a child." Her eyes got watery. "I should have asked questions but...I-I..." Nina started stuttering and the tears fell back to back from her face. It was like she knew what to say, but she needed to take a deep breath. "I...I was having a child of my own. I loved Marlo so much and I would have went to the end of the earth for him.

When we were on, it was amazing in my eyes and when we were off, I felt like I was missing something. I thought it was love, I thought I had found my better half. I always thought because we were so young, I was sixteen and he was nineteen that we just needed time to mature." She shook her head.

"He was never going to change. I thought once we had our son it would get him together. I finished high school with A's and B's. Full cheerleading scholarship to a university, I was handling my business. Working, no partying, hanging out or anything, it sounds awful but I was happy. I had plans and all he had to do was do his part. If—" She stopped talking and wiped her tears taking another big breath in. "If I would have just called him out for what the fuck he was, then my son would still be alive."

When she said that, my eyes bucked open big as hell. I had no idea Nina was a teen mom and I certainly didn't know her child had died. Then it came together for me; her sadness, the way she wouldn't smile. The emptiness her face used to hold, the way she wouldn't let herself believe she deserved happiness. It's like she was crying out for help, but in silence if that make sense.

"Marlo did everything from drinking, pill popping and cocaine. I hated when he did it and I never touched it a day before that night. I had tucked our son in and said goodnight to him. I needed to study and like always, Marlo and his friends came over. Abe, Reese and Mick couldn't stand me, they always said I was mean and so serious.

I brushed them off. But that night Marlo asked me to dance and come party with them. I didn't want to, I swear I didn't, but like always he talked me into it. He put a red cup in my hand that was laced with a pill. I didn't know, Angel, I swear to God I didn't. Next thing you know

I'm high, the room is spinning and I felt like I was on another planet.

I didn't stop there; I did a line of coke and the trip took me higher. Marlo's friend yelled his name, he yelled that our son was on the floor." Now she was crying uncontrollably, but she kept talking.

"The image of seeing my beautiful baby boy on the ground passed out." She touched her nose. "White powder all on his nose, mouth and little hands. That was the end, the end of my life right there. I got arrested and the next day, my son died of a seizure in his sleep." When she said that, she almost fell over.

I was right there to catch her as she broke down beyond her control. It was like she was reliving her past all over. I mean aside from her tears, you could hear her tremors and whimpers. I have never seen someone cry so hard before.

"Shhh, let it out baby, I'm right here. Let it out," I

said to her because this cry was held in so long, I could feel it.

She looked at me with soaking wet puffy eyes. "I just gave up Angel, I gave up on everything. I secretly hated Marlo but I still stayed. I stayed because there was no starting over for me. I didn't protect the one gift God blessed me with. I should have said no to Marlo. I should have! I should have!" Her break down made me hold her tighter.

By now, I had tears coming down my eyes seeing how hurt she was. I didn't know someone could hold in so much pain, I mean I mourned my brother and mother. But this was on a different level. Nina felt God punished her in a way. For years, she was stuck in her own prison. How the hell could she even feel this way but had a man? The father of her son. Where the fuck was that pussy nigga to comfort her? Let her not go through this on her

IN LOVE WITH A LAS VEGAS OUTLAW 3

own... he truly wasn't shit and I couldn't wait til' I get my hands on him. Right now, I needed to get Nina right. I lifted her up and set her on top of the high bench that raised her to my height.

Her face was red and puffy from her crying. I looked at her and grabbed a cloth napkin from the bin and wiped her face clean.

Shaking her head slowly she said, "You don't want me Angel, I'm a mess and I'm—"

I cut her off by giving her a kiss so deep she'd be feeling it for days. "I want you more than I ever have. I never doubted if I wanted you, Nina. The only thing I needed to do was wrap my mind around the fact that I finally knew who killed my brother. I should have communicated with you and for that, I apologize. But Nina, I need you to not keep shit from me. I want it all, bae. All the trauma, the memories, the fears, I want it *all*. Because it's what makes you, *you* and it make me love you more. I couldn't imagine going through that shit but none of it was your fault. God wouldn't punish someone like you and give someone like me everything. Naw, that ain't how he works; what happened was terrible, but God loves you still."

Even with me talking to her, she still was in disbelief, shaking her head with tears back in her eyes. I gently grabbed her face and made her look directly at me.

"What is it that I always tell you, Nina? Come on and let me hear it." Placing her soft hands on the side of my face, her thumb wiped my tear.

Sniffing and with sadness in her eyes she said, "I'm the gift, not you."

I smiled at her and kissed her lips, then hugged her tightly. "That's right chicken nugget, you're this outlaw's gift. You, Nina. *Everything* about you." I looked at her again and kissed her lips.

"Come on, I'm going to ask if Burt can give you today. We need to go home," I told her while helping her down.

"Ok, he'll let me go. It's not much happening today and I was pretty much done with work." Her sweet voice said. I grabbed her hand before she could walk past me.

"Put your ring on, Nina." I grabbed her chin and brough her face close to mine. "Do not ever take it off again or we gon' have some big problems." Pecking her lips, I grabbed her hand so we could go home.

**

"Damn Nina, he looks just like you. All that pretty hair and them eyes are a perfect match of yours." I smiled at her and then at the pictures. We were home laying in the bed while some music was playing low and the TV was off. I had her put on that sexy two-piece silk pajama set she had on when she cooked for me. I just put on my boxers and she was telling me all about her son, Nicholas. He was a handsome baby and Nina loved him so much. When she would tell me stories about him, her face would beam. In every picture, she was so happy, like she celebrated being a mom.

"Thank you, he was perfect, my little Nicky I called him." Looking at the picture in her hand, her smile was from ear to ear. The box of pictures she kept in her car was filled and I wanted to see them all. I loved how she was letting me in, she told me he was three years old when he died. Sad as hell and I wish she didn't have to go through that.

"Would you do it all again, be a mother?" My eyes shifted to hers and I really wanted to know how she felt about this. "Before you answer that, Nina please think. I don't want you to tell me what I want to hear. Live in your truth and talk to me." I made sure to keep my voice calm to let her know I wasn't about to judge her based off her answer.

Nina sat up and folded her legs. Looking down at her son's picture, she smirked and touched it as if she was really touching his face. Then she looked up at me and smiled. "I would love to be a mother, again. You did mean with you, right?"

Wrinkles formed in my forehead. "What? Fuck you mean—"

"I'm just kidding, baby." She giggled. "If you would have asked me that question some months ago, I would have broken down and said hell no." Straddling my lap her body rested on me and her arms went around my neck.

"You have changed so much in me Angel and we haven't even been together very long. You love me so right in a way I never thought was possible. You show me so much affection but yet you give me space at the same time. I've not only fallen in love with you, but I've fallen back in love with myself. I don't even know how to begin to repay you for that."

I put some of her hair behind her ear and licked my lips, examining her sexy face.

"All you gotta do is keep that ring on your finger. Marry me, have my babies and stay with me beyond death. You think you can do that?"

Giving me a sexy closed mouth smile she nodded her head. "Definitely My Angel, I can do that." We kissed and I flipped her on her back.

"Let's get started on the baby making." I licked her neck and she giggled while reaching her hand inside my boxers.

Christian

"Quest, oh my gosh, would you shut up." I threw my head back while standing in front of my dresser, getting so annoyed with this man.

He had spent the night over my house after I spent three nights at his when I got discharged from the hospital. When the man said he was going to make sure I took my medicine, he meant every word. If he wasn't texting me then he was calling me or coming to my house to make sure I took my medicine and was well rested.

I would be lying if I said it didn't feel good. Quest was so involved in my health, he even went to my follow up appointment with me. He asked questions to my doctor and always told me he would be right here with me through all of this. I believed him and my heart finally was confident in our relationship. Now, the relaxing was over, and I was ready to return to work. That meant seeing Kamila's boney ass and I low key couldn't wait. I haven't seen her since I beat her up at Quest's house.

"Christian, if you talk to me like that again, you gon' be back in the hospital tryna remove my foot from yo' ass." He said to me, standing up from putting his shoes on.

I was laughing because me and him stayed threatening each other. After I put my earrings on, I walked up to him and put my arms around his neck. He was so fine, standing here looking all mad at me, pink lips on that coco skin complexion with that long black beard. I grew to love his small gauges he had in his ears. It gave him a hard edge and his hard-muscular body in tattoos made my mouth water.

"I'm sorry, but you keep asking me the same question over and over. I am fine bae, I'm ready to go to work. I took my medicine and I'm not about to go there looking for Kamila. We don't even work on the same floor. I'm going to work, having a good day. You'll have a good day, you sure you don't want me to go with you to handle your mom's affairs?" I was rubbing his back gently while still looking up at him. I knew Quest was still hurting about his mom, I was so glad he finally told Dominick and Angel.

"I'm sure bae, me and my aunt got it. I want you in my bed tonight. I hate sleeping in that damn queen-size. You got a big nigga Christian, my damn legs be hanging all off." We both chuckled.

"Ok, I can do that." I poked my lips out for a kiss and his touched mine.

"I love you, chocolate."

"I love you too." We kissed again and then headed out my room.

"Quit babying that Viking lookin' nigga." Quest joked when we walked in the dining room to get to the kitchen.

Dominick was sitting down eating and Symba was standing behind him, holding her cup of coffee. Her other hand was messing with his beard and she was kissing the top of his head.

"You always got something to say but wasn't yo' long ass sleep on my couch with your head in my niece's lap?" Symba teased and cracked back.

Me and Dominick laughed because those two were always exchanging cracks. I called them Martin and Pam from the sitcom *Martin*.

"Them pancakes look so good. Please tell me you made more," I said to Symba, looking at Dominick's plate of blueberry pancakes.

"You know I got'chu, boo." She responded and pointed to the stove. "I only made enough for the three of us, though!" Laughing and circling her finger from me, herself and Dominick, Symba made sure to look at Quest when she said it.

He knew she was playing, but he played along. "That's fucked up Symba, I'm the reason y'all even together."

"What?! How?" Dominick came in the kitchen to put his plate and fork in our dishwasher.

"I know you remember you had Tish big titty ass at—"

"Ok! Yeah, shut the fuck up, I remember." Dominick laughed and cut Quest off.

Symba had her nose turned up, giving him the stank face. I cracked up, fixing my plate and looking at him put his arms around her to make her feel better.

"Don't even do that shit. I didn't fuck because you came through snatchin' wigs and kickin' hoes. But it's all good, cause I need my woman crazy over me cause you know I'm footie socks and pajama pants over yo' sexy ass."

He kissed her and that did it for me and Quest.

We were laughing so hard and clowning them. "Auntie Sym-Sym what did he do to you!? Text my phone 'snickerdoodle' if some shit ain't right and you need help!" I said in between my laugh. Dominick had told me a while back that if a girl rides a guy's dick good, it'll mess up his head. Have him popping up at her job with footie socks and pajama pants on, going crazy over her. It was hilarious as hell.

"Harley Quinn don't need no damn help, she loves his Michael Myers actin' ass." Quest joked while putting some pancakes in his mouth.

"Y'all some haters!" Symba yelled at us, laughing as well. "Christian did you take your—"

"Yes, I did. You are worse than this one." I pointed to Quest who then squinted his eyes at me.

"What I tell you about that smart-ass mouth?" He

looked so good when he was mad or putting me in check.

I had to squeeze my legs tight so I wouldn't mess up my pencil skirt. "I'm sorry, babe." I said sweetly and then kissed his lips.

I heard Symba snicker loudly when her and Dominick walked passed us. I put my middle finger up at her. Me and Quest finished eating breakfast and talking. Dominick and Symba left out before us so she could go to work. Once we were done eating, I locked up the house and we were outside to our cars.

"I'll be fine, Quest." I smiled at him when he opened my door for me to get in.

"I didn't even say anything." He tried to play it off but I had learned him better than myself.

"You have two major things on your mind right now; your mom and me. I completely understand why she is on your mind. That's a lot to process and come to terms with, but babe. I really don't want you worried about me.

I've been living with this for years; you can't take away my ability to be independent because of your fear. I'll be fine, I'm well rested and I took my medicine."

He interlocked our fingers and then kissed my hand. "Christian, I swear on everything, I am going to lose it if something happens to you. I know I can't keep you from living, I just need you to always be good. I ain't never loved anyone the way I love you. I got faith in God, so I know he got'chu. I'll try not to worry." We kissed a few times.

"Try not to worry at all, faith and worry don't mix." I said getting in my car. He closed my door, I started it up and then rolled my window down. "I love you more, Quest." I said to him and then I blew him a kiss. Watching his fine ass go to his ride, we both pulled off at the same time blowing our horn at each other.

It was October and we were in the middle of that

bullshit weather, I called it. Hot during the day but then cold as hell at night. I let my window down so I could get some air and then I turned my radio on. I usually always rode to Rihanna playing, but since her ass has decided to become the damn Avon lady, I've had to pick other music. I missed my work wife Molly even though I saw her twice when I was in the hospital, but I missed playing around with her at work. I enjoyed the drive in a good mood all the way to work.

"Oh my goodness I missed you." Molly hugged me like we'd been apart for years.

I soaked up the love, though. "I missed you too. What all has gone down since I've been gone?" I asked her as we walked to the elevator so we could go to our floor.

"Girl same ol' same ol'. Oh, and Kamila made top sales this week." We both rolled our eyes getting off the elevator.

"I'm so glad you beat her ass. Every time I see her, I

just laugh." Molly told me clapping her hands, laughing.

"As long as she stays in her lane, then we all good." I told her and I noticed the office eyes were on me. They were looking like they were shocked to see me, and I felt they had a hint of disgust as well. I brushed it off and me and Molly parted ways to go in our office.

I missed my office. It was so cute and I couldn't help but grin once I closed my door. This wasn't my dream job by far. I wanted my own realty company, but Kelin's Realty was a good place to make contacts and rub elbows with important people. I sat down at my desk and turned on my Apple Mac book laptop. Moving all my jumbo twist to the right side of my neck, I put in my username and password so I could access the company files and get to work.

"What the hell." I said to myself when my password wouldn't work. I tried it again and then again. I picked up my office phone and was about to call Molly to see if the passwords were changed when there was a knock at my door. Getting up to answer it, I figured it was one of the aids from personnel coming to give me the new password.

"Jerry, umm what is this?" I asked him when he was at my door with him, two police officers and this bitch Kamila behind all of them. Her face looked like Angela Bassett in *What's Love Got To Do With It*. Remember that scene when she ran her ass across that street to the hotel? Yeah, she was looking jacked and Kamila's face matched hers. Now, I did beat her ass, but not that bad. Those bruises were fresh and new. Like she got her ass beat last night or something. Our fight was almost three weeks ago.

"Christian, I was trying to catch you before you came in the building, but I was in a meeting," he said as they walked inside. One cop went and grabbed my laptop and the other one took handcuffs from his side.

"Christian Curwin, you are under arrest for assault and harassment." The officer said to me.

My mouth dropped with a mixture of confusion, dismay and anger. "What the hell? I didn't harass anyone. That bitch is fucking lying and her crazy ass probably did that shit to herself." I said while getting handcuffed.

Molly came out her office and was looking like I was. "Hell no, she didn't do any fucking thing!" She yelled out in my defense.

"Molly go back in your office or you will be fired too. The harassment emails and threats came directly from her laptop," Jerry said as he was shaking his head looking at me. "I knew you were a slut, but damn Christian, all so you could fuck her boyfriend?"

"What?!" I looked at Kamila who was smirking and I snapped. "That stupid hoe is a liar! I swear hoe, I hope you drop dead!" I yelled out as I was escorted through the floor to the elevator like an actual prisoner.

"I'll feel better when you're behind bars and me and

Quest can move on with our lives. He just lost his mother, we don't need you and your drama." That trick had the nerve to say to me before I got on the elevator.

Everything stopped because how in the hell did she even know his mom passed away? Nothing was on social media. Quest had to have told her. Chuckling low to myself, I shook my head. I couldn't believe this nigga; nothing went good for us since I've met him. I should have known a leopard always shows its spots.

"You're too gorgeous of a girl to be in some mess like this." The cop who was holding my arm said to me.

I didn't even say anything. My mind was packed, and I was trying not to break down right now. I have never been handcuffed, in this way at least, arrested and actually placed in the back of a police car. I just kept thinking there is no way Quest was playing me, everything we have shared and how we had a bond just had to be real.

The kisses, the talks, the hugs, the way we look at

each other. It was real, no damn way. Kamila is crazy to the point of no return. I kept telling myself all of this. But then I thought about how many women are naïve and blind by how fine a nigga is, how good the sex is. How many women were left just like I was, looking stupid.

"One phone call." The officer said to me after my fingerprints and picture were taken.

I picked up the phone and called Nina because her job wasn't like Symba's, so I knew she would answer.

"Christian?! Why the hell are you calling me from jail?" Nina asked after she accepted my call.

"It's a long story. Come get me out, but please don't tell Angel because he will tell Quest." My tone was so flat, all I wanted to do was get out of here.

"Ok Christian but—"

"No Nina, don't even ask, just come get me out and don't tell Angel." I repeated myself. "I know you want to know what happened and I will explain but come to Clark County and get me."

"I will, however—"

"Please Nina, I'm trusting you." I hung up and then was escorted to a holding cell.

I sat down in the corner. Two other women were in here with me. One was sleep and the other was just sitting there with her arms folded, looking like she hadn't slept in days. In jail. I just kept saying that because I couldn't believe I was actually in jail. Now, if it was for something that I did or was guilty of, then I would sit in this bitch with pride.

But we all know that ain't the deal; I swear I'm hunting Kamila down and that hoe is going to wish she was dead. I kept looking at the clock. Ten in the morning turned to eleven in the morning. Then eleven turned into noon and then twelve-thirty came.

Where the hell was my sister? Maybe there was no

bail and I had to see a judge or something. One o' clock came and then one-thirty. Every time a cop would walk by, I assumed they were coming for me. Two o' clock came, and I was about to ask for one more phone call, but then the cop who arrested me came.

"Curwin, let's roll." He said, unlocking the cell. "You got some friends in high places," he said, smirking and shaking his head.

I rolled my eyes and grew angry because I knew that meant Nina didn't do what I asked. After signing some papers and my possessions were given back to me, the loud buzzer opened the door for me to leave. Just like I fucking knew, Nina was standing outside with Quest. But I saw she drove here in her car, so I was walking straight to that.

"What the fuck Christian. You get locked up and don't call me?!" He walked towards me but I continued walking to her car.

"Yo' you ignoring me, what is your problem?!" He grabbed my arm and I snatched away hard.

"You're my problem! Look, this day has flipped upside down. I need you to fuck off and just leave me alone." The moment I turned around to walk off, this nigga picked me up in the air.

"Quest, put me the hell down! We're in front of a police station you idiot!" He threw me in his car like I was some groceries. I looked at Nina and put my index finger up to her, telling her to wait.

"You think I give a damn about a police station? How the hell you think you got out of jail?"

"I'll pay you back," I scoffed.

Quest laughed and shook his head. "It didn't cost a dime to get you out or to get all of this to go away. You just have to know the right people. Look, tell me what the hell happened."

I turned and looked at him. "How did Kamila know your mom passed away?"

His face was looking like the question was beneath him. Shrugging his shoulders, he said, "I told her but—"

When he said that, I tried to get out, but he locked the door and grabbed my arm.

"It ain't like that—"

"IT'S NEVER FUCKING LIKE THAT WITH YOU! WHY ARE YOU EVEN TALKING TO HER!?" I was shouting at the top of my lungs because I was so mad and hurt. I don't care who thinks I'm overreacting; Quest would hit the roof if I was talking to an ex.

"IT AIN'T FUCKING LIKE THAT! I just wanted to tell her my mother died. They had a relationship, I was just being respectful. On God, Christian, look at this shit." He went to his phone and went to a 702-area code number in his call log. "Her fucking number not even saved, and the call was a total of thirty fucking seconds." He held his phone in my face.

I nicely moved his hand. "Unlock the door, Quest." I said in a calm tone.

"Christian, I'm telling you right now I will crash this car right into this building if you think we about to break-up. We can do anything but that. You wanna beat her ass again? Torture her. You want me to fuck up the cop who arrested you? Beat your boss' ass?

Hell, we can go pick out a building first thing in the morning and you can start your realty business. I don't care what you decide but breaking up isn't an option." The way he was talking was scaring the hell out of me. I wasn't Symba's creepy ass; I didn't fuck with that crazy talk. However, I love the hell out of this man, but I was mad at the moment.

"We're not breaking up Quest. I just need some time by myself to just...I just need time." I got out before his words had me spreading eagle at his house.

"I'm sorry, Christian, I tried to tell you Angel was next to me when you called. He was doing business with Burt and he heard me on the phone." Nina explained when we got in her car.

I put the seatbelt on and put the plastic Ziploc bag in my purse. "It's cool, Nina. I just wanna go home, shower and go to sleep."

"What happened?" Nina asked me while she drove.

I took a deep breath and began telling her what happened from the moment I arrived at work till she came and got me. I even told her what me and Quest talked about in the car.

"Christian I know you're going to get mad, but I believe Quest. I don't think he has anything going on with Kamila."

"I don't care, he shouldn't have called her at all. It

will always be something. If he has a major surgery, then what? He has to call her because of their history, then you didn't see that bitch's face. She was beat the hell up. Either she did it herself or she had someone else do it. That's some psycho shit and I don't know if Quest is worth it."

While I talked, Nina pulled over on the side of the street.

"What are you doing?" I asked her, looking lost.

Putting the gear shift in park, she turned towards me. "It's me and you in the car, Christian. Stop lying and tell me why you really want to walk away from him?"

I was about to speak, but she held her hand up. "Remember who you're talking to. I was living in the dark and denial for a long time. I know what it looks like Christian, tell me."

I was quiet for a minute and then the tears started. Nina undid her seat belt and reached over to hug me. Once I let it out and she showed me some love, I confessed the truth.

"I took pride in knowing I was destroying marriages, making someone's husband want me. I made myself believe it was the best thing in the world to be a temptation or to be that forbidden fruit. I feel like this is karma and I just can't take that, Nina. I love Quest so much and I don't want him to be my karma." I sniffed and wiped my tears.

Nina reached in her glove compartment and gave me a tissue. "I don't think he's your karma, Christian. I think what you're going through may be the karma. I might be wrong, but I believe it wasn't going to be easy for you to have your happy ending because of all the stuff you've done. But I don't think Quest is *not* meant to be yours, you just need to put in a fight for him. You'll win Christian, because you love him and he loves you. Don't let that bitch win. You know me and Symba will ride with you and fuck her up." We both laughed and she wiped my face.

I just looked at her and smiled. "You're so different, Nina. Everything about you is elevated and you're back to yourself." I hugged her again. Nina dropped me off at home while she went back to work.

**

"I should be in here making greens with you," I said to Symba when I came in the kitchen and sat down to watch her cook.

"Girl, here." She sat some apples in front of me. "Get to slicing so I can make an apple pie."

"Oh auntie you baking? What did Dominick do this time?" I asked her, picking up the knife.

"My baby didn't do anything, he's perfect." She smiled and I playfully rolled my eyes. "It's Lanail. I've been worried about her; she's back in school now for her senior year but I've been watching her IG story. I don't think she's even in school. Every time she posts, she's at the mall or on the strip. I text and call her, but she doesn't answer. I don't even recognize the group of friends she's hanging with," Symba voice and face was laced with concern.

"Auntie, I know you might not want to hear this, but you might need to let go. Even if you think she is falling with the wrong crowd, what can your really do? Think of how you were at seventeen and eighteen, if you push you may lose her for good. You made it clear that she can call you if she needs you. Give her that chance; all you can do is pray for someone and be there if they need you." I told her honestly. I knew she had a bond with Lanail, but to me, I didn't want her stressing out. Unless she knew for sure she was in trouble, I didn't want my auntie out here putting herself in danger. Symba loves different, she is fearless with it, that's why she guarded it so hard before Dominick.

"I know you're right, I just keep thinking about her. I think I need to unfollow her so I won't keep lurking like a creep," she said turning off her pot of greens. I'm telling you if you ever wanted to get Symba a gift, just get her ass a big bag of collards!

"Let's get out the house and go to the mall or we can walk the strip. I need to take my mind off things and you need cheering up," Symba suggested.

"Why do I need cheering up? I'm fine." I played it off and of course, she saw right through it.

"Say it again and then try to look convincing. Put the apples up and let's leave for a few hours. Nina is at home with cramps so it's me and you today."

It did sound fun and I did need cheering up. It had been two days since the drama with Kamila. Me, Symba and Molly drove over Kamila's house to see if she was home and that hoe was nowhere in sight. Molly quit Klein's Realty once they made that bitch Kamila a manager. Man, I swear that hoe was sucking them brothers' dicks real good, but I swear she will get hers.

Anyway, I was still taking my time from Quest. The longer we went apart, the longer I knew he was with Kamila. Guys like Quest, or like me I should say, don't like being left alone for long. Especially because Quest already thinks he doesn't have any family. He always talks about him and her having history; I bet they were rekindling their past as we speak. The thought made me want to pop off, so it was best I just walk away.

"Yeah let's leave. We look cute today, let's hit the strip." We both got up and went to put our shoes on.

We were kind of dressing the same and not on purpose. The light wash jeans we rocked were the same. Symba had on a long sleeve white sheer bodysuit with a black studded bra under it and some white and black Adidas. I had on the yellow wrap around top with some yellow and white Chucks. After we grabbed our purses and locked up the house, we headed to her car so we could leave.

"I feel like since I'm not single anymore, I run into about two or three fine men a day." Symba said just as two guys walked past us, eyeing the hell out of me and her.

"Bitch you betta hush before Dominick hears you somehow. You saw how he acted at *Lust*, don't nobody need him walking the strip boppin' muthafuckas on the head." We both laughed, but she knew I wasn't lying.

"Oh, speaking of my baby Dom, I think he be stealing my panties."

I looked at her because she said it so nonchalantly while sipping on her Coke-Cola Slurpee. I had a Cherry one.

"Ooook, and what made you come to this conclusion?" I pulled my sunglasses down from my head and on my face because the sun was shining bright. But, we both made sure we were off this strip by the time the temperature dropped because we didn't bring jackets.

"Because I know what I buy. I have three missing and unless you got something to tell me, then I know it's him."

I laughed before I asked my question. "Do you think he's wearing them—"

Symba made a loud scream mixed with a laugh. "No, Christian! I think his freaky ass keeps them. He's that obsessed with me." Her retarded ass actually started blushing. "It's cool though, because I have three of his tanks that he wears under his shirts. I love that it smells just like him so when he goes in the shower, I take them." Again, she was talking as if what she was saying was normal while putting the straw in her mouth.

"What the fuck did that white dick do to you!? Y'all

stealing each other's undergarments and being weird like it's normal." I was laughing but looking at her like she was crazy.

"Did you just say undergarments like we in 1823!?" She teased and we both cracked up before the Hershey store.

"Still loud and ghetto I see."

Me and Christian turned around when we heard some rude ass make a comment.

"Tucker?" I said his name, looking just as shocked as I was to see him. After our break up and he left school, I got word he moved to Philadelphia. I didn't care if he moved to Alaska and froze to death, I was just glad I didn't have to see him.

"I expect you to always remember my name, seeing as how you fucked my life up," He said and his friend he had with him chuckled while looking at Symba like a snack.

"Boy I—"

"Relax, Christian. That's water under the bridge,
besides, I found a new career." He put on a slick smile and
dabbed his friend up. Tucker was still fine, I'd give him
that. Dark skin, medium size beard that lined his jaw. He
was bald and that head was shining bright as hell, tall and
I could tell he gained some weight, but it was good
weight.

"I thought you moved?"

"I did, but my parents are still here so I'm visiting
them." He was looking me up and down like he liked what
he saw.

I looked at his friend. "What'chu gay now?"

Symba snickered and covered her mouth.

"Yo' homegirl know damn well I ain't gay." He said,
looking at me like he wanted me.

I wasn't scared of shit. My mouth too slick. "What's

that supposed to mean?" I asked his friend.

"Girl, we went out before." Symba admitted like the big deal that it wasn't.

"Yeah, I was tryna get her on my team, own that pussy but she played me." He licked his punk ass lips still looking at her.

"I didn't play you, it's just your credit score was too low to own this property." When she said that and had that 'bitch' look, I laughed my ass off.

He had that 'I gotta shit' look back on his face.

"Well, this was fun, but if you'll excuse us, we would like to get back to our day. If you see me again, Tucker, just keep it moving." I said with a stuck-up smile.

He clearly didn't like that because he grabbed my arm.

"Get the fuck off her." Symba said and Tucker boy moved towards her.

I looked up at Tucker with my face pissed mixed

with disgust.

"Ya'll talk a whole lot of shit to be alone. All the disrespect is unnecessary. We could have had a nice four-some and enjoyed the day together. You owe me at least that much." His nostrils flared a little and the way he was looking at me was like he had some secret hate.

"Let me the hell go." I snatched from him hard.

Tucker laughed and so did his friend. "Vegas is small Christian, I'm sure we'll see each other again."

We walked into Hershey's leaving them outside.

"I just got the chills when he said that." Symba said looking at me.

"I did too." I turned around to see if they were still outside the door, but they were gone.

"Ugh, I'm so glad I didn't give that nigga no

pussy. If I see either of them again, I'm letting Dom know. Weak ass fucks."

We stayed in Hershey's on our BBW mess and then continued shopping at a few stores. Walking back down the strip to leave, I did pull a number. This fine ass married guy who looked like the singer *Mario* but with some dreads. Honestly, I didn't even want to do it because I felt it was beneath me. But I was listening to that devil sitting on my shoulder telling me to get the old Christian back.

The one who gave no fucks and who wasn't hurt. Symba didn't want me to do it either, but I pushed her voice out as well. Once we got home, Symba ditched me and went over Dominick's house. I picked out my clothes for tomorrow morning because no matter what, I was going to be there for Quest even though we weren't in a good place.

"What if he tells me to leave?" I asked Nina as she put her arm through mine when we got out the car.

"Baby sister, that nigga loves you and you love him, y'all just ain't seeing eye to eye right now. He ain't about to tell you to leave." Angel answered, hitting the alarm on his car.

Dominick and Symba parked behind me and approached us. We all looked nice in our grey and pink, which was Quest's mother's favorite color. I was so nervous because we hadn't talked, and I didn't know if he would be upset to see me here. More and more cars started pulling up just as we arrived.

Quest was already inside with his aunt. He didn't have a car for us, which I found to be odd. But Angel explained to me that Quest never liked to show his true feelings. I thought back to that night he showed up at my house drunk.

He was so vulnerable, like a child; Quest broke down in my arms and it was bittersweet to share that moment with him. Bitter because I hated seeing him in pain and sweet because he trusted me to be the one to let it out with. "Quest's Mom knew all these people?" Symba asked as we walked to the entrance of Eternal Peace.

"Naw, all these people are here to show respect to Quest," Dominick answered.

My eyes opened wide when I saw the Governor and Mayor sitting on the left side of the funeral home.

"What the hell?" I whispered, loud enough for us to hear.

"The Law deals with people y'all wouldn't

imagine." When Angel said that, the three of us girls looked at each other appalled.

I know we all didn't know how much pull they had. Now, we were all the way inside and my eyes went to Quest. He was looking so hurt and almost like he hadn't slept. The woman sitting next to him had to be his aunt. She was crying in her tissue with her pink and grey on, too.

The man sitting next to her was probably her man because he was rubbing her back and kissing her hand.

We went to view the body in the casket, and she looked so beautiful and peaceful. I knew Nina worked on her from head to toe. Her casket was grey with pink handles all on the sides, She had so many gorgeous pink flowers, it was insane. Some from the Governor, Mayor, Las Vegas D.J.'s, Casino owners and restaurants.

Me and the girls bought her a gorgeous arrangement as well, and it was in the front. The fellas had her picture in the middle surrounded by dozens of pink rose pedals as the backdrop and it was beautiful. We walked to the row behind Quest that was reserved for us.

Dominick and Angel stopped and hugged his aunt then showed Quest some love. It was us girls' turn, and I was so scared, I didn't want him to snap on me. I was here because even though I met his mom once, I liked her because she was like a helpless soul. I was also here because I loved her son immensely and I wouldn't want to be anywhere else right now.

It was my turn. I looked at his sad eyes and hugged him tightly. He didn't hesitate to hug me back just as snug.

"Sit with me," he said in my ear and it pulled at my heart.

I pushed my tears down because I had to be strong for him. His voice held so much pain and his request was the least I could do.

"Of course," I responded and we finally pulled apart.

"Get up, let her sit here." He told his auntie.

She looked up at Quest with wet eyes and said, "What? But Quest—"

"Get up." He squeezed out between his teeth so hard it would have put fear of everyone in this room if they could hear it.

"It's fine, Quest, I'll be right behind you." I said because this was so uncomfortable and awkward.

He didn't say anything, and his aunt and her boyfriend moved down. I looked at Symba and Christian and they were looking just like I was. Angel and Dominick weren't even acting like anything was wrong. I sat down and the service started. It was really nice, and although no one had any remarks to say when the preacher spoke, when the choir sang, it was so moving. God was definitely in the midst of the room and everyone felt it.

Closing the casket, Quest took a deep breath and I grabbed his hand. He didn't shed one tear. He didn't speak to anyone aside from Angel and Dominick, and even then it was just a few words. We followed out, all carrying a flower, and then drove to the cemetery. Quest rode with his aunt and her boyfriend in their limo. I followed behind Angel and Dominick as we were able to go through the red lights. We arrived at the cemetery and it was just as many people at the funeral home.

We all got out of our cars and I saw Quest's eyes dance like they were searching. When they landed on me, it was like he was telling me to come here. I sat next to him again as the preacher and Burt, the funeral director, said some words before everyone walked up and paid their final respects, taking a single flower from her casket. I got up and did the same, but I kissed my hand and touched the casket. Walking through the crowd of people, I spotted Nina and Symba.

"My gosh, that was like a beautiful church service instead of a funeral. The message was well received by everyone in the room." Nina said and we agreed.

"Where are the guys?" I asked them and they pointed behind me. I turned around and it was so sweet to see Angel and Dominick just sitting with Quest in front of his Mom's casket. They weren't talking or anything, they were just sitting with him, looking at the casket. It was like an unspoken brotherhood that you just knew the three of them had. All three were looking so handsome and just showing how true friendship between men should be.

Me, Symba and Nina were talking amongst each

other for a minute. I ain't gon' lie, we were being typical black people and talking about some of the wigs and shoes worn. Even though we were talking at a low tone, it still was funny. We had to hide our laughs, which was so hard. Soon, Angel and Dominick walked up on us.

"Baby sister—" Angel said, then he stopped when he looked at the three of us. You know that face you make when you are really trying not to laugh. It's almost like you're trying to hold in a fart.

"You three standing here talking about people, right?" Dominick asked, smirking. He and Angel were giving us the look of shame.

"Y'all wrong as hell," Angel said while scratching his nose trying not to laugh himself. "Baby sister, he needs you right now." Angel's words caused me to get serious real fast.

Walking over, I sat in the chair next to him, staying just as silent as he was. The crowd of people were leaving and before long, it was just Angel, Nina, Symba and Dominick standing by their cars. They were far from us, so we couldn't hear anything they were saying, but we could see them. Quest and Angel took off their suit jackets, Nina and Symba were sitting on Dominick's truck. I looked at Quest and could tell that he was so sad. Then his eyes watered, and tears fell back to back.

"I just wanted to fix my mama...ever since I was six years old and saw her trip out. I just wanted to take care of her and fix her. I'm out here making money, chasing bitches and living life while my mama was being poisoned. It's fucked up because the person who did it, she trusted. Edith had no reason to do this shit." Now he was crying in his hand, covering his face.

I felt like I was one of the distractions he mentioned, but I would never say anything about it. This just cemented the fact that me and Quest didn't need to be together.

However, he needs someone right now, so I turned to him and hugged him tightly. He didn't hug back, but that was ok. Quest was hurt, and death is nothing to play with. I knew that much from my nephew dying.

"You proved to her every day in every way that you loved her. You never abandoned her, not once, Quest. Think of it like this: her mind is finally at peace. Mental illness lives in the mind and for years she probably had trouble doing things that you and I take for granted. Now, she's on the throne, peaceful mind, body, and soul." After I said that, his arms hugged me back with the same pressure. We stayed like that for about five-minutes.

"Thank you, Christian. I'ma just chill here for a while. You can tell them I'll catch up tomorrow," he said to me.

"Ok, call me if you need me to come back, ok?" I told him, standing up and fixing my dress. I started walking away and he called my name.

Looking back at him, he said, "You my family." He may have said something sweet, but his face wasn't matching what he said, and I felt like a threat was hidden in his words.

I didn't say anything back, I just turned around and finished walking towards my car.

**
—

"I hate this, I'm used to going to work. Did you know Klein's Realty ruined my rep in the business? It's all over about me harassing Kamila. Every interview I go on, I'm turned down or get that bullshit 'we'll call you' line. I am so damn pissed; I swear, I wanna kill Kamila," I said to Nina while we ate at In-N-Out Burger.

I got a call from Nina to join her to eat on her lunch break. I of course accepted and met her here.

"If you would let Quest help—"

"No Nina, I can't ask him. I think we're really done. We haven't talked since his Mom's funeral." I took a sip of my milkshake.

"Angel told me he's stressing out over her death and finding that Edith lady. Stop playing with the man, Christian, and get his ass. Y'all two will never escape each other, especially because of me and Symba dating his friends." Nina was right and I knew it.

"I have a date tonight, nothing serious, just some drinks at a bar." I admitted.

Nina shook her head and chuckled. "My goodness sis, you're so annoying." We both laughed as the door opened. Nina's back was facing the door, but I had a clear view.

"Ew, that's the guy who was with Tucker that day we ran into them." I said to Nina.

Wiping her mouth, she faked it so she could turn to

see him. He was with two white girls who had on clothes that left little to the imagination.

"He looks slimy." Nina said, looking at me with her nose turned up.

His eyes roamed and when they landed on me, he smiled showing that bottom gold grill. Then the nigga and his girls had the nerve to come over our way.

"We told you Vegas was small," He said and then looked at Nina. "Well, well who is this?" He asked still looking at her.

"My name doesn't matter and if you don't mind, we're trying to eat." Nina responded and the two white girls smacked their lips.

"My girls don't like when their King is being disrespected." He had the nerve to say to us. He had on this baby blue Nike track suit with a sideways blue fitted hat.

Me and Nina stood up. "We don't give a fuck what

they don't like, you could have come in her and let us be. You so fucking lame that you'll come try to fuck with two females." I chuckled looking at him up and down. "And you claimed not to be gay."

Oh, I definitely struck a nerve because he came towards me with that 'slap a hoe' expression. I just knew he was getting his hand ready.

Nina picked up the tin napkin holder ready to swing, when two cops walked inside. I mean they may have saved a bitch from needing plastic surgery.

He looked from the side of him and then at us with enlarged nostrils and a tight mouth.

"You bitches and the hoe ass Law niggas gon' suffer. Count yo' days down, you dusty sluts." He snapped his fingers at the two white women, and they headed out without getting any food.

"I'm telling Angel what just happened." Nina said,

balling her bag up and putting it in the garbage.

"I don't blame you, he a sick ass nigga." I said as we got up and left out a little after his punk ass did.

After Nina and I parted ways, I stopped at DSW to grab these cute heels I saw when I was in here with Mama. I really didn't care for this store, but I really needed these heels for my outfit tonight. I wasn't wearing anything special for Terry because I didn't want him to get the wrong impression. I went out for yogurt with him at U-Swirl Frozen Yogurt yesterday and it was ok. I didn't feel a connection or even sexual chemistry. But Terry was nice and he had a cool personality. I went home, showered, and let Symba re-twist my hair.

"You look good, niece." Symba came in my room.

I had on a black and white two-piece jean set from *Fashion Nova* and the heels were these cute black and silver heel booties. I had on a pair of white gold, square shape earrings and my Pandora charm bracelet.

"Thank you, auntie." I sprayed myself with some Dior perfume and someone knocked on the door.

"I thought you said you were meeting him at the bar?" Symba asked as we both made our way to the door.

"I am, I ain't tell that nigga where I lived." I watched her look through the keyhole and this girl smiled so wide, her ears were damp.

I rolled my eyes laughing because I knew who that was.

"Why the fuck you not answering your phone?" Dominick came in practically taller than our door.

"It's dead on the charger." Symba responded and then kissed him. They were beyond sexy together and it was still crazy seeing her be in a relationship. But I couldn't have picked a better guy; Dominick was big brother for sure and I loved how he loved her.

"How you doing, baby sister? Where you going?" He

asked me, sitting on the couch and pulling Symba on his lap.

"Umm, I don't think I remember you being my father." I laughed and joked.

Dominick just shook his head and said, "Footie socks and pajama pants." Him and Symba laughed hysterically.

I smacked my lips, grabbed my purse and headed out. It was around eight o'clock at night and I was set to meet Terry at eight-thirty. I hit the alarm to my car and as soon as I got inside, a familiar smell hit my nose. I actually stopped moving because I got chills. *I just know damn well I'm not missing him so much that his scent is hitting my nostrils,* I thought to myself and then my passenger's door opened. Before I even realized that it was Quest, I froze and thought I was about to either get robbed or kidnapped. He closed the door and looked at me like he was about to chop me in bits.

"I'm mad as fuck, but not all at you. I gotta own up to some shit as well. I wouldn't like it if you talked to your ex. So, history or not, I shouldn't have said a fucking word to Kamila. That's on me and I apologize, but I can't apologize about putting my focus on what's on my plate." His eyes bore hard into mine.

I sat there with my hand on the wheel and looking at him, a little scared and shocked that he actually was in my car. His voice was so calm, but it was solid and filled with sternness.

"I think you got the assumption that because I gave you a little room, that you were single. You going out for punk ass yogurt dates like you in a damn sing-a-long movie. And what the fuck is this?" He asked, moving his index finger up and down towards my outfit. "You getting all sexy for someone else Christian, like yo' nigga don't have mental illness in his blood? I may not be diagnosed, but I am indeed not the one to fuck with. You think this a game, sugar tits?" He asked me and waited on me to answer.

"It's far from a game, Quest, but you have your affairs to handle and I have a date." Ugh, I just had to say some smart shit.

He grinned and I melted with how fine he was and looked tonight. He didn't have on shit special, but holy shit if this nigga didn't have on a black t-shirt and some plaid black and red pajama pants. Quickly, Dominick's voice came in my head (*footie socks and pajama pants*) when Quest reached behind my seat, still smiling widely. The next thing that took place will be something I will never, ever forget. This nigga sat Terry's head on my dashboard like a car dash ornament.

"Ahh!" I screamed and covered my mouth. I looked at him with bucked eyes and a wide-open mouth.

I felt like I was in a *Jordan Peele* movie, especially because he still was grinning. "Did you know a twenty-four-inch heavy machete knife will give you that clean, perfect cut? I mean, it's so sharp that the bone will cut like butter." He told me this like he was sharing a recipe. Then, he pointed to Terry.

"Tell him y'all date is cancelled, Christian. Tell him you didn't want to waste his time, but you were being stubborn. Most importantly, tell him you have a nigga who loves you more than he loves himself and you love him, too. Tell him that until now, you didn't know how far yo' nigga will go over what's his.

And in case you are confused, Christian; you are fucking *mine*. Also let him know that after today, ain't no more break or time apart. Me and you will be joined by the hip and if I don't get what I want, then you need to move far, far from me because I'll be giving you presents like this all the time, every time you think you're moving on."

I swear I heard all that he said and trust me if I didn't get it then, I definitely get it now. My nigga was crazy as fuck. I mean the kind of crazy that isn't heard of. But I was stuck on one thing.

"Quest, there is a head on my dashboard. I...why...he has a family." I looked from the head to Quest.

He squinted his eyes at me. "If you that concerned, I can sit his family up here too, so he won't be lonely."

My mouth fell back open and I shook my head at him. "Please don't do that."

"I won't, if you tell me right now who you belong to." He looked at me with a mellow expression. His long beard was French braided and he just looked so damn good. This loose cannon of a man was all mine. I mean did I really have a choice. Hell, I didn't even want one. I knew what the answer was.

"I belong to Quest." I said to him in a sweet tone.

Licking his lips, he leaned over and kissed me. "I love you so much, you're my family, always and forever." He whispered close to my lips.

"I love you too, and I'll always be your family." I responded. He tried to kiss me again, but I stopped him.

"Will you please get rid of this head on my dashboard?" I asked him and he cracked up like this was actually funny. Why y'all didn't warn me he was this crazy?

Dominick

"So it seems we have a problem, fellas." Burt said to us as we met in the basement of his funeral home. His African accent came in and out, depending on what he was talking about and right now, it was on thick. He called me, Angel, and Quest to meet with them, which is cool because we had a job to do and Quest got a lead on Edith.

"We got a solution," Quest spoke.

"Word spread about the complex going up in flames. I spoke highly of you three and assured my associates that you had the situation under control. Buyers are fearful of doing business with you now. However, I did let them know that you insured yourselves before it happened. You've set up shop elsewhere, you're still in business and have the same support from the Mayor, Police Department and Governor." Burt turned the two furnaces on to burn the bodies, then he turned towards us.

"I also found out something else that might help you. Seems your Philly enemies have a few important clients who like their share of pussy. The same way you've developed your list of famous clienteles from secret abortions, and some STD testing. They don't have nearly as many as you all do, but it's enough that if their list was made public, it could shake and make a lot of noise.

They have been using that list as leverage. Basically, they've blackmailed to get the things they want. You'd be doing a lot of big names in Philadelphia a favor by handling them. That's a whole other state that you'll have in your pocket." Burt put his hands in the pockets of the slacks he wore.

We each were sitting on a stool, listening and taking in what he was saying.

"Why the hell no one hasn't killed these fucks a while ago, it has to be more to the story. If someone is blackmailing me, I'm killing them, simple. Unless that same person has ways of my secret coming out, even beyond death," I suggested because it was making no sense to me. If they got a small list of powerful people that they were blackmailing, how are they still breathing?

"That makes sense, Dominick." Angel agreed. "We met Tucker, Gunna, Sincere and Money. Who else do they have on their team? It gotta be somebody who they trust to keep the receipts that could expose their list."

Quest shook his head and said, "Naw, I think it's someone who doesn't know that they have the receipts. Think hard y'all; if someone else knew they were holding that kind of power, they would use it for themselves. I mean I know I would. Money, fame, whatever I could squeeze out, I'm doing it. Gunna calls Tucker his boss, so we know it's somebody Tucker fucks with heavy. He got family here, we need to start there."

Burt smiled while looking at us. "This is why I spoke so highly of you three; you think before making moves. Anyway, I told my associates that you'll be doing your sales here. That way, everyone is comfortable, and they trust me. Here." He gave Angel the file that says what organs were a hot commodity on the Black Market right now. We were all reading it.

"We have an AB-negative kidney, but unfortunately, that's going to a twenty-year-old who is having a hard time finding a match," Angel told Burt.

Even though we weren't doing surgeries anymore until these Philly hoes were dead, we still looked out for those less fortunate. A married couple came to us pretty much on their knees begging to help them. They gave us their daughter's name and we had Mrs. Newman's son look her up. He showed us the long fight she's been having. Me,

Angel and Quest may be some lunatics, but we have hearts still, so we agreed to take care of her.

"Understood. What about the liver, pancreas, lungs and heart? O-positive is very common. That's about forty million. Split three ways, that's a nice ass payday." Burt stated.

"I thought we give you and your associates a cut too?" Angel asked.

"We decided it made sense to charge the buyers a fee instead of you all." This was why we respected Burt so much. His business smarts and knowledge was like Angel's pops. We think he looked at us like his sons. Mary did too.

"Shit I like that new arrangement." I chuckled and said.

"Well, I know we are all busy fellas. If I hear or have any more information, I will let you know," Burt assured, shaking all of our hands.

"No doubt Burt, good looking out." Angel told him.

"If shit gets too hectic, you let me know and my people will be ready to battle." Burt told us, giving us that serious look.

We headed outside to our blackout van and pulled off with me driving. "Cyrus looked up Tucker and his boys. He couldn't locate an address where they lay their heads, so he is running a check through that nigga Gunna's hoes. Maybe they brought places in their names as a precaution." Angel told me and Quest. He was sitting in the back and Quest was in the front.

I happened to glance over at him, and he was looking like some heavy shit was on his mind and it was pissing him off more and more.

"You good bro?" I asked him.

"Yeah I just keep thinking about when I went to Edith's house after finding out she poisoned my Ma. Her house was completely empty, as if she already had made a plan to do it. A woman is not about to pack up a whole house alone, let alone a woman over forty. Someone helped her, but Cyrus said he checked every moving company in Nevada and nothing was scheduled for her address. Meaning, whoever helped her was probably in on it too. I just don't get why, that's what keeps me up at night."

Me and Angel were quiet just listening to him. What he was saying was wild as hell. What would be the reason of Edith killing his mother? What was in if for her? Still though, I didn't like seeing my boy like this.

"We hot on that bitch ass Q, we always get our targets and everybody that was involved days are numbered," I told him nodding my head in reassurance.

"Hell yeah, whoever we find tonight is about to die as well." Angel added.

"My brothers." Quest said lowly, but we both heard

him.

I pulled up to the apartment complex address that Cyrus gave us. He told us Edith's daughter lived here. She's twenty-eight and fucked with some knuckle head car thief, but she didn't have any kids so that was good. We hated dealing with social service, they were a pain in the ass.

"What's her apartment number?" I asked putting my revolver behind my back, then I put my brass knuckles with spikes on them on.

"Apt 122." Angel answered picking up his big black hammer.

You already know Quest had some crazy ass knife, that fucker was all steel with a sharp point. Had to be about twenty-two inches. The apartment complex was set up like motels, which worked in our favor. She was on the first floor. I found the fool's BMW and matched the license plate with the number Cyrus gave me, confirming it was her boyfriend's car. Once I nodded at my boys, Quest and Angel waited on the side of her door and I threw the brick through the window. Making my way over to them, the alarm started going off and in no time, the door flung open. He didn't even step all the way outside before we rushed his ass and slammed the door closed. I had him pressed on the wall with my closed fist by his eye, searching him to make sure he had no gun on him. Quest and Angel walked through the two-bedroom apartment.

"D, I swear to God whoever told y'all I disrespected The Law in anyway is lying. I swear I don't even speak on y'all!" He started pleading and swearing on his dead ass aunt that he didn't do shit.

I could hear screaming in the back and Quest came back to the front with Edith's daughter. She had a robe on and her hair all wild like they just got done fucking. Angel was in the second bedroom. I could hear him ransacking the place looking for any clues as to where Edith was. Quest slammed her daughter against the wall.

"Where the hell is your mama... and before you lie, I know who your Mama is. She magically moved off the face of the map. Where is she?" He asked her and you could tell his ass wasn't going to ask her again.

Doing the ugly cry she said, "I-I don't know—" Quest looked at me and gave a quick nod.

"Urgh!!" Her boyfriend yelled when I hit him hard as fuck in his eye with my brass knuckles on.

"No! Oh my God please don't!" She pleaded and I smiled at her.

"One more time, where is she?" Quest asked her.

Her eyes were stuck on what I was doing because I still had my fist lounged into his eye. I pressed deeper and you could hear my spikes digging in his eyeball more and more. I had strength for days so I knew when I took my fist out, his eye was going to be done for.

The bitch wouldn't say shit, so I turned to face her boyfriend. Using my other hand I grabbed his jaw tightly and until she answered with something useful, then I was going to keep squeezing his jaws and pressing that eye.

"I'm the least of your worries." Quest told her. "That crazy ass white boy enjoys that shit. Now tell me what you know."

"O-Ok! Ok! My Mama came into some money and she moved. We never were that close, but I would stop by since my lazy ass brother only cares about his friends and bitches. Last month, she said she was moving but not out the state. I asked if she wanted any help moving and she said she was all set. I didn't think anything about it, I wasn't even shocked that she didn't offer me any money because like I said, we aren't that close. Whatever she did, I swear I have nothing to do with it, he doesn't either." She cried all that out.

"Brother, who is your brother?" Quest asked her.

"Mick, his name is Mick. He is heavy in the streets so he would know more about any of this then I would. He lives on Lawry Avenue; he hangs with Marlo, Abe, and Reese's raggedy asses!" The chick was spilling everything, and she dropped some familiar names.

Quest and I looked at each other when she said that.

"She's not lying." Angel came up front holding her phone. "I just read their text messages. Edith came into twenty-grand and then moved. Someone paid her, but I don't think it was that nigga Marlo. He ain't got that kind of bread sitting around, he a junkie and reckless. We need to pay Mick a visit tonight." Angel told us, putting the daughter's phone in his pocket.

"No! Don't touch my brother!" She yelled at Angel loud as hell.

Quest pressed her head against the wall hard with

his palm and then he put his knife in her throat. He always talks about me being sick in the head, but he ain't far behind. He twisted the long knife in circles, silencing her completely.

Her boyfriend gagged out when he saw her die. I looked at him and squeezed his jaws so hard, his teeth started ripping from its gums. Pulling my fist out his eye, I hit him twice then snapped his neck, making his body drop to the floor. We didn't even stay to talk it out, we called clean-up. Lori was at the new complex, so we told her to get ready for two new bodies coming in. She knew what to do after. Once we made it back to the van, we went and did the kill job we were paid for. We visited Mick's house at the exact address Cyrus gave us. While I was driving, I got a text on my phone.

Anika: *We really need to talk.*

I ain't never seen or known her to be this thirsty.

That's one of the reasons why I fucked with her so long. We would go weeks without talking but one word of communication, but as soon as I tell her we done, she starts tripping.

Me: *About??*

I texted back and my phone chimed soon after I sent it.

Anika: *After all the history we have, you owe it to me to meet with me face to face.*

My patience was too thin for games and bullshit, but I see the warning I gave her the first time didn't take.

Me: *Ok. I'll let you know when I'm free.*

Anika: *K*!!

This muthafucka was becoming a thorn in my rose garden and I was going to pluck her ass in the most gruesome way if she's on one.

"Aight, we stripped that nigga Marlo of his whole crew. Now we got him, Philly and Edith to focus on.

Something is telling me that Edith is not connected to them, but twenty G's is a lot for her old ass to get at one time. Cyrus is getting her bank information so he can trace where it came from." Angel told us while we were outside our new complex leaning against our cars. We made thirty-three thousand apiece, took out Marlo's crew and found out more information on Edith. All done by ten o' clock at night.

"Hell yeah, I swear I got something real good for that bitch when I get her." Quest said, rubbing his hands together.

"That's how I feel about Marlo. I wanna make that nigga scream louder than a starving baby." Angel added.

"I got plans for Gunna as well. Ever since I ran into him and Symba at the mall. I want that muthafucka to bleed from his knees and his ears." I was so serious, and these two idiots laughed.

"I swear on my mama, you say some of the most off-putting shit, my nigga." Quest cracked shaking his head.

"Why I'm the crazy one when you just hung a bitch on the wall with one of yo' magical knives? Then you." I pointed to Angel. "You just used your two-ball flail as a cheese on ol'dude's face. But I'm the sick one?!" I looked at both of them, offended as hell.

"Yeah we do things in the moment, you sit and say shit like *making a fool bleed from their knees and ears.*" Angel's punk ass mocked me and tried to speak in my tone. "I don't even know how you make someone bleed from their ears and knees, but I bet yo' ass will show us. That's what makes you more twisted! You actually mean and do the crazy shit you say out loud!" While they laughed, I waved them off and hit the alarm on my custom Viper.

"I hope mosquitoes filled with West Nile bite y'all asses up." I got in my car and left their clueless asses standing out there. Damn fools.

I walked in my palace and the first thing I did was look down to see if her shoes were by the door. I smirked when I saw they were; she actually had two pairs that were left here, but I knew if there was a third one then that meant she was here. After I took my shoes off, I walked through my hallway and headed straight for the stairs. I could hear the TV on from my master bedroom and I knew she was up because Symba loved sleeping in complete darkness. I walked in my room and there she was, looking gorgeous as hell in my oak wood king size bed.

"Hey Dom baby." Her face beamed at me.

"Sup Sym baby, you still up?" I asked her as I took my shirt and beater off, throwing it in my walk-in closet while walking to her side of the bed. I didn't want to sit on my bed with these jeans on that I just did some killing in, so I leaned over her and kissed them juicy ass lips she has. I hadn't seen her all day; work had me out all evening, so I missed dinner with her.

"Now you know I'm a vampire. I put your plate in the microwave." Her sexy voice said to me then she kissed my lips again.

"You are too good to me, let me take a shower and I'm all yours."

Nodding her head, Symba licked her lips looking at my chest and then my face. I headed to the bathroom so I could take a steaming shower and wash my hair.

"I'ma kick this girl ass." I said to myself, picking up this damn shampoo/conditioner she bought me. I wasn't into all that, I used to wash my hair with my Dove for Men soap but Symba swear that was awful. Her ass gave me a long lecture about shampoo and conditioner and some shit about luster.

What the fuck is a luster? Anyway, I told her to shut her ass up and that she can buy the shit as long as it wasn't bright colors or no sissy name. Leave it to my woman to not listen.   Coconut Milk shampoo and conditioner. I washed my hair mad as hell and used that weak conditioner shit too; this was my first and last time using this. I don't even feel like a man. After I was done, I got out and dried off, including my hair. After I dried my hair with the towel I smelled it and damn it smelled good as hell. Putting my hands on the ends of my hair, it was soft as shit. Damn girl was right, that brittle feel was gone.

"See, I told you that shampoo and conditioner was the truth." Symba said smiling at me and sitting up in the bed.

I didn't even say anything, I just smirked and put my deodorant and boxers on. Heading downstairs I went to the kitchen and opened the microwave. My stomach got excited when I saw her spaghetti and meatballs. Symba stuffed her meatballs with three cheeses and it was good as hell. She fixed me a big ass plate of it.

While it heated up, I grabbed a bottle of water and some parmesan cheese. Sitting down at the nook, I threw down on my food and downed my bottle of water in minutes. I had two big burps while I put my dishes in the sink and I felt way better.

"That food was good as hell." I said to her, getting in the bed naked of course.

She didn't have any clothes on either and that thick ass body was looking perfect. Her hair was in this curly ponytail on top of her head and she had a scarf wrapped around her edges. I sat up with my back on the headboard and reached over in my nightstand next to my side.

"Put this on for me." I said to her, giving her that sexy ass thong I took from her house some weeks back.

Symba gasped. "I knew your ass was stealing my panties!" She was laughing that infectious laugh. "Why are you just sitting there looking like you have no shame?!"

"Why should I be ashamed because I steal my

woman's panties? Are you ashamed because you steal my beaters?" I asked her with a leer expression.

Her mouth dropped and she turned red. "Oh my goodness, how did you know that?"

"Because I also know what the hell I buy. I'm flattered though because that means you ain't too far from me on the obsession scale."

I licked my lips watching her put the thong on. That thick band went around her small waist and wide hips. Just like I knew, that pretty phat pussy sat plump as hell in the see-through part. Symba had some double -D titties that were just fuck me sexy. They were real and had that fluffy softness; they sat up perfectly but had that mini drop that I love on big titties. Her caramel nipples were big and I loved watching them form hard when I was around.

"Turn around." I told her and when she did, I squeezed my dick. My woman was so thick with a peach shape ass I called it. That perfect slide in the middle that separated them ass cheeks, her thighs that had no gap between them shook when she walked. Her body was perfect, even her stretch marks that matched her skin tone turned me on.

"Come here, gorgeous." I watched her climb back into bed and my dick hopped when her thighs made that slap sound. I paid attention to every fucking thing about this woman.

When she got close to me, I put my arms around her waist and pulled her in my lap. Then I put my face all in her neck and inhaled her scent, *HER* by *Burberry*. It was infused in her and even when she wasn't around me, it would hit my nose randomly throughout the day. When I got my fill of her smell, I leaned back on the bed and just looked at her gorgeous ass. Her hand went on the side of my face and then she messed with my beard.

"How was your day?" She asked me.

"It was informative and bloody." I answered honestly because I didn't want to lie to her, ever. I told her about The Law and what we did a few weeks ago before we were even official.

"Dom please don't get hurt or die on me because I swear, I will set your funeral on fire." She turned around and laid on my chest with her thick thigh between my legs. Her skin pressed against mine was something I couldn't explain in words, but it lit my insides up.

"Damn, why would you light my shit up?" I chuckled and asked while rubbing my hand up and down her back.

"Because I'd be out here alone back on the market picking through the litter box."

"No you wouldn't."

She sat her head up with an open smile. "Dom, I am not about to be single forever. I'd be done for a minute from mourning, but not forever." The way she talked and explained had me laughing to myself, because she really believed what she said.

"Symba even if I was dead, you would have to be single. Angel and Quest would kill whoever you tried to settle down with." I caressed her jaw then brushed my thumb lightly across her bottom lip. I stayed doing things like that to her because I was obsessed with the being of her. Men today don't get as deep as they should with their woman. Not me, I loved to touch every part of her, even the odd parts.

I told Symba when I first brought her back here that I love different. I've said those three words to a woman before, but I never meant it like I do with my Sym baby. I was beyond gone; I'd do anything she asked or required. Everything about her I love, even the flaws she had. But I was at a point where I couldn't imagine life without her or imagine her with someone else. Footie socks and pajama pants.

"That is so not fair." She pouted and had wrinkles in her forehead.

"See, you can have yo' little thot fun, but when it comes to building, settling down, marriage and kids." I shook my head. "Homeboy gotta die."

She fell out laughing and it was magnetic, so I laughed too.

Reaching her head up to my face, we kissed. "You are insane Dom baby, but I love you so much."

"I love you too, Sym baby." I pecked her lips again and squeezed that thick thigh that was laid between my legs.

"So, I have something to ask you," she said, looking up at me and resting her chin on my pec.

"Go ahead, then I have something to tell you."

"Ok. You have two walkie-talkies on your dresser, why?"

I had never talked to Symba about Denise. Actually, I have never talked to any woman about her. That was a part of me that I just didn't speak on, but I had no plans on me and Symba being apart, so I figured why not.

"I bought them for my baby sister, Denise." It had been a while since I said her name out loud.

"I didn't know you have a little sister, will she be at The Fling tomorrow?" She asked me all excited. My parents' trailer park was having their wild ass hoe down tomorrow and I figured its perfect timing for Symba to meet them. Since I was little and lived at the trailer park, they have an annual event called The Fling. Loud music, good food, a shit load of keggers, cars parked all around and a good time.

"Naw she won't be there. Denise died when she was nine."

Symba covered her mouth. "Oh my goodness, Dom baby I am so sorry. We don't have to talk about this if you don't want to."

"It's cool Sym, I don't mind. It's about time that I shared this with someone else aside from my family and boys." I started telling her about the person Denise was before she got sick. I told her how my parents were growing up and how I always looked out for Denise. I then told her how Quest and Angel loved her as well. Finally, I told her when she was at her gymnastics game and she fainted.

"If I was her blood type, I swear I would not be sitting here with you today. I would have done anything to save her, It was all about money. Her doctor was a rude fucker who treated us beneath him because we didn't have the money for her surgery. After all the hope he gave us, it all came down to money.

My favorite person took her last breath on New Year's Day and it broke me. I went to her doctor's house that night, waited for him and killed him. Me, Quest and Angel weren't even The Law yet so the resources we have now, we didn't have then."

Symba wiped my tear that fell from my eye. "I would have had her right, paid for any college she wanted, a car and all. I didn't understand how someone like her could be born with a bad heart. Denise was in the hospital so long sometimes, she would get lonely, so I brought her those walkie-talkies and told her no matter what time or day, if she ever wanted to talk all she had to do was hit me up.

I learned how to play the guitar for her because it used to drown out the arguing our parents used to do. It would always sooth her and put her to sleep. I played one last time for her over the walkie-talkie. My favorite person." I said as a wave of sadness hit me.

"I never really knew how much I actually missed Denise. I had so many plans for me and her and I just knew she was going to the Olympics one day." I smiled at the thought and so did Symba.

"Wow baby, I never knew you were holding all of that in. How you loved her and looked out for her is amazing." She wrapped her arms around her neck and hugged me.

"Yeah it was dope having a sister, I felt important to someone. Not saying our parents didn't love us, but some of the decisions they used to make didn't make me feel important. But I was important to her and when she died, I had the feeling of being less again." I told her honestly.

Symba's big eyes bore into mine and I felt her love through them. "You're important to me Dominick. After God, you're right there. I don't want you to ever have that less feeling again, ok?"

I looked her gorgeous face over then nodded my head. I kissed her deeply and she pushed play on her movie she was watching on Xfinity OnDemand.

"Can you start it over? I never did get around to seeing this." I asked her as she got comfortable laying on my chest. Those big titties pressed against my skin. I knew I was getting inside her before we closed our eyes. This was our thing, though. We'd watch movies until about five in the morning and then go to sleep.

"I sure can, I was only ten-minutes into it." Symba restarted *Aquaman* and we got started watching it. Symba started looking from the movie to me and then from me to the movie. I watched her do it about five times.

"Don't even say it." I said to her in a annoyed manner. "Angel and Quest use to get on me all the time when we use to watch *Game Of Thrones.* I don't look shit like that damn man," I said, keeping my eyes on the TV. I could feel her silly ass grin on her face.

"I knew it was a reason I was feeling a tingle between my legs when he came on the screen." Symba cracked up.

My eyes shifted downward, looking at her. "That pussy bet' not tingle for no damn body but me or I'ma scrape the fuck out of it." I told her calm as hell.

"Oh my goodness! I swear Dom, you need help. How do you scrape a coochie?" She could barely get her question out because she was laughing so hard.

"Repeat what you said and find out." I grabbed her pussy from the back since she was laying on me and my arm was long enough. "This reacts to who, Symba?" I asked her, biting my lip because just that quickly, she got wet.

"Only my Dom baby." Her voice was packed with seduction. On purpose, I slid my fingers down her pussy and brushed against that clit making her let out those low moans she does.

"That's right, and it'll always be that way." I told her and we went back to watching the movie. After we watched *Aquaman,* we were stuck on the superhero flicks, so we watched *Batman* with *Jack Nicholson* as the joker.

"Oh, you said you had something to tell me." Symba said after we got about twenty-minutes into the movie.

"Hm?"

"Earlier, remember you said you had something to tell me after I asked you my question."

Shit, I forgot. I gotta tell her about Anika's text message. "A chick I used to fuck with before you hit my phone up and said she needs to talk to me." I wasn't even halfway through my sentence before Symba sat all the way up with her big breasts bouncing like sculpted jello.

"How long before me?" I knew shew was going to ask that and I also knew she was about to be pissed at my answer.

"The same day you snatched the other chick's wig off." I scratched the side of my eyebrow, trying not to laugh because her face looked like she wanted to blow up.

"Ok, so you fucked this bitch who said she needs to talk, the cheap wig bitch, and then me all in the same day!?"

"I know you betta stop fucking yelling. You getting them titties all hyped up for no reason. I didn't fuck all three of y'all that same day. I only fucked you, I hit Anika with dick the day before and if you recall, I didn't fuck Tish because of yo' wild ass."

Symba rolled her eyes. "I wasn't acting all wild, I was acting like your woman."

I chuckled and tilted my head slightly to the right, looking at her. "But you *weren't* my woman, and if I remember correctly, you made damn sure to keep reminding me of that."

"I can't fucking stand you. It's ok for you to tell me not to fuck the guy I was with at the mall. But you can take Ms. Cheap Wig to your slut house and almost fuck her? Well I should have—"

"Symba muthafuckin' Reed, I swear I will break yo' ass in half if you don't shut the fuck up." I wasn't playing with her and she knew it based off my intense stare. "Stop trying to pick a damn fight with me and appreciate that I came to you and told you the truth. I didn't go meet with her secretly or any foul shit. I want you with me when I go see Anika. I don't want to keep anything from you." I was calming down now because she had me fucked up and ready to snap talking like she ain't got no sense.

Symba looked to the side with this stubborn expression on her face, then looking at me. "My last name is not Reed, it's Greene."

I chuckled to myself because there she go with that attitude that only black girls had. That type of sassiness kept my dick on swoll.

"It will be Reed eventually, and I triple dog dare that sexy ass mouth to not cooperate." I told her.

"It's only one thing any girl has to tell a man they

haven't fucked in weeks. I'm not playing step-mama to no kid, I don't care if it was before we were *official,* Dom."

I chuckled and shook my head. "When you gon' learn that I wouldn't let shit stay in this world or come into this world that would jeopardize you and I? What you expect me to tell you some bullshit about she ain't shit but a vessel crap? Naw, if my kids not coming out that pussy," I pointed between her legs. "Then I don't want it. Ain't no way Anika is pregnant because I strap up every damn time I fuck her. I mean *every* damn time, swear on my baby sister life and I never do that. But let's say by some form of magic my nut slipped in her, she'd come with us right then and there to our complex and get that removed. Either that, or I kill her where she stands."

Her eyes were so wide. "Wow, I uh...wow. I wasn't expecting you to say that; you love me that much?" Her face had so much fear over it, but not fear of me. More like she hoped I really did because she was invested into our relationship. Like it had become her new comfort and right now, she needed me to seal her insecurities.

"No, I don't love you that much, I love you beyond that, Symba. You need to get that through your head." I pulled her to me by her arm so I could kiss her deeply.

While our tongues danced together, she straddled me. Then she moved her thong to the side and slid down slowly on my hard dick.

"Uhh." We both moaned out loud looking at each other. Symba's pussy was so tight, wet and warm inside that she made me moan. I even closed my eyes for a second while my dick made itself at home. I sucked on her bottom lip then trailed my tongue from the side of her face to her neck and I sucked on it. Her grinds were life. I loved when Symba would ride me and it was my new favorite position.

"Ahhh yes, Dom baby." She cried out and threw her head back while picking up her groove a little.

I sat up and grabbed her titties so I could have a field day with them in my mouth. Her pussy had grip and it was squeezing my shit for dear life. I put my hand around her neck, making her lift her head back up. I needed her to look me in my eyes; our breathing was rapid and we were so close that our noses were touching.

"Mine." I said, staring so deep into her eyes, it's like I put them in her head.

Symba gave me a sexy smirk that made my dick grow inside of her. "Forever." She leaned back a little, putting her hands flat on my thigh. Her feet were flat on my bed and I knew she was about to get loose.

I laid back on my fluffy pillows and rubbed my hand up and down between her titties while she bounced.

"Do them circles I like, baby," I told her.

Symba put some of her weight on my thighs some more and stretched her body out with me still in her. She then started grinding in circles, smearing her cream all over my dick and her pussy. "Fuck, Sym. Fuck." I loved seeing her body shake while she kept the circles going. Them thighs of hers and titties would be jiggling all over and I couldn't wait to cum all inside of her.

**

I bet I shake the room (ay, woo, woo, woo)

Swerve (skrrt, skrrt, skrrt)

Go 'head, shake the room, yeah

Symba and I pulled up to the trailer park backyard Fling and it was hype like always. You could see guys outside the park playing dice and drinking. The kegs were lined up with cups over cups on the sides of them. There were about six big grills going with any kind of meat you could think of on them. Now that I'm grown, I don't fuck with everyone's cooking, but when I was a kid I used to because sometimes, it was either that or I wouldn't eat until my parents sobered up the next day.

"Damn, it's a mixture of everybody up in here." Symba said, looking around shocked.

"Hell yea, poor don't discriminate." I chuckled and grabbed her hand so we could walk inside.

"Sup, D!"

"D, my nigga what's up!"

"D! How you doing!?"

I nodded my head and gave the deuces to all who was speaking to me.

"I think it's so funny how they call you nigga." She laughed.

"It's been like that for some time now, I don't mind it because I know it's a form of respect. It's better than what I used to be called as a kid when no one knew how I was coming." I told her honestly.

"Hey, sweetie." My mama spotted us and smiled with her arms out. She was surrounded by a few of her friends; all of them had a red cup in their hand. It was around seventy-five degrees out with some bright sun.

"Sup, Mama." I kissed her on the cheek and hugged her. Her dirty blonde hair was half up and half down and she had some shorts on with an American Flag shirt.

I grabbed Symba's hand. "This is my girlfriend, Symba." I said then I kissed her hand.

"Hi, nice to meet you." She smiled and hugged my Mama who also smiled and hugged her back.

Then she looked at me. "Define girlfriend, because don't get me excited and you disappoint me." Mama said with lips perched together.

"Naw Mama, it's not like that." I looked at Symba with my bottom lip in my mouth. "This is my everything right here." Symba blushed as I turned my eyes back to Mama.

"Well, hell yes! Let me hug you again!" She said and the rest of her friends hugged Symba as well.

"Your dad is across the yard on the grill cooking gator meat." She told me and I looked through the crowd and saw his loud ass tie-dye shirt.

"I can wait here while you go talk to your dad if you want." Symba's soft voice said.

"Hell no, you see how wild it is in here? You coming with me." I furrowed my eyebrows while interlocking our fingers.

"Dom, you really think I'm about to run off with someone here?" She laughed and joked as we walked over to Dad.

"Not even a worry about that, no one here is crazy enough to touch what's mine. But I can't stop people from sneaking a look at you or their thoughts, especially if they got alcohol in them. You betta be happy I let you wear them tight ass jeans and half top."

I looked at her from head to toe. We had on the same cream and pink Air Jordan 13's on our feat. I had some light jeans on with a cream and pink Jordan Polo shirt. Symba did my hair in the man bun she like and I had my diamond studs and Rolex on. Symba wore her hair down and wavy with the part in the middle that I love. She had on some diamond studs and bust down pink diamond Rolex I bought her.

That peach shaped booty was sitting up in them jeans like a hoe in charm school. I didn't want her walking around this bitch without me. I wanted everyone to know she was mine, off limits and not to be fucked with. I've brought women here to the Fling before, some I called my girl and some I didn't. But I wasn't protective of them like I was with Symba. I wouldn't let anyone disrespect me or them, but I wasn't on their ass.

"Dad." I called his name.

"Son! Hey Hey!" He turned around and hugged me smelling like beer and weed. Then he looked at Symba and back to me. "Well got damn boy, you hit every jackpot in Vegas with this one."

She laughed and so did I.

"This is my girlfriend, Symba." I introduced them.

Symba hugged him and if this weren't my dad, I would break his hands off.

"Don't lose her Dominick, you'd be a dumb ass." He said putting his attention back on his grill.

I put my arm around Symba's neck. "Never that, Dad." I told him as he opened the grill.

Symba gasped and stepped back a little.

My dad noticed it and laughed. "Aw shit, girl! Don't tell me you ain't never seen no baby gator's on the grill!?"

I laughed when Symba put this fake forceful smile on her face. "No I haven't, oh my gosh you flip them!?" She asked, looking shocked and mouth wide open.

Dad cut a piece of the tail, blew on it and ate it. Symba covered her mouth looking as if she was turning green. I was rolling, but I didn't want her uncomfortable, so we made our exit. "Pops, we about to chill and enjoy the Fling."

"Alright, well get her a drink and make sure you make your way back around here, I'm putting some rabbit on the grill next!" He yelled out to us.

Wasn't no way we were coming back over there to see that. Time went on and we were having a good time. We played two rounds of horseshoes, balloon darts with the giant, cards and of course, we had some of the many beers. Symba kept it simple and drank a StrawberRita. She was having a blast hanging with my people. My mama loved her, especially when Symba played a good hand of Spades.

"Ok, let me have a picture of you two so I can put it

with the others." Mama said as she took out her phone. They always took pictures and then she would go to Walmart and print them.

Symba was on my lap while I was smoking and talking to some of the guys I fucked with. We both stood up and she put her hand on the side of her hip with her ass out.

"If you don't bring that shit all the way back in." I looked down at her with a stern look on my face.

Smacking her lips, she stood in front of me with her back to my chest. As I was putting my arms around her waist, I noticed the guys were staring at Symba like a damn piece of gator meat. When they saw me looking at them, they all looked off in every direction but hers.

"Take the damn picture Ma, before I snatch these muthafuckas' lungs out," I said, making her and Symba laugh and shake their heads.

Mama took a few pictures of us and then answered her phone when it rang.

"Yup, just park anywhere you like and come inside." When she hung up she looked at me.

"Remember Dr. Ahuja, the one who worked on Denise's case?"

You mean the one I killed is what I wanted to say. My stomach turned sour just hearing his name, I hated that man. Had I been in the mind frame I'm in now, I would have killed his whole family if I knew he had one.

"Yeah I remember him." I guess my face read something different. Symba grabbed my arm and put it around her neck, bringing her close to my chest.

"Dominick please be nice. It wasn't his fault Denise passed. I ran into his wife and daughter at the store and I invited them."

I laughed to myself because what the hell does a doctor's wife and child look like being at a place like this?

"Here they come, behave." Mama scowled at me.

"I am so sorry, my Mom isn't feeling well so it's just me. I hope that's not a problem?"

That voice was familiar as I turned around and saw Anika smiling big and hugging Mama. I almost flipped the fuck out. I never knew much about Anika's family, except they had money and she was spoiled. This entire time, she was Denise's doctor's daughter!? This wasn't no coincidence and I thought about the letter that was sent to my parents. That hoe was behind it; some way she knew I killed her dad. Anika's smile went away when she saw Symba standing next to me.

"It's ok, I'm glad you came." Mama said to her.

"Dom baby, you ok?" Symba said close to me but I couldn't answer because I was heated.

"Anika, I want to introduce you to my son Dominick and his girlfriend Symba." When Mama introduced us,

Symba's face changed and she looked from me to Anika.

I couldn't hold my shit in anymore. I grabbed Anika by her arm and practically glided her ass to my parents' luxury trailer home. I was looking like a mad person, I already know it. My Mama was calling my name so loud and I saw some people who were around us looking at me like I was crazy. But no one was stupid enough to stop me; funny thing is, I had Anika by her arm with my right hand, and my left hand was holding on to Symba's hand.

"Close the door Symba, and lock it." I told her once we all got inside. I slammed Anika against the wall so hard the entire big ass trailer shook. "What the fuck are you doing? You think you can play me with these games? Your dad was the same muthafucka who worked on my sister. Did you send that note to my parents' house?! Answer me!" I looked at my hand around her neck and realized she couldn't breathe, so I loosened it.

Anika started coughing and gasping for air. "Is that

how you killed my father?" She asked me with tears coming down her face. "Hm, is that how you did it on the side of our home like he was trash? I was the one who found him, but what you didn't know was we had camera's around our home. I was responsible for turning them on and off. I saw you do it. But when I got a look at you, I fell in love and figured, I couldn't send you to jail.

My dad was hard on me, my Mom and my brother. He was stern, abusive at times and controlling so we were glad he was gone. I erased the tape and it went unsolved. I searched for you and found you in that bar. I knew you were broken. I tried to be everything you wanted in hopes of us being together. But days turned into weeks, months and years!" She shouted and looked at me with tears and anger.

"You started seeing more and more women so I sent the note to your parents, hoping you'd come to me for help or something. But you didn't, you pushed me to the side and even worse." Her eyes went to Symba. "You fell in love, you took her to a place I imagined and prayed for you to take me!"

I grabbed the bridge of my nose then looked at Anika's retarded ass. "Anika, you get one chance to leave here and put all this shit behind you. I don't love you, I will never love you; hell as of this moment, the sight of you disgusts me. All you did was waste time, but I thank you, because I would have never met her." I pointed to Symba. "That's the only reason I'm giving you a chance to walk out of here. I owe you, and this is me paying you back." I balled my fist up tightly because if she objected, then it was game.

"I am not the only one who has proof of what you did. I said I erased the tape, but it was only from my mother's eyes. If anything happens to me, you are going to jail and there's nothing you or your fucking friends can do to save you. So, as quickly as you think I made a way for you to get to her, is as quick as I'll take it away." Anika stood there, trying to look hard with now dried tears on her face.

"What the fuck do you want?" I asked her, trying with all my might not to lunge at her.

But I couldn't risk being away from Symba; even with all my money and connections, I killed a respectable surgeon in cold blood. The proof alone will give me about ten years, a bunch of appeals. Eventually I'd get out because I had money, but not without serving anytime. I couldn't do that to Symba. I couldn't put our life on hold. I couldn't be that long without her, I'd go crazy in jail, pick up more cases from killing someone for even walking past me. I'd lose My Sym baby for good and the thought of that tore me up.

"I want to get married."

"What!?" Me and Symba said in unison, looking at

this hoe like the looney head she was.

"You heard me, I want to get married, move out of the country and have your child. You may not love me Dominick, but you can. I promise you can, with a fair chance you will see I can be all you need." She walked closer to me and before I could say anything, Symba was on it.

She picked up the Colt45 bottle on the counter and gripped it. "I wish the fuck you would touch him." Her face looked worse than when she snatched Tish's wig off.

Anika smiled and then looked at me. "I'm going to go out there and tell your Mom I'm leaving. Get your affairs in order Dominick because when I put everything together, we will be on a first-class flight out the country as husband and wife."

When she turned her back and walked out, Symba walked fast towards her, raising the bottle. Real smooth like, I grabbed her hand in the air, and locked the door back.

"You should have let me knocked that bitch out!" Symba was going crazy and I could think of one way to calm her down.

I yanked her juicy ass to me and shoved my tongue down her throat. Her entire body surrendered to me and she was instantly calm. "You can't do shit to her because that will pull me away from you. I will never marry anybody if it's not you, but right now you need to chill and trust me. Anika is spoiled and used to getting what she wants. Her mind is on a different level of thinking right now. Do you trust me, Sym baby?" I looked her in her big pretty eyes.

"Yes I do but Dominick, you bet not touch or kiss her. I swear I will go out and fuck some one so we can be even."

I squinted my eyes at her, and my nostril flared at

what she said. Symba didn't look fazed, she held her ground.

"Take your jeans off." I told her, taking my Polo off.

"What, we are in your parents' mobile home I—"

"Take your fucking jeans off, bend over and grab them ankles. Now Symba, on my life I won't ask you again."

I watched her do as I said. She was so thick, taking and putting on her jeans was always a struggle for her. But I didn't give a fuck, I was about to tear that smart mouth pussy up, then take her home and make her knees beat up her face while I plow her deep. I bet she won't threaten to give my pussy away ever again. Footie socks and pajamas.

Symba

"Let's look that bitch up and go fuck her up!" Christian said after I told her and Nina what happened the other day at the Backyard Fling.

I still couldn't believe that bitch Anika and I swear every time I thought about it, I wanted to kill her. Me and Dominick were taken all the way back when she walked in the trailer park. Then to find out her sick, twisted mind has been working all to get Dominick is disgusting.

"No, I promised Dominick I would trust him." I said as I stood over the pot of greens stirring them. I called the girls over to Dominick's house so I could give them this crazy ass update. Dominick left and said he had business to take care of, so I did my usual, cooked my stress away.

"Well give us her information, we didn't promise Dominick shit." Christian's crazy ass went on.

"I agree, we'll say you had nothing to do with it." Nina agreed.

I shook my head laughing at them. "Nieces no, trust me, I would have been had us pull up on that hoe strong, but I can't. Dominick broke it down for me as far as if she was to go to the police. I can't be away from him for any amount of years, y'all both know if it was Angel or Quest you'd do the same."

They both calmed down then because they knew I was telling the truth.

"What the fuck is with bitches like Kamila and Anika? They hate to see another woman bring out the best in a man that she failed. Like hoe, fuck off." Christian said, picking up her glass of wine.

I loved Dominick's kitchen because it had stone-pebble walls with this rust color, chrome appliances and his chairs around the bar were a rust color metal. I loved his home, well *palace*, he called it; it was enormous and so comfy. I also loved that he told me he would send his designer over if there was anything I wanted to change. I appreciated that but honestly, I wouldn't change a thing. I loved his taste and this cabin like feel, very cozy.

"I don't get that shit either, like with Marlo. He sees me happy with someone else and I know that's what really fucks his head up. Had I done my usual like went to Mama house and stayed a few days he wouldn't care as much. He refuses to believe that we were toxic and he even further refuses to believe he's gay." When Nina said that, she broke out laughing so hard it made us laugh.

"That nigga all fucked up, like how we both throwing ass in a circle, homie?" She joked some more.

This was the real Nina: silly, cracking jokes and playing with us. I know me and Christian missed this so much and we were loving it.

"But for real y'all, you know what really bothers me?" I asked them while sitting down across from both of them and picking up my glass of wine. "I don't like that when he leaves my mind...I never felt this way towards a guy before, but with Anika and him telling me to fall back and just trust him..."

"You feel like you'll get played, like what if he's with her right now." Christian filled in the gaps of what I was trying to say.

"Exactly. I don't know this feeling. Jealousy, insecure. I so be wanting to text and call him all day to see what he's doing, but I don't like coming off vulnerable. Our normal is like a few texts and maybe a phone call until we see each other. Like I haven't been home since meeting his parents and that's not like me. I get scared that if I go home, she might come over even though he's never had her over but..." I let out a long breath. "See how my mind is all over the place?" I said putting my glass to my lips.

"I feel you auntie, that's how I used to be about Quest."

"Really, how did you get over it?" I asked Christian adjusting myself in the chair.

"The crazy nigga put a head on my dashboard."

All three of us laughed hysterically and clinked our glasses together.

"So, I have something to tell y'all and you can't say anything till after the barbeque at Mama's tomorrow. Grandma is revealing her new man and I want the attention to stay on them." Nina told us while grabbing her Hermes Birkin purse. When she looked at us and smiled then held her left hand in the air flashing a big ass diamond, me and Christian went crazy.

"AHHHHHH!!" We both jumped and ran to her, almost knocking her down hugging her.

"Oh my gosh Nina-Bina!! When?! How!?" I screamed with a gin so wide I could feel air on my gums.

"It happened after the fire, and I said yes. But then the drama with Marlo and finding out he killed Angel's brother. I thought we were over and I gave him his ring back. Angel almost hit the roof and told me to never take it off. We agreed to wait till after the barbeque to tell everyone, but y'all know I can't hold water."

Me and Christian chuckled because she was right.

"Congratulations Nina, if anyone deserves this, it's you." Christian said and her voice cracked while she hugged her.

I went over and hugged her as well. "I couldn't pick a more perfect man for you than Angel. You two are so perfect for each other."

"Thank you two so much. I absolutely love both of you to pieces. I can't believe I'm at this point in my life, if you would have asked me this some months back I wouldn't believe it. I truly love that man so much because he makes sure I love myself. I'm genuinely happy." She told us with tears coming down her eyes.

Mine and Christian smiles were so bright. We were genuinely happy for our Nina-Bina.

**

"I don't know what feels better, this perfect temperature water or your skin on mine." Dominick's deep voice said to me. He had those honey golden eyes piercing mine with his arms stretched across the ledge of his pool.

It was the perfect evening to go for a swim; his in-ground pool was temperature controlled. The big stones he had built all around it with the dim lights made it so romantic. The view of the Las Vegas city was perfectly placed in front of us. The sounds of *Sade* were playing over his outside speakers. I had a tray of strawberries and whip cream for us and a bottle of Cristal Champagne on chill in the wine bucket.

I figured I'd wear a sexy thong two-piece bikini and do something romantic for my man. I had my hair in a high bun and just some diamond studs in my ears. Right now, I was feeding him a strawberry and kissing on his neck and chest. Dominick was so fine from his eyes, beard, long blonde-brunette hair, his voice and of course, his body covered in tribal and Egyptian tattoos. His big, muscular arms had my pussy ready for him all the time.

"I think I got the water beat." I joked with him.

"Hell yeah you do, I appreciate this tonight. I needed it. This shit with these Philly pussies and the beef with and Nina's ex is annoying as fuck. Then Anika drops this bullshit on me; I'm telling you right now Symba. So many people are going to die, but I promise it won't be us or anyone we love."

I looked his handsome face over and caressed the

side of it. "I know Dom baby, I trust you and I know you'll handle your business. We'll all come out on top," I said kissing his lips.

"Do you mean that?" He asked me while I fed him another strawberry. It was some whip cream on his top lip, so I of course licked it off.

"Mean what?" I asked him.

"When you say you trust me, do you mean it?" His thumb traced the bottom of my lip.

"Hell yeah I mean it, Dominick. I mean I want to fuck Anika up right now. But I trust you to handle it. I uh...I do sometimes think like, you know." I couldn't get my words right.

"You think what?" He asked looking curious.

I bit the corner of my lips. "I sometimes think about what you are doing when you're not with me. Like not with random girls, but with Anika. I hate this feeling because I am not an insecure person. But I can't help it with this situation. I saw her face; she loves you and is determined to get you to see that. It was scary." I dropped my head at the fact that I was actually admitting this out loud.

Dominick lifted my head up by my chin. "Thank you for sharing that with me. I'm so in tuned with you baby, I knew something was wrong. Let me tell you right now, I ain't the one. I don't gotta stick my dick into no pussy to see shit through. If I tell you I'm working, believe me, that's what I'm doing. You got all I need: beauty, smarts, attitude, body." He bit his bottom lip smiling and grabbing my booty. "All this ass, pussy and all the heart I need is all in you. I'm set for life, Sym baby."

I couldn't help but grin so big and he did too. "I love you so much, Dominick." I said grabbing his dick since he was naked in the pool.

That intense look was in his eyes as he roughly grabbed my legs and put them around his waist. I loved when he was like this, just handled my thick ass so good.

"Nobody does me like you do Dom, you stimulate my fucking soul baby. Ahhh...Uhhh." I moaned out because damn his dick felt so good. The water was making mini waves around us. My head went back a little while he sucked on my nipples.

"Argh shit, shit Sym you control my every being. Ugh fuck, this pussy."

Mm, I enjoyed him grunting and moaning whenever he was inside of me.

"Mine, all fucking mine." He said as we both picked up speed. I could feel my orgasm building up and so was his.

"Uhhh yes baby, all yours." I told him through my moans.

Dominick squeezed both my breasts with his big hand while his other one gripped my ass cheek, fucking me so good.

My body got warm and that tingling feeling came; it was elevating with each thrust.

"Ah! Ah! Ah! Ah Dom oh my gosh! I'm cumming baby, cum in me! Cum in me!"

"Ugh fuck!" Dominick filled me up with nut then he pushed his big tongue in my mouth. We were kissing so nasty, I got back went and I felt his dick grow. He picked me up and walked towards the wide steps of the pool.

Putting my left leg on his shoulder, Dom had me in a V shape position while he fucked me. We both looked down at his big dick pumping me, it had my lips opening so wide and it felt even better. I love when he would take it out, hit my clit with his dick then ease back in me. I didn't think I would ever stop cumming, I called out his name and he called out mine as we had a full-on fuck fest in his pool.

You make me happy

This you can bet, yeah

It's clear right beside me, yeah (come on, come on)

And I won't forget (come on, come on)

My sister was such a *Frankie Beverly and Maze* fan

so I wasn't surprised when we pulled up and she had it

blasting outside. I was glad Dominick decided to invite his

parents. I told him they weren't too ghetto for my Mama

or sister. He picked them up then we headed over.

Everyone was outside talking and laughing. It was a

different mood from the Backyard Fling, but it still was in

the hood.

"Hey everybody." I said as we walked into the gate.

I introduced my sister to Dominick's parents. My Mama

wasn't here yet; I couldn't wait to see her because I was

definitely going to see if I liked her new man.

Angel's pops was here and my sister invited a few

of her neighbors and Mama's card playing buddies. They were all at the long connecting tables playing cards, smoking cigarettes and drinking. Dominick's parents fell right in and everyone was getting along. There were lawn and folded chairs spread out. Dominick took my hand and we walked on the left side of the yard to his boys and my nieces.

"My nigga, I'm glad you're here." Quest was laughing as we sat down.

I was in the chair next to Dominick, but he still pulled it closer and rested his hand between my legs. I had on some jeggings and he wasn't touching my kat, but it still gave me goosebumps.

"Tell my crazy ass woman that pussy is a bigger deal over getting some head!" Quest said, sitting up in his chair still laughing.

"It's not a bigger deal, y'all will leave a bitch if she doesn't give good head." Christian added her opinion.

"I feel the same way." Nina said raising her hand.

Angel kissed it and said, "I love you bae, but you lost ya mind." He laughed.

"Sorry baby sisters, but I gotta agree with my boys." Dominick said and I looked at him with my mouth open.

"So you mean to tell me you don't like good head?" I asked him.

He chuckled and said, "I love head just as much as you love how God is good." We all fell out cracking up. "But you can teach a bitch how to suck dick, you can't teach her how to have good pussy."

"Exactly! That's what me and Angel were trying to tell these women."

Me and the girls waved the guys off.

"What if I had obese dick, but I could lick your pussy real good, would you fuck with me?" Dominick asked me and we all laughed loud again.

"What in the world is obese dick?" I asked him through my laugh.

"You know them 400lb men with that thumb-size dick, I'd be sittin' my big ass belly on the top of your ass while I fuck you." He cracked up while actually explaining his crazy antics.

I thought of that dick he has that I cradled like a proud mama then I thought about that big wide tongue he has, I needed both to live.

"Would you still have the same skills you do now? Because I could get some toys and we'd be good." I told the truth and the guys laughed while my nieces smacked their lips.

"Oh you'll switch up that quick auntie?!" Christian asked and I shrugged my shoulders.

"Fuck that, I would have to get a toy too." Nina said crossing her legs like if 'period pooh' was a person.

"No the hell you won't!" Angel quickly killed that shit making us all cackle. "You betta take this weak dick, pray over it and sleep tight every night."

"I'd cheat." Christian raised her index finger.

I laughed and high-fived her. "Okkkk niece!"

"I see yo' ass ain't learned the last time I left a body part in your car." Quest looked at Christian with his nose turned up.

I was laughing but when I looked over at Dominick, I laughed harder. "You know I would never cheat on you Dom baby, so stop looking at me like that."

He nodded his head slowly and said, "It's all good, I'ma scrape the hell out that pussy when we get home." He sat back in his chair, drinking his beer with his hand still rested between my legs.

"Did you just tell my auntie you'd scrape her pussy, Dominick? Oh my goodness!" Nina laughed, clapping her hands.

"That nigga a crazy ass white boy," Quest added.

"Leave my Dom baby alone," I said in his defense, putting my hand on the side of his face and kissing his lips.

"Yours." I said against his lips.

He did that light chuckle and eye squint I liked and said, "Mine."

"Ughhhh y'all are gross!" They all clowned us.

A horn blew and we saw my Mama and her man pull up in a red 2020 Chrysler 300.

"Don't even start, you getting the best dick of yo' life. Let your Mama get her coochie tossed," Dominick's annoying silly ass said in my ear.

I couldn't help but laugh and nudge him in his side because I was kind of disgusted of anything involving my Mama's coochie. As they walked in the gate I must say, she had a brightness to her that I'd never seen. Mama was gorgeous and still had a bounce back body for a sixty-three-year old woman, a medium BBW would be more precise.

Her guy though, had all us girls looking like *what thee entire fuck!* The man was so fine and from head to toe, he looked just like the guy *Jada Pinkett* was fucking in the movie *Set It Off.* No lie, he was identical to him, the only thing different was his facial hair and the hair on his head was salt & pepper. I was glad because that let me know he was in her age group.

"Hi, Mama." I was the first of us girls to snap out of the lustful trance. I hugged her and she smelled good, like a new perfume.

"Hi my baby girl." Smiling big she then hugged both her grand daughters and then her daughter. We all introduced her to Angel's dad, Dominick's parents and then to our guys. Then, she grabbed her man's hand and looked at us.

"Everyone this is Harvey, my fiancé."

All of our mouths dropped, especially mine. "Is he an American? He doesn't need a green card or does he have a creepy mama waiting to store you in the basement!?" I don't care how I sound, I seen that Tyler Perry movie.

Christian and Nina snickered, and Dominick pinched my booty on the low.

Mama laughed and looked at me, "No Symba it's nothing like that. We have been dating on the low for a year. I just didn't want to tell anyone, and I wanted to do things different this time around. We are picking up my ring tomorrow from the jeweler and we decided to have an outside wedding around April or May" Looking at me, my sister, Nina and Christian with a grin, she continued. "That leaves us with some months to plan everything." She explained and everyone else seemed ok with it, but I was skeptical.

"How are you, Symba? Your mother talks about you all the time and it's an honor to finally meet you. She's so proud of you; I've heard every accomplishment you've had and all about the school you want to start. I have some buddies on the education board who would like to hear your plan whenever you're ready."

Harvey shook my hand and said to me. His words had suave written all over it, but I felt some sincerity in them, too. He didn't have a sly smirk or look in his eye, his face was serious, and he looked me in my eyes when he talked. He then shook all the guys' hands and talked to them for a minute while I side talked with my nieces.

"I like him." Nina said looking at him.

"Me too, got damn Grandma picked a good one. Old ass is fine as hell. I bet his balls haven't dropped yet." Leave it to Christian to say something crazy and making us laugh.

"I still have to feel him out, but I'm open. I like how he is in some Nike gym-shoes, jeans and a simple shirt. He is definitely older; look at his watch, ring and necklace. Who the hell wears gold anymore?" I joked. Gold was cool, it's just not typically a young person's go to.

"Let's go talk to him and feel him out," Nina said and we made our way back over there.

In thirty-minutes, Harvey had every woman from me, to Dominick's mom drooling over him and listening to him tell us all about him. He has been divorced for ten-years, has three children and he showed us so many pictures of them on his Facebook page. His ex-wife is remarried, lives in Europe and comes to America to visit their three-children who live in Boston. Him and her are cordial and only come together for the children.

His oldest son has two kids, so he is a grandfather and a proud one. Harvey is a plastic surgeon and has his own practice. He is an outdoors person but loves fine dining. He had a few flaws as far as he said he used to date young girls, but I mean if you can see him, you would understand. I know I would have thrown it back for him if I met him first, for sure. But overall, he was good and really loved Mama.

Only time will tell if it will last, but I prayed it did. Us ladies were surrounding him talking and laughing for so long I forgot about the guys. I looked around and all of them, including Dominick's and Angel's dads were standing in the yard holding a beer and scowling expression, talking while looking at all of us.

I grabbed Nina and Christian to the side. "Look at them." Grinning, I pointed to the guys. "They are heated as fuck."

Christian and Nina broke out laughing and we were all shaking our heads. My sister went in the house to get all the sides for the grilled meet and I went inside to help her.

"Do you like him?" I asked my sister while she took the potato salad out the refrigerator.

"I been liked him when I met him back in January." She smirked at me.

"Am I that bad that Mama has to hide her relationships?" I put my hand on my hip and asked.

"Yeah you are Symba, but I get it, because of the way our dads did Mama. And the way Christian and Nina's dads did me, but you have to let Mama do her own thing."

I knew for years Christian and Nina had separate fathers. One day Mama and my sister were arguing when I was around eleven and it came out. I promised to never say anything, and I kept it because I didn't want to destroy anything. I believed and at least hoped my sister had her reasons.

"I'll try, but the minute he hurts her, I'm fucking him up." We both laughed but I was for real.

Going back outside, we all started having a good time. My sister put her foot in the meat she grilled and the sides she cooked. Her music really gave it a barbeque vibe, they guys played cards and us ladies even got in on a few hands as well with our plates on our lap. I had glanced over at Christian and she was looking like she was in a daze. Her purse was on the ground between her legs and she had what looked like napkins peeking out of it. At first, I didn't pay it any attention until she got up and headed in the house, taking her purse with her. Everyone else was talking and enjoying themselves, but I got up and followed her inside.

"Are you ok?" I asked her when I came all the way in the house and into the kitchen.

I scared her because she jumped and stood in front

of the garbage, like she was using her back to block what she was doing.

"Yeah, I'll be out in a minute."

I went around her and she moved the same way I did. "Christian, what are you doing? Tell me you're not a crackhead now." I breathed out tiredly. "I really don't feel like dealing with crackhead behavior right now."

She laughed and turned around. "No auntie, I am not a crackhead." She opened up here purse and took two napkins out and threw them in the garbage.

"It's potato salad."

When she said that, I looked at her confused as hell. "But that's your favorite."

"It was before I found out I was pregnant, and the texture makes me want to throw up."

I was about to jump and scream but she stopped me. "I have not told anyone yet, not even Quest, so please don't say shit."

Her hand was over my mouth. I nodded my head up and down real fast and she moved it.

"Why are you keeping this a secret? You know Quest won't be upset." I asked her.

"Because I'm still taking it in, I never thought of having kids." She leaned against the counter.

"I understand that. I would be the same way. Take your time but at least let Quest know, he'll be so excited." She agreed and we hugged. "Oh my gosh, you're going to be a mommy." I squealed out smiling big.

"I know right." I hugged her one more time and we walked back outside.

Before we could even close the door all the way, an all-black Charger with deep tinted windows turned the corner so hard its tires screeched. Then it zoomed down the street and as soon as it got close, it intentionally ran over my sister's street-side mailbox then went back down the street, turning the corner hard as hell again.

"What the hell! I just brought that damn mailbox, fucking young hoodlums!" My sister shouted, about to go out the gate, but Angel stopped her.

"Just in case they come back, let's wait." He said to her.

"That wasn't hoodlums, that was Marlo." Nina said and we all looked at her. "I know that car, it's his Mom's car." Her sentence wasn't even finished before Angel flew out the gate to his car.

"Angel!?" Nina yelled out to him.

"Don't do it, man!!" Quest shouted to him too, but Angel was on a mission.

Dominick and Quest ran after him, but they weren't quick enough. Angel's tires burned rubber as he took off down the street. Dominick jumped in the passenger seat of Quest's car and they took off after him.

"Oh my gosh. Oh my gosh. Oh my gosh." Nina

hurried back to her purse, grabbing her phone calling Angel.

"He's not answering!" She yelled and stomped, dialing again.

"Calm down Nina, Quest and Dominick will track him down and it will be fine. Just try to calm down," Christian told her and I was rubbing her back.

"I hate that extra crispy ass fucker, Marlo." My mama said, looking down the street hoping to see something.

"Don't worry darling, them two won't let shit happen to Angel." Dominick's dad told Nina.

We were trying to get back to having fun and take Nina's mind off of the car chase. Every car that rode past had her hopping up and looking to see if it was them with Angel. It took about an hour before all three of them came back. By then, Dominick's dad lit some wood and paper inside the grill to start a knock-off bonfire. They were

tipsy, playing blues music and still playing cards. Even

Harvey was down with them.

"Are y'all ok?" I asked them when they came

through the gate.

Dominick and Quest were looking like they were

shocked a little. Angel came in, walked passed all of us,

grabbed Nina's hand kissing it and they walked back out

the gate to his car. We watched him open her door, let her

inside and then get in the driver's side and pull off.

"He's out for blood. I ain't never seen him like

this." Dominick said to me and then he kissed my

forehead.

"Will she—"

"That nigga will never hurt Nina." Quest told us, putting

his arm around Christian's waist. "It's about his brother,

so it's personal."

"Did he track down the car?" I asked Dominick and

he shook his head no.

We all felt for him and knew Marlo was going to get his.

**

After the barbeque, we ended our night around nine at night. The old people were drunk as hell, but I was glad everyone had a good time despite the whole mailbox thing. Nina video chatted me and Christian on three-way to tell us she was ok. Angel wasn't mad at her, he just wanted to be alone with just her. I couldn't believe all that was going on, good and bad things.

Anika, Marlo, Kamila and a bunch of other shit me and my nieces probably didn't know about. But in the midst of it all, we have so much good news. Nina and my Mama are engaged, and Christian is pregnant. I couldn't believe it. In the course of a few months, they are about to have life changing experiences. Even me, I couldn't believe all the shit I talked about love and no relationships.

Here I am, so madly in love with this sexy ass man who was lying between my legs kissing all on my stomach and belly button. We took a shower when we got home, put on a movie and now were laying in the bed. My hands were massaging his scalp while he just kissed on me.

"This is all mine." He looked up at me and said then kissed my stomach again. I love how intimate we were with each other.

"Forever?" I asked him, giggling because the tip of his beard was tickling my stomach.

"Fuck yeah, Symba. You. Are. My. Everything." He said in between kisses on my thighs.

I was looking down at him smiling at how silly and cute he was being. My phone started ringing and he moved his way down to my kitty. I tried to move so I could grab my phone, but he locked me down with his long arms around my thighs. I was going to ignore the call, but it rang again.

"Ugh Dom baby, let me answer the phone." I moaned out and Dominick shook his head while still licking me so good.

I stretched all the way over with my strength and finally got a hold of my phone. When I saw Lanail's name and looked at the time, I answered with hesitation.

"Hello." I had to do my best to speak normal because I was on the verge of cumming.

"Symba?" Her voice was cracking and I knew she was whispering.

I sat up. "What's wrong?" When I said that and Dominick heard my voice, he stopped and looked up at me.

"I'm sorry to bother you, I just didn't know who else to call. I'm in trouble and really need your help." Now she was crying hard, but still whispering.

"It's ok, I told you to call anytime. What's wrong?"

"I'm in the bathroom hiding out and I am really scared. I got into some stuff and I just want out, I don't want to do this anymore."

I was getting up and going to Dominick's closet to grab some leggings and a shirt. I had some clothes over here because I was here a lot. Dominick was behind me asking me what was going on, but I had to ignore him.

"Just tell me where you are, Lanail, I'll come and get you."

"I can text you where I am, please hurry." She pleaded.

"Ok, just stall and play it cool. I'm coming," Hanging up, I put some gym-shoes on.

"Symba what the hell is going on?" Dominick asked me, fully dressed in sweats now.

"One of my students is in trouble and I need to get

to her." I held up my phone and to show him her text message.

"What the fuck she doing at this Motel? Ain't shit over there but hookers and junkies. Let's roll," he told me, grabbing my hand.

When we got to the address Lanail texted me, Dominick was right. It was filled with hookers outside whistling down every car that rode by. There were dark alleys where cars were turning into, probably about to fuck. This was a whole other side of Nevada I've never seen.

"Stay close to me and do as I say," Dominick told me as we both got out.

"Ok." I said, looking around with disturbance all over my face. I held his hand while he kept me behind him.

"Bitch! We didn't pay for you to stay in the bathroom all night!" We heard some guy say when we made it to the room number Lanail texted me. I used my

other hand to cover my mouth because I didn't know what

kind of shit she got herself into.

Dominick took out his chrome revolver gun,

twisted the silencer on it and looked at me. "Squat down

and don't come in until I say so. When I knock on the door,

you say, 'It's me, Lanail' when you hear them ask who it is."

His face let me know he wasn't bullshitting, so I agreed and

did what he said. He knocked on the door and like

Dominick said, one of the guys asked who it was.

"It's me, Lanail." I said.

"Hell yeah, she called another girl." The guy laughed

and when he opened the door, I couldn't believe my eyes.

It was like a scene from a damn action movie. Dominick

shot the guy in the head then I heard four more shots.

"Come on, baby." He called out to me.

I came into the room and gasped when I saw five

dead bodies. There was a camera standing on a tripod

stand. They were about to gang bang her and record it. I saw the bathroom door and knocked on it.

"Lanail, it's me Symba." When I said that, she opened the door crying and ran into my arms.

"It's ok, shhh, it's ok you're safe." I rubbed her back and kissed the top of her head.

"Come on, let's go." Dominick said and he led us to his car.

"You can take us to my house, Dom." I told him when we started driving.

"Hell no, I don't know who is after her or what she's into. The safest place for y'all to be is at my house. Give her a guest room, tell me what all she got going on and then we can handle everything else in the morning." He looked from the road, then to me.

"Ok, thank you." I gave him a half smile, crossing my legs. He rested his hand between them the whole ride back to his house.

"No need to thank me."

We got back home and I set Lanail up in a guest room. I gave her one of my grandma gowns I had over here and let her take a shower. While she handled her hygiene, I went to Dominick's room.

"You were amazing tonight, how do you know what to do on queue like that?" I asked him while taking my clothes off.

Dominick was in his closet with me, taking his clothes off as well. "In my line of work, you gotta be quick on your feet. But it also comes from growing up like I did. Me, Angel and Quest were some bad ass kids. Even before we all met, I grew up around a lot of dope dealers, thieves and criminals on every level. You pick up shit along the way, how to be smart and how to survive.

It also teaches you a lot of what *not* to do. I watched a lot of people demise themselves from being stupid. I refuse to be one of them, I'm human so some shit may slip pass me. But I always figure it out and when I do, I show no mercy." He was talking, but looking like a different person. Everything he said was the truth and I believed it. Dominick didn't walk around playing a 'wanna be' part. This was really him and he was only different with the ones he loved.

I put on some boyshorts and one of Dominick's beaters. "I'm gonna go talk to her and then I'll come back and tell you what I know."

"Ok." He responded and kissed me on the lips.

The guest room was down his long hall and to the left. I knocked on the door and she told me to come in. She had the TV on, sitting in the middle of the bed. Her eyes were still puffy from all the crying she was doing. I sat down at the edge of the bed and turned to face her.

"Start from the beginning."

Taking a deep breath, she began. "Remember I told you my friend was making all this money? New clothes, shoes, purses and jewelry... well I asked her what she was doing and she told me her cousin's boyfriend had a way we can make a lot of money. He had a friend who you know...managed girls."

I looked confused. "Managed girls? Like a pimp?"

"Yeah, like a pimp. I started out doing good, I made money and everyone was nice. I make good money and didn't care about anything. I haven't been to school not one day and it's the middle of November, but I didn't care. My mama put me out and I still didn't care because I was living with my friend and the guy who was in charge. Then my friend started sleeping with him and he tried to sleep with me.

I denied him and everything changed. I started getting johns from bad neighborhoods. He told me I didn't have a choice and tonight, I was supposed to meet with someone at that Motel. When I got there, his friends were there. I played it off like I had to use the bathroom and I called you." By now she was crying. "I'm sorry Symba, I let all the material stuff cloud my judgment, I've messed up my relationship with my Mom and I have thrown away my senior year."

I felt bad so I hugged her. "You can always start over, Lanail, it's not too late. But let me ask you this, who are the guys that are in charge and drives y'all around?" I didn't know if she would tell me or not, but it was worth the shot.

Wiping her eyes she said, "Gunna, Money and Sincere."

I literally had to tell myself to hold it together and not wear my emotions. Forcing a small smile, I stood up and told her to get some rest. Walking out her room I went back to Dominick's at a lost for words. I can't believe I went out with someone who pimp's girls, underage one's at that. I got in bed with my man and saw he was watching *Mall Cop*. I laid next to him and told him what Lanail told me.

"Damn, man I would kill every fucking body if my daughter got caught up in some shit like that." He said with his hand rested between my legs.

"Gunna, Sincere and Money." I said their names.

Dominick looked at me with his eyebrows furrowed. "What?"

"That's the names she just gave me, I think Gunna is the pimp and Money and Sincere are his errand boys."

"Please tell me you fuckin' with me, Symba." He closed his eyes for a second then pinched the bridge of his nose.

"I wish I was, but I seen the guy Money pick her up from the dance school in August. He didn't see me, but I saw his tattoo. To think I could have sle—" I stopped talking when I realized who I was talking to.

"I would have killed him and put yo' ass in the hospital."

I laughed but he didn't crack a smile. "I would never talk to you again."

"Yes you would have, trust me you would have. I'd nurse you back to health, you'd learn your lesson and then we'd move on." His hand lightly squeezed my inner thigh. "I love keeping my hand right here, it's always warm as hell." He admitted what he just said before that was nothing.

I wasn't even about to go back and forth with him because my Dom baby wasn't right in the head.

"In the morning she is going to give me an address for Gunna. Right now, I need you to give me her number so I can have my boy Cyrus keep a track on her phone."

I reached on the nightstand and grabbed my phone and the DVD remote. Reading the number off to him, I got up and walked to the DVD collection he had in the case on the side of his TV. While he was on the phone, I picked out *Ride Along 2* for us to watch. Dominick hung up when I walked back over to the bed.

"Let's watch a DVD," I was about to hit the button on the remote for the TV to go to HDM2 but Dominick freaked out.

"No! I mean, my BluRay doesn't work." As he was saying it, he was reaching his arm out for the remote.

It didn't take a rocket scientist to know he was hiding something, I turned my nose up and stepped back from him. "Why are you so jumpy?" I asked him.

"I'm not jumpy Symba, just give me the remote."

"No." I put it behind my back and stepped back some more.

Dominick got out the bed on his side and slowly walked around to me. "Give me the damn remote, Symba."

I moved to the right the more he moved closer to

me. "I said no! What are you hiding, is it porn? Ah!" I laughed while jumping on the bed when he ran towards me. I was too fast and he missed me, now I was on his side.

"Oh hell naw, if you're willing to chase me, then I gotta see." I looked down at the remote and his muscular ass jumped over the bed like fucking *Scar* jumped through the fire on *The Lion King*. I was still too quick and while I ran around the bed, I hit the button to go to HDM2. When I looked at the TV, I saw *The Aristocats* movie title on the screen.

Dominick ran towards me again and I jumped on the bed, cracking up. "Awww you watch *The Aristocats?* It's a good movie, my Dom baby is sensitive...Ah!" I yelled out when he grabbed my ankles and made me fall back on his colossal ass bed.

"Would you give me the damn remote, woman!" He said, trying to wrestle me, but I was putting up a fight.

"Nope! Let's talk about this, I'ma start calling you O'Malley!" I got out between laughing.

It was so sexy and fun seeing and having him laugh and play back with me. Then he got me by wrapping his arm around my waist and pulled me into his hard chest, kissing me so deep I dropped the remote on the bed.

"You cheated." I said once we broke our kiss for some air.

"I never play fair when it comes to you." His sexy, heavy voice said to me. "Don't be thinking I just be home watching Disney movies." He chuckled and said. "This was Denise's favorite movie and I like to go to sleep with it on."

Kissing his lips again, I put my arms around his neck. "I think that's really sweet. Let's watch it, come on." We both laid down in the bed and got comfortable while he pushed play.

Quest

"Cyrus, tell me you got something?" I answered my phone when I saw who it was calling me.

"I have a credit card purchase under her son Mick's name on Amazon and I have a delivery address."

I hit the air, geeked as hell. "This is why we pay yo' ass bank. Text me all the info; I'll meet you at your house tomorrow with your money."

"Can do."

When he hung up it turned my day from good to great. "I got a location on Edith." I told Dominick and Angel. We were loading bodies up in Burt's furnace. It was only the three of us down here. Suddenly we heard a loud thud and then Burt and his buddy came down, dragging three bodies.

"Here, throw these in there too." He said to us.

"Who the hell are they?" I asked him, looking at the faces to see if any of these people looked familiar.

"That's Marlo's Grandma, cousin and aunt." When he said that, the three of us looked at Burt with our eyes open.

You see, Burt was about his business. Designer tailored suits, always a nice piece of real gold jewelry. He reminded me of a dark skin version of the dad from the movie *Coming To America*. We knew he had another side of him because the nigga is African but got damn we didn't know he would just off someone.

"You gotta strip away the layers to expose the rot." He said and then him and his boy walked upstairs.

"Shit, I think that nigga worse than you." Angel said pointing to Dominick who then gave him the middle finger.

"So, how are we gonna handle Edith?" Dominick

asked me when we got outside. "I say we hang her upside down til' she bleeds from her ears and knees."

"See, I normally would clown you about your psychotic ideas but that actually sounds good." I said to him, really thinking about that. "But I wanna get at that tomorrow night, today I need to be with my woman. Something is up with her, I think it's the loss of her job, but she's been acting a little different lately." I hit the alarm to my car.

"Aight, just let us know. I need to go pick me and Nina's shoes up for Dominick's party Saturday night." Angel added getting into his car.

"Bet, I'll text y'all." I said and after they agreed we all pulled off in opposite directions.

I was slowly coming around to accepting my mom's death. I think what Christian told me really helped; Ma's mind had been clouded all day, every day. Hearing voices, switching personalities, having break downs and only being able to sleep with heavy medication. That's no way to live, now she was at peace and sleeping with a sound mind.

I stop beating myself up and started celebrating the fact that I was a good son to her. I loved her so much and would give up any and everything so she could get the proper help. Christian made me see all of that. I loved that woman so much and she wonders why I cut a nigga's head off for her. All of her belonged to me, and I was so glad she finally got with the shit and accepted it.

That's why I didn't like that something was bothering her. I called my housekeeper and she told me that no one was at my house, so I was headed over to Christian's house to get her. I normally would just spend the night wherever she was, but I really wanted to be in my bed tonight after we go to dinner.

"Hey, Q!" Symba's loud ass opened the door and

greeted me.

"You just loud for no reason, ghetto ass." I joked. I like fucking with baby sister because she could take jokes like a nigga and dish like one, too.

"I'm no louder than you when my niece be putting it on you." Her ass started imitating me. See what I mean? Symba was one of the homies.

"Why you talking like that in front of children?" I looked at the young girl sitting on her couch. "How you doing young mama?" I spoke to her.

She seemed to be in her teens, probably, and she waved back "I'm fine."

"Get you a new role model." I told her jokingly and Symba pushed me, making me crack up. I walked to Christian's room and opened the door. She was laying across her bed, fully dressed and with the TV on. Her shoes were off her feet and she had some navy-blue leggings on and a grey off the shoulder shirt. That round soft booty and them long legs were looking good even though they weren't exposed. I laid next to her and brought her close as hell to my body.

"Sugar tits, wake up bae." I said in her ear, then I kissed it and her neck.

"Mmm." She moaned so sexy that my dick twitched.

"Stop moaning like that before I slide up in you," I whispered in her ear.

I guess she didn't believe me because she tooted that soft booty against my dick. "I miss you, Quest." She cooed out to me with her hands going inside my Nike track pants. Her back was to me and when her soft hands grabbed my dick, it grew.

I loved this shit about Christian. She would whip my dick out no matter where we were and either suck it or put that pussy on it.

"I miss you too, Christian." I told her while pulling

her leggings half down. It took no effort for my dick to get between them cheeks and inside that warm kat.

"Fuck bae, yo' pussy so wet and snug, shit." I moaned low in her ear. She was so wet you could hear it and I was pumping her slowly. I couldn't speed up because I swear I was going to bust and I wasn't trying to be no two-minute nigga. I put my hand around her neck and kissed her jaw, then I slid my two fingers in her mouth and she started licking on them. Her tongue was wet and felt good as hell. We were both moaning and breathing hard while she just gushed all over me.

"Why the fuck you feel this good?" I moaned in her ear. I mean she always felt bomb but got damn today was different. I was literally on another planet, eyes closed and all.

"Mmmm. It's probably because I'm pregnant, bae."

I stopped moving when she said that, dick still hard

as a brick inside of her. I had to process what she just said. Once I replayed it in my mind about three times, I grabbed her jaw gently and turned her face to mine. Looking at her gorgeous chocolate face, I smiled.

"You're gonna have my baby?" My smile stretched further, making hers appear just as big.

"Yes I am. Ahhh." She moaned out when I started moving again.

"Say it bae, tell me. Ugh, fuck."

"I'm gonna have your baby Quest." I gave her a sloppy kiss so deep it made her get wetter.

"I love you. You my family forever now Christian." I spoke in her ear.

"We love you more, bae."

Man I will never forget those words or this moment. After we both got off, I cleaned us up. We went to eat at Golden Star Steakhouse and then I took her back to my house and made love to her all night.

"Congratulations, nigga!" Angel gave me a pound and hugged me.

"Man, that shit is dope as hell!" Dominick followed behind him and gave me some love.

"Thank you, I appreciate it y'all, for real. I can't believe this shit, seems unreal."

I had been smiling since Christian told me she was pregnant. I never thought about being a father again after Kamila cheated on me. I figured I couldn't really trust any bitch but with Christian, I could see it all. Our kids, a home, her being pregnant and getting all round driving me crazy with her weird cravings. I saw it all and we were making it real. Her first doctor's appointment was in a few days and we both couldn't wait.

"So you the first one of us to be a daddy, that is wild as hell. I thought for sure Angel would have been the first, especially when he was fucking with that bitch with the gap." Dominick said as I drove us in our blackout van.

"Why the hell would you think me and Becka would have a baby?" Angel asked from the back seat.

Me and Dominick looked at each other and laughed. "Homie that bitch used to be up yo' ass. You couldn't do shit without her wanting to know every detail," I spoke.

"That's how you knew I wasn't about to get her pregnant, she had trust issues."

Dominick looked at him quick as hell. "Muthafucka you was cheating like you ain't never heard of coochie before." We all laughed hard as hell.

"Yeah but she didn't know that, the fact that she didn't trust me made me cheat more," he laughed and said. "Naw but for real, I would never do that shit to Nina. I can't wait till I knock her ass up."

Dominick nodded his head. "Hell yeah, that's how I

feel about Symba, I want a beautiful baby girl with her."

"You having a boy my nigga, another creepy you with them crazy eyes." I told him laughing.

"I bet you have a boy, I have a girl." He looked at me and said.

"Aight let's put money on it, ten-grand that I have a girl and you have a boy." I held my closed fist out to him while I turned down the street.

"Wait, I want in on that." Angel added.

"Whose side you on?" Dominick asked him.

"Yours, I don't think God will give you a junior psycho and he gon' give Quest a mini him." Angel pounded our fists and we sealed the bet.

"That ain't Edith's car." I said to them when we parked some houses down to where Edith was.

"Also, this nice ass neighborhood costs more than twenty G's that she got deposited in her bank. Cyrus said she didn't have any other big deposits and she only had

thirty-grand total in her account. How the fuck she afford

this house and a 2020 Audi Q8?" Angel pointed out to us.

"I don't know, but we about to find out." I told

them as we started walking.

The two of them had a gun and I had my Tapanga

knife, two inches of sharp blade. Each of us had a small

picking kit so we can each pick the locks. I was taking the

front door, Angel was taking the back and Dominick was

taking the side door.

Her new house was a one-story home with a curve

driveway and white and black brick. Getting inside was

very easy and I just shook my head because she didn't

even have an alarm. Making my way through the living

room, it was some open boxes which showed that she was

still unpacking. All her furniture looked like it didn't

belong in a house this nice, that's how I knew she didn't

pay for it. Getting to the kitchen, we saw Angel down the

hall. You could hear moaning and my stomach tossed thinking of Edith's ugly ass fucking.

Phew! I shot the old nigga fucking her from the back in the head.

"Ah—" *Punch!*

I hit her straight in her face before she could scream, causing her mouth to bleed.

"Ugh it smells like icy hot and prune juice in here." Dominick said, holding his nose. Fool ass.

While Dominick and Angel disposed of the dead body, I handled Edith. "Now you know damn well I was going to find you." I leaned against her dresser and threw her the robe on the floor because her body was disgusting.

"P-P-Please, Mr. Foster don't kill me, I swear I didn't want to do it." She had the nerve to cry out for me.

I chuckled and looked at her. "Yeah you did. You

wanted to because of the house, car and money you got. You were tired of your job and your no-good kids would never be able to take care of you this way. But you knew you could have came to me and I would have given you more, just for turning over the muthafuckas who asked you to kill her." I got angry just thinking about it.

"I made sure she didn't suffer, I swear, she didn't suffer." She was shaking with blood dripping from her mouth and snot coming from her nose.

"You made sure she didn't suffer?" I asked her while I pushed off the dresser and walked towards her. When I got close, I grabbed her around her neck, lifting her off the bed and slamming her against the wall.

"You think I give a damn that she didn't suffer? My woman is pregnant. You took my child's grandmother. They will never have a relationship. All for what, something you could have gotten from me had you just asked?" I was in her face with my eyes bucked and my mouth tight.

"Because my mother loved you, I will give you the opportunity to live. But, you betta tell me who the hell paid you to kill her. Think carefully because if you play with me, I will kill you. You understand?" I asked her and she nodded her head slowly. I loosened my hand a little and waited for her to talk.

Tears were pouring from her eyes, but I didn't give a damn. "It was K-Kamila."

I had to blink fast so I could make sure I wasn't hearing shit and that what she said was real. "Why would she have you do this?"

"You left her and she knew how to get back at you." Edith's voice struggled out.

I looked around the room then at her again. "Kamila can't afford no house and car like this; who else was helping her?" I asked through gritted teeth.

"I don't know, I swear I don't know. I got money wired in my account, a new house, car and she told me to lay low until she could get me out the state."

I never imagined that bitch Kamila to do me this dirty. When I get my hands on that hoe, oooh my goodness I was killing her. I looked at Edith and squeezed her neck tighter, lifting her back off her feet against the wall.

"Do you wanna go home to your kids or die?" I asked her.

"My k-k-ids, please let me go with my kids."

I smiled at her and said, "As you wish." I slid my blade between her eyes and snatched it out, doing it two more times. When her body hit the floor, the clean-up crew walked in just in time as I walked out.

"You find anything out?" Angel asked me, him and Dominick were standing by the van waiting on me.

I threw Dominick the keys and opened the back

door so I could get inside. "Yeah, Kamila had her do it." I said then climbed inside.

I know the both of them were thrown back when I said that, but right now I wanted to head to her house and end her.

**

Fill 'em with vibes (yeah), get in and ride (yeah, yeah)
And no, a nigga not blind (uh-uh)
But I keep the stick and I'm firin' (bitch)
I ain't met a nigga in life
That's fuckin' with me, say he did, then he lyin' (mmh, mmh)

Dababy-Vibez was blasting loud through Lust night club. It was my boy Dominick's birthday and we were in here on another level of lit! Everything was luxury from the red carpet we had laid out all over VIP, to the expensive champagne we had, fresh lobsters and crab legs flown in from Maine laid out buffet style to how we were all dressed. Me and the fellas had on designer three-piece tailored suits.

Everyone in the club had on black and white except for Dominick and Symba. They rocked gold and red. He did have his colors yellow and blue, but he changed them. I dug my nigga's custom Armani red and gold shoes. He had him and his woman iced the fuck out. I was proud of him because he did it big. The big ass tower of a cake had the number '31' on top of it.

Christian walked over to me in her fitted long black dress that squeezed her body and had a high slit on the side. Her stomach wasn't showing yet, but I always rubbed it like it was. We were all looking fly and having a good ass time. I needed this tonight; Kamila was no where to be found and I was getting pissed. That hoe moved on me and because I was with her for five years, she knew how I moved, so she was smart.

Cyrus couldn't find any trace of her, bank account, credit cards, even health insurance. I even staked out her job and still never found her. But it was all good; I was coming for her and it was no place she could hide. Dumb bitch really took shit to another level and killed my mother. I kept eyes on her Mama and brother twenty-four-seven and they still came up with nothing. That hoe was being wise, but I knew she would slip.

"You look so good tonight, chocolate ass. Mm! I'm eating that booty good as hell tonight, you gon' be the definition of a wet ass." I told Christian in her ear. I was drunk and high as hell, but I knew what the fuck I was saying, she looked beyond sexy tonight.

"You need help." She said giggling at what I said then she crossed them long legs and ran her fingers through my long beard.

Symba and Nina came over to us, looking like some queens as well. "Come dance with us." Nina said to Christian, pulling her up.

It was cool with me. I was about to smoke and kick it with my boys. "I'm surprised you let Symba go dance with that dress on." I teased Dominick then I poured some Cristal in my glass.

He blew smoke from his blunt out his mouth. "My woman know not to get to crazy unless she want me to fuck up everybody night."

Me and Angel laughed. "How you holding up after finding out everything?" Angel asked me.

I knew he was talking about the mess with Edith and Kamila. "I'm good, I know what it is now. I was hurt as fuck when I first found out because you know I got history with that bitch. But it is what it is, until my last days, I will hunt for that hoe every day until I take her head off."

They both nodded their head in agreement.

"Did you tell Christian?" Dominick asked me.

I lit my blunt. "Naw, I just want her to focus on being pregnant, but I might. I don't know yet."

After we smoked and chatted it up some, we got up and stood at the top of the steel rail overlooking the entire club. We could see our ladies on the floor dancing and all I could see was Christian's chocolate legs peeking from the long slit of her dress. It was all good because she was dancing with Nina and Symba; niggas knew not to fuck with our women.

"Dominick!?"

We turned around when someone called his name like he was in trouble. I think we were all surprised to see Anika standing there with a scowl on her face and her hand on her hips. There was another chick standing on the side with her, who was looking at Angel like she wanted to pull his dick out.

"You ignore every call and text as if our last conversation was a joke. Now, you don't invite me to your birthday party?" Her loud ass voice was up for no damn reason because the music wasn't as loud as it was downstairs.

"I swear, I'm killing my fucking security." Angel said since this was his club.

Dominick walked over to her, looking like he wanted to drop her right then and there. "What the fuck are you doing here? Take yo' stupid ass friend and get the hell on."

"No! You're my...Ahh!" Anika yelled when Symba came out of no where, grabbing a hand full of her hair making her lean back further than *Fat Joe*.

"He ain't shit of yours!" Symba yelled in Anika's face.

Me and Angel had to grab Christian and Nina when

they swung on her friend, knocking that bitch literally out her heels.

"You are fucking pregnant; if something happen to my baby I gotta go through the club and cut every woman's uterus out! Why you wanna put all that stress on me!?" I yelled at Christian when I had her ass in the corner.

"Fuck all of that, I got my baby. These bitches over-stepping!" Christian was trying to look over me, but I was like a brick wall blocking her, so she wasn't going anywhere. Angel was next to me doing the same thing.

"I got her bro, go check on Dominick." Angel told me and I gave Christian a 'don't fuck with me' look and went to make sure Dominick and Symba were good.

I got back over there and security was carrying Anika and her friend out the club, all in the air. Anika was calling Dominick's name so loud and dramatic like the nigga was holding her life in his hands. It was funny as hell, but he wasn't paying attention, he was making sure Symba was ok and calm.

"I'm sorry, but I'm fucking not. She shouldn't have even tried this shit." Symba said as the girls came over and fixed her dress.

"Why y'all always gotta fight in my club?" Angel joked and said to Dominick and Symba.

"She started it when she was all in my Dom baby's face." Symba put her arms around Dominick's waist then he bent down and kissed her.

We all got sick to our stomachs and started talking shit. We ate some more food, danced with our ladies then the D.J. had the entire club sing happy birthday to Dominick. He let Symba blow out his candles and all of VVIP had some of his good chocolate-vanilla swirl cake.

"You ok, bae?" Christian asked me when she came and sat down next to me with a black fluffy comforter around her.

We were at my crib, freshly showered and I wanted to step outside under the dark sky for a minute. It was three in the morning and I had some shit on my mind.

I watched her get comfortable. Her hair was bone straight for Dominick's party, but after our shower she put it in a ponytail. When she caught me looking at her, she opened her arms so I could get in the blanket with her. I wrapped my arms around her waist and kissed her for a minute, then I decided to be real with her.

"I found Edith and killed her."

Christian turned to face me all the way. "How do you feel?"

"I would feel better, but she told me who had her kill Ma; it was Kamila."

Her eyes almost fell on the floor. "Wow, wow. I'm so sorry Quest, I know that hurts you to know that she would go that far." When she hugged me I was shocked. I thought she would flip or have an attitude because this bothered me so much. I was so used to Kamila popping off no matter what came out my mouth, if it involved another woman then she was tripping. But Christian held me and just showed me nothing but love; that's how I knew then that I was marrying her.

"I'm killing her bae, I just want you to know that. She's moving smart though and basically wiped herself off the face of the earth. Even Edith's house and car she put in another name."

Christian sat looking at me like a green light went off. "I think I know how to find her, or at least I can see if she's still in Nevada. You said she moved... I can get a list of all home sold within the past four months and the names they're under. I bet you she put it under a name that is important to her. My friend Molly can get the list for me; she quit but I know she still has her access information."

"Hell yeah bae, if you could get that for me, that would help me out a lot." I told her. "You the shit you know that? I'm glad I got'chu on my team." I kissed her again and my hand went between her legs. She had on a short night gown. "I want you to cum for me before I fuck you," I said in a low tone while my fingers tickled her pearl.

I propped her legs on the lawn love seat we were sitting on then I slid the thin straps down her smooth shoulder. Her C-cup breasts with those Hershey nipples were revealed and I started licking and sucking on them like a never-ending sweet piece of candy. My fingers were fucking her nice and slow and she was wetter than wet. I licked all the way from her breasts to her neck, then I shoved my tongue so far in her mouth her head went back.

"Cum for me bae, make that fucking kat cum." I said, then I sucked on her bottom lip.

"Ahhh Quest, shit. Ahhh." While she moaned, her breathing changed and I knew shew was getting closer. "I'm cumminggg, ah." She licked them sexy lips of hers and her face had that relaxation on it.

"Yeah, mm!" I said kissing her cheek and sliding my two fingers out her. Of course, I licked my fingers clean then I stood up and dropped my basketball shorts because it was my turn.

"Arch that sexy back and cross them legs." I told her and I enjoyed watching her do what I said.

I slowly slid my dick up and down between her ass cheeks and before I went inside her kat, I swirled the head all around her juices. I was teasing her, getting her even more wet then I slid inside. After we both moaned out and were still for a minute, I started fucking her at a medium pace.

"Quest oh my gosh, oh my gosh." Her moans were so damn sexy, I had to bit my lip hard as hell and lean my head back so I wouldn't cum right now. Once I gained control, I stopped moving and let her fuck me. Looking down at that luscious chocolate ass, I slapped them ass cheeks.

"Look at'chu makin' a mess on this dick. Yeah bae, fuck yo' nigga back, fuck yo' nigga back. Oooh, shit."

Slap! Slap! I hit them cheeks again.

"Slow the fuck down for a second." I grunted out to her.

She slowed down and started rotating that ass like some tires on a car. I was just enjoying the sight as I squeezed her booty.

"Look at that." *Slap!* "Look how wet that pussy is, why I be having that pussy so wet?" *Slap!* I hit her booty again and she cried out. "Huh Christian, why Quest be having that muthafuckin pussy so wet?" My voice was husky as hell, and I was in paradise. Once I was done with the nice and slow shit, I grabbed her soft booty roughly with my nails and started pounding her shit.

"Ahhh! Uhhh, bae!" Christian was loud, but that farting pussy was louder.

I leaned my head back and had my tongue out like a dead dog all while fucking her until we both came hard as hell.

Angel

"Will you please tell me the surprise?" Nina was smiling, bouncing around in the car like a kid, but it was cute as fuck.

"Nope, I'ma make you wait like I make you wait to cum." I looked from the road to her and gave her a wink making her giggle.

While I drove us, I was actually more excited about the surprise than I led on. I needed a getaway with just me and my chicken nugget. This shit with her ex and these Philly niggas had me on edge as fuck. I mean the slightest thing would tip me off if it didn't have anything to do with Nina.

Even Pops told me to take a mini break and just

IN LOVE WITH A LAS VEGAS OUTLAW 3

clear my mind; he said I'll think better and handle my enemies. Then I kept thinking about Quest and finding out his ex killed his Moms. I don't know what the hell I would do if one of my old bitches actually took out my Pops. Man, I'd kill her entire blood line and they damn pets.

"Oh my goodness, we're going somewhere far!? How far!?" Nina squeezed my hand with that smile that I would bleed out for wide on her face. "You never told me you had a plane, it's gorgeous." We both sat down in the soft seats and buckled up.

"It's a lot of amazing things about each other that takes time to learn," I told her kissing her hand. We both were dressed chill. I had on some grey sweatpants, a sky-blue t-shirt and some grey Nikes.

Nina wore some tight jeans, a simple white shirt that stopped above her bellybutton and some white Adidas. She went to the shop the other day and got this long hair in her head that stopped at her round booty. Her flawless face had no make-up. I told her to ride with me and bring nothing but her purse.

"What if it's things about each other we don't like?" She asked me as the flight attendant put a bottle of water and warm towel on the tray in front of us.

"We're human Nina, so it will be things about each other that will annoy us, It'll definitely be times when you cuss me out. It'll be times when I wanna put my foot up yo' ass." We both laughed.

"But the way we build is to learn each other's limits and never go to sleep mad. I'm not worried about anything when it comes to me and you, and I need you to feel the same." I made sure I looked in her eyes whenever we talked about us.

The history and amount of hurt Nina has been through, I knew she needed the comfort and security of knowing that our thing was real and forever.

"I love everything about you Angel, even when you keep the A.C. up too high." She joked.

I pulled her to me by her arm and kissed her tender lips. It never takes me long to get into kissing her. My hand went on the side of her waist and I squeezed it, then slid it behind her back.

"Mmm." That moaning in my mouth thing she did always turned me on.

The captain spoke over the speaker and when he said our destination, Nina broke our kiss smiling so hard.

"We're going to Barbados!?"

I cracked up because she was so damn excited.

"Oh my goodness, I've never been outside Nevada! Thank you baby, I am so ecstatic!"

"Anything for you chicken nugget, four days to relax and just chill. After I sort all that shit out at home, I'm taking you on a real vacation, I promise." I told her as our plane took off the ground.

"Anywhere I go with you is paradise," her sweet voice said and then we kissed again.

The light flash to remove seatbelts, so I unclicked hers and pulled her in my lap. My hands were on the side of her face through her hair and then under her shirt. I pulled it over her head. I started licking and kissing on her neck and she pulled my shirt over my head. My flight attendants better stay back there unless they wanted a show.

Me and Nina both couldn't wait; the hunger we had for each other was insane. I told her to stand up in front of me so I could pull her jeans down. The white thong she had on was so sexy and when I turned her around, I tongued that sexy ass booty of hers down while I slid her thong down. We took our shoes off and once we both were naked, Nina sat down on my dick with her back facing me and her hands flat on my thighs.

"Oh my Angel, you feel so good," she called out while going up and down slowly.

My right hand was massaging her wet clit and my other one was rubbing up and down her back.

"Hold them ass cheeks open and be my porn star on that dick." I told her, opening my legs a little wider to give her room.

Her hands gripped her booty so tight I could see her nails indent. It was the sexiest thing, especially when she bounced and that long hair trailed down her back. That squishy sound her pussy made was loud. I just put my hands behind my head and watched her cum like crazy.

"Gimme my fucking pussy, Nina. Don't play me, give it all to me. Sssss yup, just like that, chicken nugget." I then put my hands on the sides of her waist and slowed her down. I loved seeing her cum smear all over. Closing my legs some, I put hers across mine, leaving all that kat exposed, then I started fucking her hard. Nina put her hand over her mouth to hide her screams.

"Move that damn hand, don't be hiding shit, Nina. Let me hear you, tell me where you want me to cum.

"Uhhhh...in me, cum in me."

Those words were the icing on the cake and I did just that. When I released, Nina still was grinding on my dick. She was making sure she got all my nut in her.

11-hours and 43-minutes later

"Good afternoon Mr. Mckay, Ms. Curwin." The concierge welcomed me and Nina when we got out the Rolls Royce.

"Good afternoon." I gave the valet my keys and then grabbed my woman's hand.

I booked us to stay at Villa Isla Cozumel, the best of the best. The sky was a beautiful crisp blue and the palm trees all around gave it that exotic look I wanted. This was my first time in Barbados so me and Nina were sharing a first together. The Villas were two stories, cream and white with a crisp lawn and brick pavement in the front.

"Angel, oh my goodness." Nina looked around our villa when we got inside with her mouth wide open. It was beyond five-star quality; fully furnished, the colors were midnight blue, cream and grey. Every room had a big window with a beautiful view of outside to it. My favorite was the backyard. Me and Nina walked the trail hand in hand. There was a crystal blue pool with a fresh lawn and patio.

Then the part that made me seal the deal on picking this villa, the trail to the rest of the backyard. It took no more than five-minutes to walk and when you reached the end of it you'd probably need to take a deep breath at the sight. The beach was engaging with white sands, water, palm trees and the sky was like the finishing touch on the painting. There was a jacuzzi and just a lot of space to do whatever you wanted. It was perfect, just like the woman holding my hand.

"I feel like I am in a dream. This is just, wow." I looked at her and wrapped my arms around her waist.

"Now you see how I felt when I first met you." I told her, then I kissed her neck making her blush. "I love you."

She turned her head slightly to me. "I love you, too." We kissed and stood there, taking in the view. The rest of the day we relaxed, ordered room service, took a bath, I got in them insides and then we slept.

**

"Hell no, Angel, it's way too dark down there, let's go back." Nina's face had fear all over it while she stood there, practically shaking in her gym-shoes. It was our first full day here and today was all about being outdoors and active. We were inside an actual cave, Harrison's Cave to be exact, and my chicken nugget was freaking out.

"Come on Nina, we'll just go in a little and then come right back." I reached my hand out to her.

She started doing this cute wine and pout. "Nooo, it's dark and scary." Her face was so sweet, but I didn't like her being scared. I had our size taken and clothes delivered to us from the hotel assistants. Nina had on these black stretch shorts that had the Chanel logo on the side, a matching sport-bra, some black and white Chanel gym-shoes. I like how she wore a jean jacket tied around her small waist.

I wore a pair of Raw Men jeans with a black beater and some white and black Retro Jordans. I walked back to her and grabbed her hand kissing it; she was still shaking her head.

"Trust daddy and let's go in a little, I promise we'll come right out." I started walking still holding her hand.

Nina was whining every step we took.

"I got'chu chicken nugget, daddy got'chu come on."
When we got to the part that looked like gold all around us,
she calmed down. It was bomb as fuck and we both took
plenty of pictures.

"Ok, let's go back." I held her hand tight while we
walked back through the darkness.

"I hated that." She said, looking serious when we got
back outside.

I laughed and brought her close to me, "No you
didn't, I like how you trusted me and followed my lead." I
pecked her lips.

"I'll always trust you." Her sexy ass said then
smiled.

We continued our day doing some of everything. I
did body surfing while my scary ass fiancée watched and
cheered me on. Then we both went jet blading and then

swimming in the ocean. We rented bikes and went bike riding in the village, did ocean tours and kitesurfing, which I had to beg like *James Brown* to get her to do. I traveled all the time, but it was always alone or with my boys. Now I'm here enjoying my time and making memories with the love of my life. Shit was wild, but I was here for it.

"I wish yo' ass would stop looking at the tag of everything you pick up," I told Nina while we walked through this boutique of women clothes.

"I know I just...I like to make sure I'm not going crazy." She shrugged her shoulders and put the wallet she had down.

It was the second day in Barbados, and we were having the time of our lives. Today, we did what I knew she would enjoy, shopping. However, my woman was annoying me because she was being timid while shopping. I've brought her plenty of things before, but it's been all stuff I picked out or Lori grabbed.

I picked the wallet up and gave it to her. "Money is never an option. There's always more money. Get whatever you want and stop playing with me, woman." I kissed her cheek and squeezed her booty. I was holding the dress she just brought from this other store; it was in a black dress bag and I had no idea what it looked like. While she was shopping for her dress, I went to the men's store and got me something to wear. I had dinner plans for us tonight and I told her it would be fun if we got ready separately and she met me in the backyard of our villa.

"I'll miss you." Nina giggled and said to me after we took a nap and woke up so we could get ready for dinner. I was getting ready in the villa next door while she was getting ready here. Nina didn't know I had the works coming for her: hair, make-up if she wanted, a nail tech to do all she wanted done and a jeweler to give her a choice of whatever went with her dress. I unlocked the door for her and before she went in, I kissed her soft lips.

"I'll miss you more." Watching her go in, I was ready

to get fine for my woman.

After I got out the shower, I dried off good and put

some Dove Men lotion on and deodorant. Nina loved that

smell on me. Then I put some brown dress socks on and

my Hugo Boss boxers. I picked up my Tom Ford dress

slacks and put them on. I decided to get them in tan with a

brown pigskin leather belt. I did my line up before I got in

the shower, I even made sure my nails were clean. I put my

feet in my brown Louboutin loafers with the gold LV in the

middle of them.

Before I grabbed my shirt on, I picked up my JBW

Phantom watch on with the brown band and gold diamond

face. Then, I put my gold diamond studs in my ears and put

on my simple gold twenty-six-inch chain. Fixing my shirt

once I had it on, I made sure everything on me was good.

The shirt was a silk brown and tan long sleeve with a V

shape in the front showing some of my chest. Spraying myself with my Clive Christian Original cologne, I was satisfied with my appearance.

"Mr. McKay, your lady friend will be down in ten-minutes." I nodded to the butler as I walked outside. It was perfect timing. I didn't want to risk running into Nina. Walking to the backyard I walked the trail. It was perfect weather tonight, seventy-two-degrees, clear sky and no wind. Ten minutes passed and I was told Nina was coming, when she turned and walked through the bush covered garden arbor, her mouth dropped to the floor. Her eyes went around the yellow dim lights, flowers, the white flower covered chairs... I even had a red carpet lined in front of her. But what really surprised her was the fact that our entire family was here. Her Mama, Grandma, Symba, Christian, Dominick, Quest, Dominick parents', Burt, Mary and of course, my Pops. Burt stood up and walked towards

Nina.

"It would do me the honor if I can walk you down the aisle." He stood next to her with his arm out.

Nina was now crying, and that's when everything hit me. Every person we loved was here with smiles on their faces, so happy for us. I put this together the day after I asked her to be my wife. It was hard, but Symba and Christian being all girly really helped me out. I got Nina's favorite flowers, color and her dream place she always wanted to visit. Looking at her and how beautiful she was had tears in my eyes. I didn't even give a fuck.

Nina had her hair wavy with a part in the middle. Her lips were done up, but that was all. There was a white gold and yellow diamond bracelet on her wrist. The dress she had on was so sexy and classy. The straps were thin, and the front played peek-a-boo with her nice breasts. There was one high slit on the side, revealing her caramel leg, and these gold heels she had on that strapped up her legs. The engagement ring was stunning on her finger.

"I would love for you to walk me down the aisle," Nina finally got out and when she said that, the preacher walked in and stood in front of me. Finally, the music started.

I've finally found the nerve to say

I'm gonna make a change in my life

Starting here today

I surrender all my love

I never thought I could

I'm giving all my love away

And there's only one reason that I would

And baby it's you

Looking at her walk to me had me emotional, her

beauty enhanced the closer she got. Nina's Mama was crying and so were Symba and Christian, who had their phones out recording.

"I cannot believe you did this." Nina made her way to me and Burt gave me her hand after they hugged.

"I'll move mountains for you," I told her and I was about to kiss her, but the preacher cleared his throat and our family laughed. Grabbing both her hands in mine, we stood in front of each other with smiles, ready to do this.

"Tonight we are here to unite Angel and Nina as one under God. I didn't get to meet Nina, but I did meet Angel on a video chat for three hours. He informed me of the surprise he was setting up, but he respected my requirement to meet with the couple before I marry them. I bent the rules because after talking to Angel for hours, it was no doubt he not only loved Nina. But he adored her, he understood the definition on loyalty, commitment and a bond between two. I am honored to make these two, one unity. Angel told me he wanted to say some words to his bride."

I had the floor and I started talking. "Nina, on sight when I saw you, I was taken back by your beauty. Even though you had an attitude and practically ran through me, I had to have you. Once we met back up under nothing but fate talking to you, I felt the hurt and despair that was on you. I just had to make it stop. I saw a woman who stopped loving herself and my first thought was how in the world can she not look in the mirror and *not* love this?" My hand caressed the side of her face, which was covered in tears.

"When we were at the complex chilling and talking, I saw the person you were before the hurt. The smile, your jokes, you being silly and carefree, all the things you have been lately, I had already saw. That's what made me fall in love with you. Someone had the honor of having you, and they messed up. This perfect work of art that God made in perfection was damaged, before you fell in love with me. I wanted you to fall in love with yourself again, look at yourself the way your family and I do. I don't want anything in return, except you taking my last name and staying mine." I sniffed and she wiped my tears.

I had the women crying and my boys, Burt and my dad were looking at me and Nina with smiles and like I made them proud of my words.

"Whew, I am lost for words Angel. I had no idea God could make someone like you." She put her hand over her mouth and cried in it for a second. I rubbed her other hand to let her know it was ok.

Clearing her throat she pointed to herself and continued. "I hated this girl, I had love around me from my family, but I still hated myself. No one could get me to see that God loved me, he was never punishing me. But then you came and you listened to me talk, you looked at me like I was everything. You touched places like my ears, shoulder and you put my hair behind my ear... it was so intimate, and it may sound immature, but it showed me that you saw me beyond anyone has ever seen me before. I thought you were a trick from the devil. But I had to apologize to God and then thank him because you were the complete opposite. You're my Angel, and I promise to take your last name and wear it forever."

When Nina finished, I kissed both her hands and then the preacher finished his part.

"I now pronounce you husband and wife; please do the honor and kiss your bride." Once we got the ok, I kissed her so deeply, I forgot we were in front of a man of God.

Our family clapped so hard for us and it was time for us to eat. I made reservations at a restaurant with Barbados' number one cook. It was time to eat and have a celebration with our loved ones. Today was the start of our life together as husband and wife, and this shit seemed unreal. Her smile was on her face all night and when we got back to our villa, I made love to her so good the first round then we got nasty as fuck. We weren't leaving this island until I knocked her up.

Marlo

A week later

"If you don't calm the fuck down."

"Fuck that! I'm out her naked as fuck, these muthafuckas killed two of my homies, my Mama, Grandma, aunt and my cousin! He was only seventeen and you telling me to calm down!" I looked at Tino like he was crazy.

I was crushed knowing my peoples were dead, then to top it all off, there were no bodies. Like I'm supposed to believe all my people dipped out all at the same time. The Law could have let me bury my family. I got Abe and Reese's people all in my face asking questions. I had nothing to tell them, hell even if I did, I couldn't anyway.

"Yeah nigga I'm telling you to calm yo' ass down

getting hype all in my shit! I get you tripping but this is what the fuck happens when you fuck with The Law." Tino sat in the chair rolling his weed and packaging coke.

I snapped and knocked all that shit on the floor. He got up and came at me, but he had the right one tonight because I was on tip. He swung at me and hit me in the face, but I came right back with a hit to his face and then his ribs.

"Punk ass muthafucka!" He yelled while he pressed my head down in the carpet.

I was choking out, but my leg got free and I kneed him in the dick.

"Ugh!" He fell over and I kicked his ass away from me.

"This is the thanks I get for letting you stay in my trap house because them fuckers went in your house!?" Tino staggered to his feet with a bloody lip.

I stood up with a bloody lip as well. "My bad, I'm just fucked up with all this shit. I want my life back. I want my homies and my woman back, my family alive and everything to go back how it was before—" I stopped talking and he looked at me.

"Before what, nigga? Don't come at me with that corny ass talk. We weren't doing shit that a lot of homies do. Yo' bitch—"

"Don't call her a bitch, man." I was for real and he better shut the fuck up.

Turning his nose up he said, "Fuck her, she wasn't in that cell with us or had your back when them other dudes were locked up and tried to come at you. That was all me, now you crying because some blood was spilled and Nina left you. What you need to do is say fuck that *bitch* and come and fuck me."

Tino grabbed my dick, pulled down my pants and dropped to his knees. The head was feeling good as hell and I put my hand on the back of his head and started fucking his face. Before I came, I dropped to my knees and told him to bend over. My dick was wet from him sucking it, so I rammed it in his tight asshole and started fucking him. Our grunts were loud and I was ripping his shit harder than I normally did because I was so pissed. I mean I felt his skin ripping, but I didn't give a fuck.

"I told you not to call her a bitch." I said to him pulling my gun out and shooting him in the back of his head. Fuck Tino. He told me if me, Mick, Abe and Reese set the Complex on fire, than his boys from Philly would handle The Law. Wasn't shit done and I lost all my family in the process. I was the only one who took a loss. Fuck that.

I crawled to the coke on the floor and did more lines than *Tony Montana*. Once I was good and high, I crawled back over to Tino and stuck my hard dick back in his ass. I pumped, pumped and pumped until blood was on my dick and I nutted hard as fuck inside his dead corpse. Breathing hard, I walked to the bathroom and ran my face under some cold water. I looked myself in the mirror and didn't know who I was anymore.

My waves were fucked up, I had a nappy ass beard, and my beater had a little blood on it from my lip. My gold grill was still in but everything else was fucked up on me. All of this was Nina's fault; if she would have just heard me out and let me explain. Instead, she went and gave my pussy away then left me for good.

I ran my face under the cold water again and then stumbled back to the front. I sat at the table and put a brick of coke in my pocket and the stack of hundreds Tino had. I did a few more lines and looked at his dead body. That muthafucka was face down, ass up, dead as shit with my nut spilling out of him. Getting up, I picked up the Hennessey bottle, kicked Tino over, took his keys out his pocket and walked out the house, leaving the door wide open.

It was two in the morning. I loved driving while high because the lights and fast cars made it feel like I was inside a lava lamp. It didn't take me long to get to my destination. I parked, turned the car off and let the radio play. I didn't sleep at all, I was to wired to sleep. Sitting the brick of coke I took on the dashboard, I broke it open and started sniffing some off my long pinky fingernail. I kept that up for a while and then I started drinking. Man, I was numb, mixed with heartbroken.

I wanted my girl. I wanted Nina back and it was killing me not having her. Sitting there with the music, everything was spinning in circles. I started laughing at memories of my old life. Before I knew it, the bright sun came up. I was sweating so bad from the dark liquor. Looking in Tino's back seat, I grabbed a bottle of water and the sniper gun and set it on the seat. Opening the water, I downed it in one gulp then sniffed some more coke.

A red Bentley pulled up with Angel driving and Nina in the passenger seat. I was hoping she drove herself to work so I could talk to her one more time, no drama or hostility, just us talking. But this nigga had to drive her like she didn't have her own car. I watched him walk over to her side and let her out, as if she couldn't open her own damn door.

Once again, she was smiling so bright and when he took her hand, the bling almost blinded me, and I was far distanced. I picked up the sniper gun and looked through the scope. This bitch married him!? Immediately I started crying, I mean balling my eyes out. How could she do me this way? She was mine but she went and married somebody she knew less than a year!?

I had snot and tears falling down my face and I was sweating so badly. Wiping my nose, I grabbed a hand full of coke and snorted it so hard my nose started to sting, but

I needed the numbness to kick up. I had lost Nina for good.

She actually gave herself to someone else. Nina said fuck

our life, history and what we had, I was defeated.

Angel

The night before

"You cool man?" Quest came in my office to check on me.

I had a moment and broke a crystal vase that was on my end table. I never trip out like this, but I was frustrated because I haven't found that nigga Marlo. I didn't even give a shit about those Philly pussies and they burned the complex down. Marlo was personal; he took something form me, my family and I promised Nina I would kill who made her stop smiling. The nigga was cancer and I needed to cut him out.

"Yeah I'm good, I just want that nigga more than I want my next nut. I feel like I'm failing Axel, my family and my wife." I leaned against the front of my desk.

Quest came and stood next to me. "I know that feeling. I feel like I fucked up. Let Kamila in when I knew damn well she should have just been something to hit. I fucked her on the first night, outside of a nightclub. That wasn't shit I was supposed to wife up, especially when she still partied and stayed out all night. But I pressed and tried to make something out of nothing." He shook his head and continued.

"I kept the toxic shit around. Now, I feel like it's my fault, which is mainly the reason why I gotta get that bitch. My mother deserves to have her death avenged and I won't rest till I do it. However, Christian tells me all the time I gotta look at the person I was to my mother. Every time I do, I don't feel so guilty. My point is, you were a good big brother to Axel; he died knowing that. You were a good son to your Moms and she died knowing that. You're a good man to Nina and to prove it, she became your wife. You all good G, we gone get they asses."

I was taken back the way Quest was talking, he usually was the one me and Dominick were calming down. Seems Christian had him on a more lighter vibe, which was dope to see.

"Baby sister got'chu being the voice of reason." I laughed and told him. "I dig it, thank you for that." I gave him a pound. "I'm about to get home to my wife; she'll make a nigga feel better." I said turning my computer off.

"Yeah I need to go to her crazy ass sister." Quest chuckled, walking out my office with me.

"Hey, chicken nugget." I walked in the door and the smell of spices hit my nose. I went to the kitchen and Nina was taking my plate out the microwave.

"Hey, my Angel." Putting my plate down on the table she walked over to me, gave me a hug and a juicy kiss.

I took notice to what she had on. It was a sheer robe

thing and I saw she was wearing nothing under it.

"I want you to eat then join me on the back patio."

I watched her pull my chair from under the table and even though the seafood gumbo smelled good, I wanted the dessert right now. "I want what'chu got now, I'll eat after." I told her.

Laughing, Nina took the food, put it back in the microwave and grabbed my hand.

Nina had candles lit everywhere, soft music playing and she had the outside tub filled with red and yellow roses all in it. I loved this about Nina; she would do stuff like this that cost nothing and I appreciated the shit out of it.

I looked at her and she started undressing me. While she was doing it, she kept kissing on my chest and arms. My dick was rising like some buttermilk biscuits and I kept licking my lips. Then she stood back and took her see through robe off, her UGG house -shoes and then she stepped in the water with me, holding her hand. Once she got in, I joined her sitting across. The tub was shaped like a banana split bowl, which gave us a lot of room.

"You stay spoiling me bae, thank you for this." I told her, picking her feet up and placing them on my chest. Whether she had polish on her toes or not, Nina's feet were naturally beautiful and always smelled good.

"I love spoiling you because you always spoil me so effortlessly. I still can't believe you bought me a Bentley." Her smile was big.

"You gotta understand I want only the best around you. We working on that cheerleading camp you want, too. A business plan is a great way to bring the vision to life." I was massaging her right foot and looking at her hungrily.

"You know if you didn't have all of this," she looked around with her eyes and then back in mine. "I would still love you and still become your wife, right?"

"I know that babe, I never have doubted you pertaining

that. But I love when you let me do for you and spoil you.

I've wanted someone I can do al those things with. Beyond

a designer bag or shoes, I just want to give you everything."

I said kissing her toes.

"I love being your wife." Her sexy voice said and she put on

that flirtatious smirk.

"Oh yeah Mrs. McKay? Come here and tell me more." I

pulled her to me by her leg and she straddled me while we

kissed.

I raised her up a little and brought her back down on my

dick. I like how the rose pedals were stuck on her wet skin.

One was covering up her nipple and I licked it off. Once she

started moaning and moving up and down, I pulled her off.

"No babe, I was about to cum." She moaned and whined

out. I sat her on the edge of the tub and started licking that

pussy. I wanted that sweet taste in my mouth; her clit was

soft and wet as I sucked on it.

"Oh Angel shit, ohhhh my gosh." Her hips were grinding in

my face and I was getting every drop of her orgasm in my mouth.

I brough her back down to me, sitting us in the water and getting back inside of her.

"This will never be broken Nina, on my life, we will always be together." I told her while she came again.

"I love you so much Angel, my Angel, sssss."

"I love you more wife, my sexy wife."

**

"You don't have to work today?" Nina asked me, coming out the bathroom putting on her earrings.

"Naw, not until tonight." I looked at her switch to the closet then came out with some heels on.

"I'm getting a sexy teacher vibe from you, come here." I was still in bed with my boxers on. I loved watching her get ready for work, especially when she would lotion up and put on her bra and panties.

Shaking her head laughing, she walked to me and sat on the side of me. The skirt she had on fit her body good, but what I thought was sexy was the grey blouse she had tucked in. Her hair was in a neat low ponytail, that bare beautiful face was highlighted with her quarter size diamond earrings. After I kissed her for some time, her small hands went on the side of my face. My heart leaped every time she did that.

"Play hooky with me today chicken nugget, Burt will be cool." I begged her, rubbing my hand up and down her arm.

"I wish I could babe, but I have to finish these twins today."

I started kissing and licking on her neck.

Nina giggled. "Stop Angel, I have to go to work." She stood up and kissed my lips again.

"Let me drive you to work." I sat up and pulled the covers

back.

"That's ok, you're comfy in the bed." Nina bit her bottom

lip when I dropped my boxers and put another pair on.

"It's cool, I'm not ready to part with you yet." After I put

my shoes on, I pecked her lips and we walked downstairs.

"You want me to make you some breakfast?" I asked her

when she opened the refrigerator.

"No thank you, I'll just have a banana and smoothie

drink."

I grabbed an apple, my keys and we headed out. The

weather was chilly today, it was forty-two degrees and

the high was set to reach fifty-four today. Turning my

heat and radio on low, I pulled out the driveway.

"Christian's stomach is getting so big." Nina laughed

looking in her phone.

"Hell yeah, I was cracking up when I saw her IG pictures.

Quest is geeked as hell about being a father," I said and

she got quiet looking out the window.

I let her have her time because it was what she needed. I always felt like I can build Nina up every day forever, but she has to come to terms with her past in her own pace. We rode listening to the music and I noticed her face didn't look sad anymore. In fact, we both were being silly singing along to *The Temptations-My Girl* song. I enjoyed being with her; it's crazy because that's what most men forget to do. Just enjoy your lady beyond the bedroom. Once we got to her job I got out, walked around to her door. Helping her out I stopped in front of her before I closed the door.

"The same mother you were when you had Nicholas, the love you had for him. The way you cared for him, fed him, played with him and adored him. You'll have the same feelings towards our child; you were an amazing mother then and you'll be an even better one now." I looked her in her brown eyes with love filled in mine.

Her hands went on the side of my face. "Thank you, Angel." She kissed my lips twice.

Closing the door, I grabbed her hand so I could walk her inside. We were laughing and talking, then she stopped in her tracks and squeezed my hand so tight. When I stopped and looked at Nina, she had her hand on her stomach looking down at it.

Moving her hand, our eyes bucked when it was covered in blood. Everything happened so fast but in slow motion at the same time. I caught her when she was about to hit the ground and then I heard clear as day, tires screeching so loud and an even louder engine. I couldn't take my eyes off Nina though; I think I was in shock at what I was looking at.

"BURT!" I shouted his name out because I snapped back into reality when I realized this shit was real, Nina was shot.

"What's going...WHAT THE HELL!" He yelled when he saw Nina in my arms, bleeding everywhere.

"Oh my God!" Mary yelled, covering her mouth.

"She was fucking shot! Help me get her in the car!" I shouted while scooping her in my arms.

Burt picked my keys up off the ground, opened the back door for me and I got inside.

I didn't pay attention to shit else but all the blood. It was so much of it coming out of her.

"Nina, don't do me like this; please bae, I'm fucking begging you." I had her face so close to mine, my tears were falling directly on her. I mean a nigga was doing the ugly cry hard as fuck because of all the blood and her eyes were closed.

"Drive the fucking car faster, Burt." I cried out to him.

He was dashing every red light, zigzagging around cars like he was in a movie. "I'm going as fast as I can. Get the fuck out the way!" Burt blew the horn hard and continued driving.

"I know who did this Nina, I swear I'm killing everybody he knows. I'll do it in front of you just don't leave. COME ON MAN, DRIVE!"

Burt hit a hard turn and literally almost drove into the door of emergency room. Two people dived out the way. I tore the back door open with Nina in my arms, running inside. As soon as the nurse saw me, she pressed some button and then ran from around the counter, grabbing a gurney.

"What happened?" The nurse asked me.

"Someone shot her. Why the fuck is she losing so much blood?!" I asked through all the chaos. Three nurses rolled her in the back and I followed, then two doctors ran towards us and started asking questions.

"Name, what happened?"

"Her name is Nina, she's twenty-six and she was shot. I-I

don't know where...I...why is it so much blood coming out of her!" I shouted as they ripped her blouse open and her white bra was now all red.

My chicken nugget's body was looking lifeless as they stuck all kinds of shit in her arm and talked medical tearms to each other. My eyes were still were wide, and I watched them work on her like a hawk. I headed towards them when they stuck this thing all the way down her throat.

"Yo' what the fuck—"

"Please sir, let us do our job, wait in the waiting room—"

"Hell no! I'm not leaving my wife!"

"Please sir, please! You will make it hard for us to save her, please." The nurse was begging me and pushing me out the room at the same time. My neck was about to snap off trying to keep my eyes on Nina while I was being pushed.

"I promise, I will update you." She said then went back in

the room.

I burst through the double doors and Mary got up, running towards me. "Is she alive?" Her face filled with tears as she looked at me in a panic.

"I don't know, they're working on her." I said like I was in a daze. Looking at my shirt and sweats, I was covered in her blood. I don't even know what I was sitting on, but I had to sit because I felt like I was about to faint.

My heart was ripped out my chest, it was back there with Nina. We were just fine, laughing, singing to an oldie and kissing. Burt was talking to me but honestly, I have no idea what he was saying. He was holding his phone and I heard him say something about Quest and Dominick. Then in a few minutes, the entrance opened and my boys along with their women, Nina's Mama and Grandma, came running in. I jumped up and when the women saw me covered in blood, they yelled and cried.

"Where is my child?! What happened to her!?" Her Mama ran to me crying and asking.

I told her what happened and it made her cry harder, then she did some shit that took my mind off Nina for half a second. My mother in-law turned around and slapped Burt so damn hard that I think all of our faces were stinging.

"Mama!?" Christian yelled, shockingly at her.

"Is this because of you and your crazy African business you're into!? Was our daughter shot and practically fighting for her life because of you!?" Her voice made the whole damn hospital tremble.

The entire room was looking like a deer caught in headlights, even people who didn't know us. I think they were looking like that because of the slap.

"No, Lakota, I swear to God this isn't my doing. I kept my promise and never involved her in my dealings! I wouldn't do that—" He was cut off when the nurse came through the doors.

"Nina is AB-Negative, does anyone here match her blood type?"

Without hesitation even though he was crying, Burt practically pushed us out the way. "I am!" Just like that, he followed the doctor to the back and it was a waiting game. I sat down for about twenty-seconds then I was back on my feet pacing the floor. I prayed and tried to do like my Moms always told me. Give it to God, trust him and rest, but it was so hard. All I saw was me and Nina getting married, how happy she was and beautiful she looked. Then I saw her on our first date, breakfast at my house. I made love to her so good, secured my position in her life. That same day was the first day I saw her smile and heard her laugh, it was the best day. I need her. I need to feel those soft hands on the side of my face, kiss her lips and hear her voice. As I paced, those memories and the ones I had for us in the future filled my head. Tears were falling

and I couldn't stop it, I wanted my wife.

Nina

<u>Two days later</u>

"Angel." I said his name low and with my right hand, I caressed the side of his face. He was in the bed with me, sitting on top of the covers sleep sitting up, with his back propped against the pillows.

He popped is head up so fast it kind of scared me. "Oh fuck Nina, you're up." He smiled at me and kissed my lips like I was made of thin glass. When I put my hand back on the side of his face, he closed his eyes and tears fell from his eyes. We stayed that way for a few minutes, I was crying too.

"Do you remember anything?" He asked me finally opening his eyes.

"Yeah, I remember going to work, getting out the car holding your hand and then a sharp pain. Like something entered my body and was burning, that's all." I watched him get out of bed. He had on some Adidas track pants that snapped on the side and a black shirt. Grabbing my hand he kissed it.

"You were shot, babe. Marlo did that shit, I already know it. He was ducked off in a car down an alley. I know how to find him now; his dumb ass was caught on Burt's cameras. I promise you, I will deliver that nigga to you and you can choose how he will die."

I wasn't surprised when he said Marlo. Since I've known him, he has tantrums when he doesn't get what he wants. What I messed up on was thinking he would just let go. I let the fact that he trashed my apartment as a sign of him letting out his frustration. At this moment, I wanted him to die; I didn't wish shit on him even after me finding out he was fucking Tino.

"We broke up because I caught him cheating, with a guy. Actually, the guy was my best friend's brother. When it happened, I went straight and got tested. Everything came back negative, but I still took another one a week before Barbados and it was negative too. The doctor told me I was fine and in the clear; she said if I had anything, it would have come back positive." I had never told Angel all of this and I hated hiding it but I didn't want him to think I was nasty or careless.

"What's your best friend name?" He asked me, still holding my hand.

"Talia, I think her crazy brother had something to do with my Mama getting attacked." I told him and he just nodded his head just as the door opened. The doctor and a nurse following him walked in.

She started checking my vitals and the doctor was listening to my heart. "Mrs. McKay, you were brought in here by your husband with a gunshot wound to your upper abdomen. On the scene, you lost a lot of blood, but we were successful in removing the bullet. However, you lost more blood during surgery and you are AB-negative, which is a rare blood type. Luckily, your dad was here and he willingly donated enough along with what we had. He saved your life." The doctor was smiling at me, but when he saw my face, he looked confused.

"Um, I'm sorry but...what?" I looked from the doctor to Angel who was looking like he knew what was going on.

"We'll talk after the doctor leaves, it's some things that happened while you were out." He told me, kissing both of my hands.

At this point, I was ready for the nurse and doctor to get out. The doctor told me it would take six to eight weeks for me to be healed and aside from a small scar, I'll be fine. I thanked God over and over in my head and out loud because I thought I was going to die. When it came to me that I had been shot, I remembered fainting and everything going black. I could hear Angel's voice slip in and out, but I couldn't wake up.

It was beyond scary and even though it felt better to just let go, I couldn't. After the doctor left, the nurse gave me some ice water. I put my order in for some soup, jello and vanilla ice cream. I could only have liquid and soft foods for a week. When she left, Angel washed my face, brought me things so I could brush my teeth and then gave me a sponge bath.

"Angel what is going on, what was the doctor talking about?" I asked when he put my sports bra over my head. I put on my diamond earrings because I was that girly and always needed to have on earrings. I could tell Lori probably brought me the clean clothes and personal products because everything had tags on them.

"I'll tell you; let me just call everyone and tell them you're woke." He took out his phone.

"No, don't. Because they'll be a distraction and I want to hear from you, my husband." I was trying to remain calm, but I was really getting annoyed because he was stalling.

Once he looked at my face, he grabbed the chair behind him and pulled it close to my bed. Of course Angel had me in a suite hospital room, so it was enough room in the bed for him to get in too. When he didn't and grabbed my hand, I knew he was about to drop a bomb on me.

"Burt is your dad, babe."

I looked at him and laughed. "What? Ok, who told you that because it's not—"

"It is true Nina, your Moms got pissed at him because she assumed you were shot because of him and his business dealings. That's when she blurted out that he was your dad. The doctor came out to us in the waiting room. He asked was any of us AB-negative and Burt jumped up with no hesitation to save you." Angel's eyes were locked on mine and he had so much sincerity in them.

I was crying before he finished his story. "How can this be? I've worked for him for almost five years. Mary, she's—oh my goodness, does she know?" I was talking through tears and my voice filled with confusion.

"Yeah she knows, it's a lot babe and I think you need to talk to your Moms and Burt and have them explain things to you."

"Explain?! What could they explain, that they are liars and he never wanted me! This whole time he's..." I stopped when I felt sick.

Angel saw my face and he grabbed the bin he used to give me a sponge bath with and I threw up all in it. The nurse walked in with my food on the tray smiling at me as

Angel cleaned my mouth up.

"Aww, don't worry, the morning sickness will end soon." She said to me, setting my food up.

I chuckled and responded, "Oh I'm not pregnant, I just was feeling woozy." When I said that, her face had an awkward smile and she looked at Angel.

Of course my eyes shot to him and he had his sexy lips pressed together. "So, that's one of the things that happened while you were sleep."

I shook my head quickly as if a bug was in my hair. "I'm sorry, what!? I'm pregnant!?"

"Yeah, the doctor told me before your surgery. The baby is fine; you're six-weeks. Our baby is a little ass kicker." He smiled and placed his hand on my stomach.

I couldn't help but laugh and place my hand on top of his. "I should slap you, that should have been the first thing you told me." I joked.

"Well shit, first I had to soak up my wife being

alive and awake." He bent down and kissed me a few times and the nurse smiled at the gesture before leaving out.

"What am I going to do about Burt and my Mama? I don't know where to start. I'm so damn angry, this is some shit off a soap opera. How long have I been out?"

Angel put the spoon of soup to my mouth. "Two days too fucking long. I swear I thought I was going to lose you. You lost so much blood and your complexion was draining." He drifted off while he talked.

I moved the tray and put my hands on the side of his face. "I'm right here, we are out the woods and we can continue our life together. We're about to be parents, nothing will keep me from my Angel." We kissed feverishly.

"I love you so much chicken nugget, I'll beat'cho ass you do some shit like this to me again." He smiled while we were still face to face then he kissed my lips.

"I'll do my best not to get shot again." I jokingly said.

"I would greatly appreciate that and as far as your Moms and Burt, it's all up to you. Your feelings are the ones that matter, you hear them out, let them know how you feel and make your decision at your own pace. You know I got your back one-hunnid fold, you ready to call everybody know?"

"Yes, let's video chat them."

**

"Your stomach seems bigger and it's only been two days." I laughed, rubbing my sister's belly.

"I gain five-pounds an hour, I promise this will be the only child." Christian said then took a bite of angel food cake.

Symba made me one since she knew I could only

have soft foods. Hers was perfect, sweet and actually tastes like a light pound cake in my opinion. It was the only one I ate.

"The devil is a lie, Pinocchio." Quest jumped in, making us laugh. Him, Christian, Symba and Dominick had been up here for about thirty minutes now.

The guys had balloons for me out the ass, Symba and Christian had presents like I was out for more than two days. But I felt so love by all of them.

"Whatever, this my body nigga." Christian rolled her eyes putting some more cake in her mouth. I was sitting all the way up, Angel was sitting next to me on the bed with his legs up eating cake. I loved having him so close to me, I felt so safe.

"Baby sister I swear you about to have a roommate right next to you in this big ass room after I kick yo' sister ass."

I just continued laughing at them two and eating some cake.

"How do you feel about being a mommy?" Symba asked me with her grin wide. She was sitting in Dominick's lap on the couch in front of my bed.

"I feel really good, I'm so blessed the baby is fine. I didn't even know I was pregnant, I haven't been feeling any differently," I said honestly.

"I did, but I just didn't say shit until she noticed." Angel added and I looked at him.

"Really, how?"

"Because that pussy was—"

"Ahhh! Ok!" I covered his mouth and they all laughed at me.

"Shit that's how I knew Christian was pregnant. Them walls were tighter and wetter."

"I should have just stayed on birth control like this one." Christian said pointing to Symba.

"She ain't been on that shit for about two months."

Dominick said plain as day while he was eating.

Symba shook her head while eating her cake

laughing. "Crazy, y'all."

Dominick was looking like he gave no fucks but he

kissed the back of her arm, laughing with us.

The door opened and my stomach dropped when

Grandma, Mama, Burt and Mary came in. Grandma came

straight to me, hugging me and kissing all on my face. I

talked to her for some time while Burt, Mary and my

Mama were looking like they didn't know how to take me.

"We need to step out and let them talk." Angel

stood up and told everyone. That's when I knew for sure

that they all knew what was up.

"Call my name if you need me, chicken nugget." He

said in my ear then kissed my lips.

Once they left, I adjusted myself in the bed sitting

up and looking at both of them. "Is it true?" I said out loud, not caring who answered.

"Yes, it's true." Burt spoke first.

Since he did, I focused on him. "Did you know before I came to work for you?"

He was leaning against the wall with some blue linen pants on, a Bill Cosby looking sweater with his typical pure gold necklace, ring and watch on. Burt and Mary were a good looking older couple. He was African and so was she. Since day one, they have been good to me and I thought nothing about it. I assumed they knew a little about my history and wanted to help.

"I knew before you came to work for me."

I closed my eyes when he said that and I felt them water. Blinking fast, I looked at him with hurt in my face. "How could you know I'm your child and not say anything to me? Did you cheat on Mary with my Mama and just not give a damn?"

I have never seen Burt's face look like it did; he had a distinguished look to him that made him demanding. Like whatever he said, you knew was final and his African accent that came in and out made it concrete. Now, he was looking hurt like me and he had tears coming down his face.

"It's not his fault, Nina." Mama spoke up while wiping her tears. "It's not him or Mary's fault, in fact, he wasn't even with her when I met him. He didn't meet her until you were three; it's on me. I was in love with Christian's dad, who is someone he was beefing with back in the day. He wanted you, but I wanted someone else, told Burt if he didn't sign his rights over then I was going to the police."

I swear I could not believe Mama was saying this to me.

"You have to understand Nina, my hands were in

so many illegal hustles, things that would have put me away for life. I couldn't be able to protect you if I was in jail, I didn't have the connections and pull I have now. I never stopped looking out for you—"

"Looking out for me! We lived in the hood, in a bullshit house that you bought!" I raised my voice, thinking about Mama working long hours, a beat-up car she drove, the many of things me and Christian missed out on because we didn't have the money.

He looked at Mama with his eyebrow raised, so I turned my head to her.

"Christian's dad bought us that house; he told me he would take care of us, but I found out he was married with kids. He left the day after I had Christian and I haven't heard from him since. This is no one's fault but mine, Nina. I was angry at my decisions and prideful. I refused to go to Burt for help, he would come by and try to see you. I made sure to keep him away, he um." She stopped talking, went in her big purse and pulled out a bundle of envelopes with a rubber band around them.

"Twenty-six birthday cards for you, he would leave them in the mailbox. I've never opened them. I am so sorry, Nina. Once time passed, I just thought I couldn't say anything without you looking at me like you are now." She was balling as she sat the cards on my lap.

To explain the way I was feeling is impossible. Fuck tears, I was angry, confused, shocked and hurt. To make it worse, I had no idea who to direct my anger to. "I feel like you didn't fight hard enough for me." I looked at Burt and said. "I was out there, in the same city as you, who the hell ignores something like that? I had school dances, plays, cheerleading competitions—"

"That I have never missed." He said and Mary stood up, giving him this album she had in her wide bag. He sat it down on top of the envelopes and opened it for me. Stepping back, he let me flip through it on my own.

There were pictures of me in elementary as an elf at a Christmas play I was in. I was the Easter Bunny in one, then on Halloween he had pictures of me every year til 11th grade when I stopped dressing up. Homecoming, prom, graduation, my eyes watered when he had pictures of me outside Mama's house playing with Nicholas. I could go on and on, it was like a memory lane of my life. I don't even think Mama knew about this because of her face looking taken back.

"You were paying my tuition for college?" I asked him when he had information on University of Nevada.

"Yes, the scholarship you applied for was funded by me. You were covered no matter what college you went to. I promised I wouldn't interfere in your life, it took everything in me not to kill Marlo when you were pregnant. This doesn't make up for what your Mama did or what I did, but please Nina. I need you to know I have always loved you before I knew what your sex was. This may be a little forward, but that is the only thing that kept your Mama alive.

I didn't fight enough for you, you're right. I was thinking of everyone I was connected to, if I would have gone to jail they could have been exposed. Believe me, they give little regard to life and they would have killed you, your Mama and your sister.

I could protect you better from behind bars, aside from you being born, when you came in my funeral home that was the best day. I got to be around you, see you every day but I hated knowing you were going through anything, I hated knowing you were sad. When I walked you down the aisle, it meant more to me than anything in my life. I know this is a lot, but please don't shut me out for good, I love you more than anybody in the world."

Burt was looking at me, pouring his heart out.

He had me crying, I couldn't hold it in anymore. I looked at Mary and she wiped her tears, with a closed mouth smile she nodded her head at me.

"I just need time to process all of this, I have to stay here for three more days and I just don't want the stress or pressure. I'm angry, confused and I feel cheated, so just give me some time." I said to all of them, wiping my face.

Burt walked over to me and kissed the top of my head twice and told me he would get the album from me later. Mary said goodbye; I think she didn't know if I would let her hug me or not. Mama stood there wiping her face after they left.

"Nina—"

"Mama how could you keep this from me, why wouldn't you want me to have a relationship with my father?"

She sat at the foot of my bed and looked at me with wet eyes. "I only have the truth for you, I was in love and

Christian's dad was who I wanted. He told me a bunch of lies and I let myself get played. I was young, angry and full of myself."

"All these I's you keep saying, you're selfish. I would never hate you or cross you out my life because at the end of the day, you did good with me and Christian. Does she know all of this?" I asked her and she nodded her head.

"She's not speaking to me. I love both of you girls. I messed up, but I don't need you two not speaking to me." She put her purse on her shoulder and walked out the room. That's how Mama was though, if she thinks she wrong she has to still maintain some type of stubbornness. It's like she doesn't like being in the spotlight for long.

Everyone else came back in and I told them what was said because it was already made public when I was passed out. I showed them the album, my sister and

Symba came over hugging me and telling me it would be fine. They chilled with me for about another hour than it was just me and Angel.

"How are you feeling?" He asked me helping me back in the bed from using the bathroom.

"I'm fine, a little overwhelmed, but I'm fine. The best thing about today was waking up to you next to me and finding out I'm pregnant." I smiled at him watching him get in bed with me.

"You should have saw my face when the doctor first told me. I can't wait to play with my kid and just watch this little person change our lives upside down."

I loved looking at his face while he talked about our future, I was excited for it myself.

Gunna

"The Law flew through Tino, Marlo and his boys. Now they will be focused on us." I told Tucker, pacing the floor of his parent's basement.

He was sitting where I usually do, fucking with his chess pieces as if he was unbothered about us having these three crazy ass fucks on our hands. I was calm and cool about it all when I assumed, we were winning. Now, I'm seeing one by one our plan to fail once I saw on the news that Tino was dead. That was my homie from when he was in Philly partying.

Him and his boys brought a lot of pussy from me. I told him I wanted to pay him and his crew to set fire to the complex. It was to distract The Law and have them believe they had other enemies. Tino introduced us to Marlo, Reese, Mick and Abe. All they were supposed to do was set the building on fire on the specific day The Law would know it wasn't us because we made sure our selves were out and about.

Me and Tucker purposely ran into Christian and Symba so they could go back and tell Quest and Dominick. You see, there was no way they would think it was us and we still moved around as if we were untouchable. We needed to make them think they had more enemies that way, they would want to have us on his team since its strength in numbers. But these fuckers took out Tino, Marlo and the rest one by one and they killed Marlo's family. Here Tucker is sitting around like everything was Gucci.

"They not about to be focusing on us because once I meet up with Christian, we out this bitch. Pack up the girls, tell Money and Sincere also."

I stopped walking and faced him, looking lost. "Wait, why are you meeting up with Christian, how do you know it's her and not Quest?"

"Because I've been video chatting with her. Dumb ass went and got pregnant by him, but he went back to his ex. When I meet up with her, I'ma fuck her good then kill her." He moved one of the chess pieces.

"What are you killing her for?"

Looking up at me with an evil face he said. "Because that bitch fucked up my life. I wasn't supposed to be here talking to you and managing hoes! I was a ball player, then that hoe fucked my hand up because I wouldn't stay with her sick ass!"

I ain't never seen this nigga face like this, he was filled with vengeance. "Was all of this for her, G? All that bullshit about Vegas would be more money and we should move here, you said you had police and some other big name connections here. Was all that bullshit to convince us to relocate, just so you could get back at a bitch who hurt yo' feelings?" He jumped up and shoved me against the wall.

"Did you hear anything I fucking said? That woman fucked up my whole life and then moved on like it was nothing. Now, after I kill her, then we can leave." He let me go roughly. I knew I was done with Tucker.

I didn't even know he moved this way, all to get back at some bullshit in the past. He could have done this on his own. I looked at Ragen, the bitch I had with me, and told her let's go.

"Leave her." Tucker said while sitting back down, playing chess again.

"What?" I said to make sure I heard him.

"I said leave her fine ass here, I need some young pussy. Pick her back up in about half an hour."

I didn't give a damn, she was a bitch I was fucking

but she wasn't mine. I didn't even have her on the level as my other hoes I came here with from Philly. Those were my bottom hoes who I would fuck somebody up over if they played them. They'd been down with me for about six years, so we were tight. Ragen was this slim, cute nineteen-year-old who I met a few months back. I had her sucking my dick and giving me pussy within twenty-minutes.

She was young and she made me a lot of money but who I wanted was her friend, Lanail. That young bitch was fine and the closest thing to Symba's perfect body. I wanted to fuck her and make her my main bitch. I thought I could have but she ran off. I sent her on this date in the hood at this rat ass Motel. I think the niggas she was supposed to fuck were beefing with some people, because they were found dead in the room and Lanail was gone.

Ragen lowkey was glad because she was jealous that I wanted to fuck her home girl. I thought about that young pussy a lot and made Rageb stay in touch with her

incase she wanted to come back. Leaving Tucker people

house I got in my ride and headed straight home. I didn't

want to be out in the street long and The Law hot on us.

Fuck Tucker, I was leaving tonight and taking my hoes with

me.

He can handle his business on his own and if he gets

killed, then oh well. I took the last pull of my blunt as I

pulled in my driveway so my nerves can calm down. I

pressed the lock door button for my car and walked to my

front door. I was pissed about leaving this house because I

liked it. I really did think Nevada would be my new home,

so I didn't just pick any house to live in. I wasn't stupid, I

knew when to dip when stuff was off and Tucker was on

some bullshit.

"Money, Sincere, get every—" I stopped talking

when I opened the hallway door that lead to the living

room. Four of my hoes were on the floor dead, holes in the

middle of their forehead.

I started going through the house and in the kitchen was my other girl on the floor, dead with the refrigerator door open. I stepped over her, went to the basement and on the laundry side was my favorite white hoe, Carol, dead. I went on my side and almost threw up. Sincere and Money's heads were sitting on my pillows and their bodies were sitting across from each other where my chess game was set up. I had eight hoes here and only found six of their bodies. Getting back upstairs, I went to one of the bathrooms.

Tasty was in the tub dead with her throat wide open, I could tell she was taking a bath. I walked to Connie's room when I realized I hadn't seen her body yet, she must have been sleep. When I got closer, I saw the hole in her head. That's a sick ass way to kill someone while they are sleep. This shit just fucked me all the way up. My damn hoes and my homies were all dead. Now I was on a

vengeance, I was beyond heated and wanted blood for

blood. I left out the house, locked it up and headed back to

my car.

Dominick

I know you love fuckin' me (Fuckin' me, fuckin' me)

I can tell by the way you in love with me (Love with me)

You can't get enough of me, yeah

Well, I guess it's lookin' like you stuck with me

You can tell by the lyrics Symba picked this song. If she wasn't listening to this *Jhene* chick, then she was blasting that *H.E.R.* girl. Anyway, we were on our way to meet with my property realtor. From the moment we got dressed, I was horny looking at Symba in this tight dress. It stopped above her knees and she had these boots on that met her dress where it stopped. The pink color was gorgeous against her skin and that peach shape ass was looking just right like always.

I kept saying I was going to save it for tonight, even when she got in the car and her thighs were peeking through. I drove with my hand between her legs like always. I let her control the music as I hit the freeway. This song came on and she kept sneaking looks at me. Her freaky ass moved my hand up between her legs and that was it. I pulled over on the freeway, cut my hazard lights on, undid my jeans and told her to get the fuck over here.

Like always, she did what I said and now she was bouncing that fat booty on me. I had my hand sliding up and down her back with my head back on the seat, biting my lip and closing my eyes. No female has ever had me like this, closing my eyes and moaning. I wasn't the one, but it was more than just fucking with Symba. Every time she let me inside of her, it was us reconnecting all over again.

I was inside of her and it was nothing more

personal than that. This was my pussy, no one would ever have it again. This was my woman, my everything and at the snap of her pretty fingers, I'd jump high as the sky for her. Opening my eyes, she was looking back at me licking her lips. See, she fucking knows I can't take when she looks at me like that. I get on brick, my heart speeds up and I get more addicted to her. Something about that look, it tips me all the way off. I let my seat all the way back, grabbed her by the back of her neck and brought her down to me so I could kiss her nasty. My dick was still in her and she started grinding her hips in a circle in my lap.

"Mine." I said to her with her face on the side of mine. I tickled her clit while she grinded faster, we were both about to cum because our breathing was changing.

"Yours..uh, I'm cumming, Dom."

I sucked on her neck while I shot all inside of her. I

felt like she just took everything out of me and then restored it all back. It was like *Popeye* when he ate his damn spinach!

"Shit!" I shouted.

Symba swirled so slowly making sure her pussy squeezed every drop out of me.

"Do that shit I like you to do," I told her.

She lifted up, opened them ass cheeks and pushed my nut out of her. It landed all on my dick, then Symba brought that pussy back down on it.

"Ughhh." She moaned out while holding still. I loved when she did this shit, it just turned me all the way on. I grabbed my gym bag and gave her the odorless wipes and a towel. After we were clean I helped her back in her seat then set my chair back up.

"Come here," I told her, meeting her before she put her seat belt on. I wanted a kiss. "Thank you for that, Sym baby."

"You're very welcome." That soft voice that made me weak said. We both put our seatbelts on and I got back on the road.

"Dom, baby this is perfect." Symba was more excited than I was.

We were at this garage attached to a two-story building. I had been looking for a property like this for three years. I wanted my garage for motorcycles attached to a building so I can sell guitars. Now that Symba was in my life, I wanted to make these decisions with her. This place was dope, modern, more than enough space and it was in a great location.

I wanted to sell motorcycles downstairs and guitars upstairs. I also loved how I could put a stage upstairs too. It was that spacious and had a full kitchen. My realtor told me someone had a burger joint and a bike shop in the garage. It's been on the market for a month and now that my baby approved it, I was going to buy it.

"You really think so?" I asked her while we were in the kitchen.

"Yes, it's amazing. Can you let me cook here sometimes?" She asked me, looking at the upgraded chrome stove.

"Of course Sym, then you can come watch me play when I have amateur night." I put my arms around her waist and kissed her neck making her giggle.

"This is so amazing, thank you for bringing me and having me be a part of your dream." She wrapped her hands around my neck.

"*You're* my dream baby, this is just extra. Now, we are about to start working on your school you want. You graduate soon so we on that shit ASAP, at least get a visual of what you want." I told her while squeezing her booty.

"I think I want to collide with the school I work at

now, I was talking to my boss about it and she loves the idea, but she wants to see a more vivid plan."

"Ok, we can make that happen. It's whatever you want Symba, I'll back you." I looked in her eyes and told her. After I kissed her again, we went back downstairs to my happy ass realtor. She got excited every time I told her I wanted a new property. I told her I was going to buy it and she informed me that in a few days, I had to come to her office and signs some papers.

Me and Symba left so we could eat and then head back to my palace. I didn't have to work today. The Law worked all yesterday. We had some organs to sell then Cyrus finally found out where Gunna was laying his head. So, we paid them a visit and killed everybody inside, I wanted Gunna to be there, but he wasn't. It was all good, he was definitely getting his, meanwhile all his people were dead.

We were slowly taking care of our enemies. I had to handle that bitch Anika tonight. I got a call from the new tenants I rented my hoe house to. Anika's stupid ass didn't know that I no longer used that house. She took her stupid ass over there and bust out all the windows then threw black paint on the side of it. I put my residents in a suite for a week and had the house redone. I was so sick of that bitch and I was glad that she didn't know shit else about my business.

This bitch texted me all day, called all day, hit me up on Instagram over and over. I try not to call women bitches, but this wasn't no woman, this was a spoiled bitch who didn't know who she was messing with. Last night she got so pissed because I wouldn't answer and she did what I knew she would. Her slippery mouth let out who else knew what I did to her dad; it was her brother.

In a threating voicemail she told me I had two

days to leave with her or her brother was going to the police. That was all I needed her to say. I knew what I needed to do to get this bitch out my life. I assumed one of her homegirls would have been the one she told. But I should have known it wasn't because at my party, Christian and Nina fucked her homegirl up. Women are emotional and when she didn't yell out what I did from anger; I knew it wasn't her.

"Dom I wish you would let me come with you." Symba walked in my closet with her hand on the back of her hip. I wasn't crazy, she had been watching me ever since I told her what I was doing tonight.

"I told yo' ass you are not coming with me, I don't need you in no danger." I answered her, picking up my deodorant.

"Why the hell are you putting that on?"

When she asked that, I looked at her like she was

crazy. "I gotta go outside with funky pits?"

Smacking her lips she said, "I'm just saying,

deodorant, your hair in a man bun...are those new socks?"

Yo', my woman had me crying laughing.

"It's not funny Dominick, I swear if anything goes

down, I'ma sit on your face and smother you to death."

I couldn't stop laughing and she was getting even

more mad, so I rushed her and wrapped my arms around

her waist. Lifting her up, I sat her on the love seat in my

closet.

"We gotta take turns on being crazy Symba, we

can't do it at the same time. Right now, I need you to be

the sane one and know what kind of man you have. Can I

live without you?" I asked her.

She had her head to the side rolling her eyes

looking mad. I grabbed her jaw and turned her to me. "I

said, can I live without you?"

Stubborn ass was trying her best not to smile and

blush. "Not at all."

"Ok then, use your fucking brain. I'm about to get dressed and after tonight, we won't have to deal with her anymore." I kissed her lips, got up and put my clothes on.

I was in our blackout van looking at her mother's big ass house. After Cyrus called me and gave me the address to my first stop, I handled that business and now I was here. I haven't been here since I killed her pops. In a way, this was my fault because I should have made it my business to know more about Anika.

But then again, I never had intentions on her being my woman, so that's why I didn't. I would have been killed her, even if she didn't know about me and her dad. But, here we are and now I was getting out making my way to their house.

"Why do I have to go through all of this drama to get you to see things my way?" Anika asked me when I got inside.

"Since you have been knowing me you know I move at my own pace." I followed her into the living room. It smelled like professional money in here, like you knew her Mama was a stay at home Mom and she cooked dinner every night.

"Does your Moms know your plans to just dip?" I asked her, standing in front of the fireplace.

"It's not her business. I have a million dollars form my dad's life insurance and you have money. I know what I want, I didn't want to do things this way, but you left me no choice." Anika was a beautiful girl; it's sad she was about to die from her stupidity.

"Anika, I am not going anywhere with you, I don't love you and since my parents' crib, I'm actually disgusted by you. I'm warning you right now to stop this shit and move on. I love Symba so much that I should be committed. You can't compete with her or that melanin pussy she got. I'm asking you for the last time, let me walk

out of here and we part ways." I folded my arms and

stood there looking at her.

She was standing in front of me by the couch; her

leggings had the word PINK in cursive, and she had a

matching oversized sweater on. Her long hair was black,

straight and she had some Balenciaga gym-shoes on.

Flipping her hair, she picked up her phone with a slick

smirk.

"You think you are so smart, like you're not the

only one who knows how to move. I knew you would

come here and try to make all these threats. But you

underestimated me, Dominick. When I say I love you, I

mean that more than you know. When I say if I can't have

you then no one will, I mean that even more.

I didn't have my brother here for insurance

purposes. You can kill me now or not, it doesn't matter

because you will be in jail by morning. But guess what, I will still love you." Putting her phone to her ear she dialed her brother. It was priceless to see her face when she heard his phone ring from my pocket.

I took the phone out and answered it. "You underestimated me." In a flash, I pulled my gun out and shot her in the head. I told Cyrus to keep eyes on Anika's brother. When he told me where he was, I killed his ass before I came here. I knew Anika wasn't dumb enough to have him here. Once I told her I would never be with her, I knew she would follow through with her threat. I had her brother's body at our complex. He was AB-negativ,e so you know that was money for us. After I shot her, I went to her body and got her ready to load her in the van.

"Don't move." Someone spoke behind me while I squatted over Anika. "You son of a bitch, why did you just kill my daughter?"

I had my hands up and was about to turn to her

but she stopped me.

"Don't fucking move! I know you, my husband worked on your sister's heart before she died. How do you know my daughter?" Her voice was shaky but I knew she had a gun on me because she cocked it.

"I met her after my sister died, I didn't know she was related to y'all. We were never together, just friends. I got a woman and she got jealous; I told her to move on, but she wouldn't.

"So, you killed my baby girl! Where is my son, he was here when I left?"

I wasn't about to lie, even though she had the advantage. "He's dead, I killed him because him and Anika were blackmailing me." I still had my hands up and had no idea what she was about to do.

I heard her sobbing and then she said, "I have to bury my children, and so does your parents."

POW!

I closed my eyes when I heard a gunshot, but I didn't feel shit. I've been shot twice so I know what it feels like. Turning around, I saw Anika's mama on the ground dead. When I looked on the side where she was standing, Symba was there in all black holding a 9mm.

I couldn't help but smile wide at her. "Symba what the hell?"

"I trust you, it's Anika I didn't trust, so I followed you. You've been teaching me how to shoot and where you had all your guns over your house."

I walked over to her sexy juicy ass and kissed her so deep that my tongue tickled her tonsils.

"Next time I tell you to do something, don't listen to me," I joked and kissed her again. I was thankful she didn't listen because I would have died, leaving her and my family heartbroken. I decided to call my cleanup crew to handle the bodies. Right now, I wanted to follow Symba home and get all inside her.

Christian

"Everything looks really good, you're healthy, the baby is healthy and it's heartbeat sounds perfect," The ultrasound technician told me and Quest.

I was now eight months and I carried all in my belly. My thighs were thicker and I'm not even about to talk about my booty; I was close to joining Symba. I ate everything under the sun and I ate meat at least twice a day. Overall, I was miserable. I just had this big belly and child inside that kicked all day.

"That's really good news." I said smiling, looking at

her clean the gel off my stomach. Quest kissed my lips and my hand. He was so excited as well.

"So, do you two want to find out the sex?" She asked us.

I looked up at Quest. "What do you think, you wanna know now or just wait til I give birth?"

He made me laugh when he ran his hand over his sexy face, smiling. "Why you gotta leave that up to me, bae?"

Me and the technician were cracking up at him because he was really thinking.

"Come on man, you the mama, so you decide!" He licked his sexy lips then held his bottom one in his mouth.

"Ok, you can tell us." I told her and my heart started beating so fast form anticipation. I really wanted a boy, but I wouldn't be hurt if it was a girl.

"Do you guys have any names picked out?" She asked us.

"Yup, Journei Alanna Foster if it's a girl, and Chance Quade Foster if it's a boy."

I have never told Quest that because I wanted to surprise. I gave our daughter his aunt's middle name because his Mom seemed to lover her so much. Quest told me so many stories of how she hated everything about herself, including her name. So, I figured why not name her Alanna. Quade was his father's name, so I thought it would be a beautiful tribute to give our son that middle name.

"Why you gotta hit a nigga in the heart like that, bae?" Quest said with an open smile. His eyes had tears in them, but he blinked them away then he kissed my lips. "Thank you, sugar tits."

I mushed his face because I hated when he called me that in public, but it was funny.

"Those are beautiful names, so Chance Quade Foster it is!" She said and we got so excited.

"Yes! I got my boy!" I shouted, crying.

"Hell yeah, a mini me first? I can dig that shit!" Quest rubbed my stomach and then kissed on it twice. "Damn, I owe Dominick and Angel money!" He hugged me and kissed my lips a few times.

"Congratulations you two, he is going to be beautiful." She told us and we thanked her while I pulled my shirt down and Quest helped me up.

"Come on let's get up out of here, I got something I want to show you." He told me, grabbing my hand so we could walk out.

"Ok cool." We got to the car and after he opened my door for me to get inside. Then he went around to his side and we pulled off.

"I am so excited about having a boy; I know most women want girls, but I really wanted a boy first," I said while we were in the car.

"I'm hella geeked about having a boy too, you said

boy first. So does that mean you'll be giving me more babies?" His fine butt looked at me with that smirk that made my kat purr.

"Bae, I would give you as many babies as you want." We were at a red light so I reached over and gave him a kiss.

"That's what I like to hear." He pecked my lips again and we finished talking about what we wanted to buy for our son.

I didn't want a baby shower. I know that sounds crazy, but it's just never been something I've wanted. I knew my family would still want to buy things for him and they can, but a shower isn't what I wanted.

"7th & Carson! Yes baby daddy you love me very much!" I got excited when we pulled up to the restaurant. Not only was I hungry, but now I was excited when he picked here to take me. They had the best chicken and waffles to me, and my mouth was watering.

"Chunky ass." He chuckled and said after he opened the door for me.

"Is this what you had to show me?" I asked him after we walked inside.

"Naw, that's what I want to show you." He pointed towards the booth that had some older man sitting in it.

I was passed confused as we walked in his direction.

"Gene, how are you today?" Quest said to him then he shook his hand.

"I'm fine Mr. Foster, how is my top client?"

Client? I thought to myself.

"I'm great since I found out my bae is giving me a boy." Quest told him while smiling and rubbing my stomach. "This is my woman I was telling you about. Christian, this is Gene Hermes, the best realtor in Nevada."

"Nice to meet you, I have heard great things about

you." He shook my hand.

I smiled and spoke as well. Quest let me slide in first and then he sat down, the realtor sat across from us.

I was still a little lost and Quest knew it, so he held my hand. "I want me and you to search for a new home together."

"A new home? But you have an amazing home already."

"No, I have an amazing house. I told you that when I first took you there. I want a home that me and you pick out together. I don't want you and our son in a house that another woman used to call her own. Naw, I ain't even cut like that." He kissed my cheek.

I was so excited and surprised, Quest amazed me how much he has changed from the moment after he found out I was sick. This man was just amazing and showing me every day that he loved me.

"I brought my iPad to show you the list I put together with your limit. I also sent a portal to each of your emails. Anytime you see a home that interests you, just hit the 'star' button and I will get the keys so you can go see it." He gave us the iPad.

When I scrolled down and saw the prices, I almost choked on my water. "Bae these homes start at eight-million." I said lowly because I didn't want Gene to hear me.

Quest was looking at the iPad concentrating hard and he responded, "I know, that's the minimum I told him to set the price. I want to see how the ten and fourteen one's look."

He didn't even see the face I had. I knew Quest had money but got damn. That's a lot of fucking zeros. After I snapped out of the fact that my baby daddy had bank, I started looking at some of the homes. They were beautiful and I got into the feel of living in one of them.

"Can we see some today?" I asked Quest. Now I was beyond geeked. I put four stars by my favorites already.

"Anything you want, bae." He said, kissing my cheek again and gave Gene the iPad back.

"Well actually, I like to give people at least a twenty-four hour notice—"

"I'm sure you can make an exception for your top client and his lady, right?" Quest said sitting back and putting his arm around my waist.

Gene gave us a closed mouth smile. "Sure, let me just make some calls." He slid out the booth while putting his phone to his ear.

The waitress brought us our food and I looked at Quest, chuckling. "You think you got it like that?" I teased.

He shrugged his shoulders. "It's my job to make sure you get what you want."

"Will you be like that to our son?" I asked putting a

piece of waffle in my mouth.

"When he's little but once he gets around ten, he'll need to start doing small chores. Nothing crazy, but like making up his bed, cleaning his room and listening to his Mama. Then he will get rewards for that. Now when we have a daughter, then yeah, I'll do her the way I do you." He put some pepper on his mashed potatoes

"I think that's fair." I started eating when Gene came back and told us it was a go for us to see the four houses. We hurried up and ate so we could get to it.

"I am in love!" I said to Quest while walking out the master bathroom.

This was the third home we went to see. Me and Quest put shopping for the baby aside for tomorrow. Right now, we were in the mode. The first two homes were great. But this one right here, this was it, I could feel it. Seven bedrooms, two full kitchens, one in the main part and the other in the basement.

It had a big outdoor pool and a basketball court for Quest, like at his first house. I wanted to make sure our home had that and a workout room for him. Ten bathrooms, two dens that we were turning into our office spaces, and we had a sauna room. The outside of the house was a beige brick with a dark red roof, wide garage for multiple cars and a beautiful garden.

"Yeah this one is the shit, that basketball court slaps hard. Come here." He held his hand out to me. He was standing on the balcony that was inside the master bedroom. "You really love this house, this is the one you want?" Quest asked me while placing me in front of him and putting his hands around my waist. The view of the neighborhood and the other mansion homes was breathtaking. What I took pride in was the clear sky and the fact that our home was the biggest.

"I am one-hundred-percent sure, I don't even need

to see another house; this one is perfect. Thank you so much Quest. I can't believe this will be our house." I couldn't stop smiling, I was that happy.

"You never have to thank me for providing and taking care of both of y'all. I'm glad this house is everything you need." He said kissing my neck.

"You're everything I need bae, you and our son." I told him with sweetness in my voice.

"Oh yeah?"

"Absolutely." I responded and I rubbed the end of his beard.

"I can think of one more thing you need." He said while kissing my neck again.

I giggled. "What's that?"

He moved his left hand and I felt his hand on my booty so I thought he was about to get nasty, but he put it back in my face with a small box in it. I thought I was seeing things. My eyes spread open wider. Then, he got down on one knee.

"Quest, what are you doing?" I asked as my eyes immediately watered.

"About to ask the most beautiful, sexy, ambitious, smart and compassionate woman I have ever met, to please become my wife. We can do this however you like. Long engagement, island wedding, just the two of us, over the top wedding...I want what you want. Just please say yes."

I hadn't even looked at the box, my eyes were stuck on his. I was so surprised and ready to kick his ass because I had on makeup today.

"I love you so much, Quest." I spoke through my cry.

He laughed, "Is that a yes?"

"Yes, fuck yes!" I shouted and he put the round shape eight-carat diamond ring with an aquamarine color center diamond on my finger. It was shining brighter than the sun and it fit perfectly.

When he stood up, he interlocked our fingers and then we kissed. I couldn't believe it, I was getting married!

**
—

"Didn't I tell yo' ass to throw them pictures away?"

"I look so good in these pictures though, look at my dress in this one." I held it up in Quest's face and he looked at me, pissed.

"Nina, get your sister before I flick her ass all the way home."

We were at her and Angel's house with Dominick and Symba as well. I showed them my ring and of course, they were so happy for us. Symba and Nina screamed loud as hell with me and were hugging me. Nina was still healing, so I couldn't hug her like I wanted. She was walking around now, but nothing too crazy. Angel stayed on her tough, making sure she wanted for nothing.

A week ago, Quest came home and put all these pictures of me and Tucker on our bed. He wasn't upset with me, but he was upset at the fact that Tucker was my ex. I sat him down and told him the story of us, he told me how he knew him. I couldn't believe he was the reason the complex burned down; he could have killed Angel.

I hated Tucker so, I begged Quest to let me help him get him. I told him I could start talking to him on Facebook, we can video chat when I'm home, make Tucker believe I was really trying to fuck him. Quest was ready to kill me when I told him the plan, but Tucker kept out-smarting him. You see his parents have been on vacation and won't be back until after the winter. So when they went to go get him thinking he was there, he wasn't but Quest had all these photos and some bookkeeping with important names in it.

I told Quest ever since Tucker got expelled, him and his parents had not gotten along. I didn't know where Tucker was living, Molly looked his name up and there was no house in his name or his parents. I bet he was resting his head in a hotel suite. But Tucker wasn't staying under his name and Las Vegas is filled with them so that was like a needled in a haystack. This was the only way so Quest finally agreed. Tucker was skeptical until we started video chatting.

I told him I was pregnant by a guy who I really didn't want to be with. Of course, he started acting cocky and telling me I shouldn't have fucked unprotected. It took so much not to snap on him, as far as Tucker knows. I have no idea that him and Quest know each other, I'm just his ex who wants to fuck. He asked if he could come over tonight and I told him ok. I think it's nasty as fuck to fuck a bitch who is about due to have another nigga's baby but to each its own.

"She does look sexy in this homecoming dress. Oh my goodness, remember I went with Brenden." Symba laughed and said to us. "That night we...Ahem. Never mind."

Me and Nina died laughing because that girl shut her sentence off real quick.

"Naw complete your sentence, I'll look that muthafucka up and kill his ass." Dominick was now looking like Quest.

We were in Angel's second living room with the big TV and movie style couches. The guys were sitting in the row in front of us playing the game. Angel had Mexican food delivered here and we were all eating and drinking except for Nina and me were drinking juice. I took out these old photos of me in college and high school. Tucker was in every single one and Quest hated it, he wanted me to throw them out.

The only reason I wasn't tripping was because I had all of these plus ones without Tucker at Mama's house. Speaking of her, I was still so mad at her for lying all these years. I didn't hate her, but I was disappointed at how she did me and Nina. I texted her yesterday and she responded. This morning I called her and told her the baby sex and that I was engaged. Her and Grandma were together, and they were so happy for me. I was pissed at her, but she's my mother and still my queen.

"Here, chicken nugget." Angel gave Nina her medicine and a bottle of water because she drank all her apple juice.

"Thank you," she said to him and he went and set back down with the guys.

"I love you, Dom!" Symba yelled to him because she knew he was annoyed.

He got up and walked over to the table display that

Angel had all the food sitting on so he could get another quesadilla. After he filled his plate up, he walked over to where we were sitting. He bent down and kissed Symba. "I love you, Sym."

It was hilarious and cute to see how Symba was now.

"How are things with you and Burt, is it weird?" Symba asked Nina and I wanted to know too.

"Him and Mary came over yesterday for dinner. It was awkward at first because I didn't know how to act with him. I just can't believe he's my dad, Mary knew after he married her but she accepted it. It's just a lot and I feel like a plot in a afterschool special. I don't even know what to call him." Nina told us putting some taco salad in her mouth.

"It will come to you boo just give it time. Mama asked if I wanted to know about my dad, I told her fuck no.

Let that nigga stay where he's at." I mentioned folding my steak taco in half so I can take a bite.

"I don't blame you, he just dipped out. Me and my dad are close but it could be better. He knows about Dominick, he said another black girl taken by *the man*." All three of us fell out laughing when she whispered that last part.

"All ya'll do is giggle and whisper, Nina you bet not be talking shit." Angel looked back at us and said and we just laughed harder.

We chilled over Angel house until around eight at night. Between me and Nina we ate almost all the damn food. I brought three steak tacos back to me and Symba house. The home me and Quest brought won't be ready until after my due date, so I had time to pack. I was still going to pay rent here until Symba figured out what she wanted to do. Quest had been on me about getting my real estate license and starting my business up. I was actually ready to get on that as soon as our son was born.

Tucker Must Die: *Send me your address*

I got nervous as hell. The last time me and him was in the same room, I fucked his hand up with a baseball bat. Now after Quest dropped me off, I was due to see him. I had showered and put on some leggings with a graphic tee-shirt. I had just taken my jumbo twist down so my real hair had a little twist pattern. I texted Tucker my address and he hurried up and text that he was leaving now.

I rubbed my belly while I sat on the couch watching TV. Chance would kick like crazy when Quest touches or talks to my stomach. I put some popcorn in my mouth and was killing it like I didn't just have a bunch of Mexican food. My doorbell went off and I got up to answer it, knowing who it was.

"Damn Christian, you fat as fuck." Tucker said when he came inside. He looked good for him. He had on some jeans, a red Gucci belt and a loud ass red sweater with a big G on it.

"And yet you're still here so you really don't give a fuck you just wanna say some rude shit." I said closing the door. "Why do you have a duffle bag?" I looked at his sit it on the floor.

"Because I'm spending the night, I heard pregnant pussy have you K.O."

"You are so silly." I faked laugh while taking the empty bowl of popcorn to the kitchen. Tucker followed me and he opened the refrigerator. I realized with him being here for all of five minutes that Tucker is annoying and obnoxious. He also is rude I think I never noticed because I was seeing him through lust goggles. Like now, he was opening shit up without even asking. Taking bites out of different stuff and he didn't even know whose it was.

"Where is your room at?" He asked me when we were on the couch watching American Dad for about ten-minutes.

Finally. I thought to myself, we got up and he picked up his duffle bag. I turned the TV and living room light off then he followed me in the back. Once we got in my room, I closed the door, turned the light on and then the TV.

"Girl you still ain't grew up?" He asked, picking up my star shape pillow.

I snatched it from him with my nose turned up. "I don't think a nigga dressed like a cherry bomb has room to talk shit. Look, can we do what you came here to do before I put you out and just masturbate?" I dropped my leggings revealing my legs which Tucker was weak for. Pregnant or not, my legs and chocolate skin still looked amazing. I was standing at the end of the bed and he was standing by the door, his eyes glued to my legs.

"You know, it's a fucking shame, I wanted to come here and fuck the shit out of you. But even with them legs that I used to be weak for all out, I still can't get the fact that I hate your fucking guts out my head." His eyes traveled up my body til' they met my face and I could see the hate in them. He went into his duffle bag and pulled put a long, steel baseball bat.

I placed my hand on my stomach and the other one on the end of my bed rail so I wouldn't pass out.

"Have you ever thought about how you fucked up my football career? I was going pro, going to be something. All of that shattered when you hit me with that bat because your bitch ass wasn't satisfying me anymore. We were in college, why the fuck do you think I would want to sit under your sick ass all day?! Missing out on frat parties, trips and have a real college experience. Instead of you just accepting that, your jealous ass took things to another level and fucked my whole life up!" He yelled some more, looking like a lunatic.

"I tried to move on and forget about it, but your

stupid face kept popping in my head. It was fate when my boy Gunna sent me pictures of The Law bitches and one of them was you. I scratched all plans of working with them to getting along with you and killing you. I thought you were setting me up, but I sat down the street and saw Quest drop you off and pull off. I even sat and waited to see if he would circle back." He had this greasy smile on his face and even though he was close enough to me, he pointed his bat to my stomach.

"I am going to knock that baby the fuck out of you. Then I'm gonna bash your fucking brains in. Your family won't even be able to have a funeral because once I'm done, I'll burn this house the fuck down."

I was so scared I couldn't even blink, then my door busted open and Quest shot Tucker twice in both his legs.

"ARGH!!" Tucker yelled and hit the floor. Before he could even grab his legs, Quest raised this big ass knife and brought it down on Tucker's hand, cutting it completely off.

I had my hand over my mouth. I have never seen anything like this, not even on television. Quest looked worse than Tucker; he looked like he was enjoying it. Then he picked Tucker's hand up and squatted down over him.

"Is this what you were tripping on my fiancée about, this punk ass hand?" He said to him.

Tucker was shaking, trembling, holding his arm. He had tears coming down and sweat all over him.

"You and them niggas you came here with were never leaving this bitch alive from the moment y'all had the balls to walk in our complex." Quest looked at me and licked his lips then looked back down at Tucker.

"You stupid as hell, I would have fucked first." He laughed then put the knife in Tucker's chest so hard. He twisted it and moved it around like Tucker was some butter. When he pulled the knife out, Tucker's heart was on the end of it. What the hell was it with this man and body parts?

"I'm about to be sick, Quest." I told him. He dropped the knife on top of Tucker and came and picked me up.

"The cleanup crew is coming, when they get done it will look like nothing happened." He told me while taking me to the kitchen. "I was about to fuck the whole plan up when it took you a while to turn the living room light off. Once you did, I hurried my ass in here. I didn't want you to even kiss him." He looked at me while giving me some of my ice tea. His eyes squinted.

"You didn't kiss that nigga, did you Christian? You already was standing there in your panties."

I laughed. "Quest, I didn't touch him, calm down. Can you go get my leggings please, then can we leave?" I asked him while putting my cup down.

Quest rubbed on my thighs, making my kat wet,

then he kissed me.

"I love you, you such a down ass for doing that shit. But never again will you be a part of anything that will jeopardize you or our child. Y'all my family and I won't be right in the head if something happens to y'all." He kissed me again and I was ready to leave, eat and get fucked by my fiancé.

Quest

"Got damn Christian, I swear we havin' two weddings. One for me and you and one for my dick and your pussy." I told her while I had her bent over the couch. She was so wet that my dick would slip out when I would go crazy in it.

"Ugh, fuck, Quest! Fuck me! Fuck me! Fuck me!"

Christian yelled out while cumming so much it was all on my pelvis.

I was loving it. I put my foot on the couch so I could go deeper. Then I slowed down and pulled out so my dick could drip. I squatted down, spread her chocolate ass cheeks open so I could see that pretty pussy contrast from the back.

"Sssss, look at that pretty muthafucka, she tryna catch her breath." I licked my lips and felt hungry, so I started licking her from the back. "Mmmm mmm!" The sweet water taste was so good, I was pigging out. Then my nasty ass stopped and let her juices spill out my mouth to my beard. I love that pussy moisturizer in my beard. Standing back up, I eased back in her gold mine and she cried out.

"Close your fuckin' mouth and take this dick, Christian. Take it all cause it's all yours. Hell yeah, bae." I held my head back. "Ughh, slam that ass back." I told her squeezing her booty.

"Oh my gosh. Yes. Yes, Quest, I'm gonna cum again. Whew!" Christian was throwing it back crucial and nutting on me.

I squeezed her waist, thrust hard in her and came so good I felt like I died a peaceful death and came back to life inside this pussy.

"Shit woman, I needed that." After I cleaned us up, I sat on the long part of the couch with her between my legs. Rubbing on her stomach, I pulled the blanket off the back of the couch and covered her up. She had this short shirt on and a thong, that's what made me bend her pregnant ass over.

"I can't believe he will be here any day now." I told her referring to our son.

"I know right, I'm glad the house is ready for us. Are you sad because this is your last night in this house?"

"Nope, I mean it's a dope crib, but I'm anticipating our new life together in our new home."

She tilted her head up to me, that gorgeous face smiling. "Me too."

I looked down at her, "You mean so much to me Christian, you changed my life in ways you couldn't even imagine. Not a day goes by that I feel alone or like I don't have a family. I'll forever willingly be indebted to you." I told her on some real shit. I loved this woman beyond words.

"I love you too bae, you taught me to trust again. I cannot wait to become your wife."

I leaned down and gave her a kiss, then we watched TV until we fell asleep.

**

"Hello, I'm Curtis Street, Comcast technician for Denny Kelin's estate." Cyrus said to the guard at the entrance of Golden Estate Mansions. This nigga had everything you needed and if he didn't believe me, he would get it. How he got a Comcast van, with tools, a badge and uniform was beyond me. But this is why we paid him the big bucks; he was the shit and he was our lawyer.

Christian couldn't find Kamila. Her friend Molly searched for any properties brought under her name, and all names I gave her. Nothing, then yesterday, she called and told Christian that their old boss Denny Kelin brought a new mini mansion. I gave Cyrus the address and he saw a Comcast tech was scheduled to come out today.

I don't know how he did it, but now he was that tech. How did I know it was Kamila's house? Because Cyrus got a hold of surveillance coming in and out this place and she was on it. Kamila was smart; she didn't move around a t and when she did, her stupid ass wore a blonde wig and ⎯des. I don't know why this dumb girl didn't just leave Nevada.

Even though I would have found her, she still would have had a head start. While Cyrus pulled up the long driveway the front door opened, and Kamila walked outside. I guess the blonde wig wasn't a wig after all because she had it in a ponytail on top of her head. It was a nice breeze outside, but she wore some workout clothes.

I also noticed she had a big rock on her finger; either she was married or getting married. Christian already told me about Kamila fucking their boss for over two years. That's a damn shame, this whore really wasn't shit but only for whatever would get her ahead. Cyrus went inside for about five minutes. I shot Christian a text telling her I love her, and I was good. Cyrus came back outside and opened the door.

"She's in the living room on the left doing yoga, no one else is home."

I nodded at him as I got out, holding my Latin machete. As I walked inside, I could hear her workout video. I was so geeked about this shit I almost felt like I was horny. I walked in the living room and her back was to me while she did this stretch move.

"You've always been very flexible," I said.

When she heard my voice, she turned around and looked like she saw the devil. Like I knew, she tried to run but she ran smack into Cyrus, who was holding a gun. He wasn't going to shoot her, but she didn't know that.

"Quest please, Edith did all of this, I swear! I wanted to tell you but her and her son threatened me." Already she was begging, lying and crying while walking backwards til' her back hit the olive-green walls.

"Kamila shut the fuck up lying. I'd respect you more if you told the truth. Look at you, new hair, house, husband." I pointed to her ring. "Why go through all of that if you are scared for your life?" I asked her, standing in her face.

Kamila was so scared I felt her shaking. She looked like she wanted to throw up. "I don't love Denny, I'm just using him for his money I only love you...I...You." She started stuttering when I held up my phone in her face. It was a video of Christian sleeping sound in my bed. She didn't even know I was recording her.

Her beauty and glow were out of this world. I got in the video, moved the covers and kissed on her stomach. Then I kissed her hand flashing that big ass diamond and aquamarine ring on her finger. The way I was grinning in the video was the way I was grinning now. Once the video was over, Kamila's tears were coming down fast and she looked at me with despise all in her eyes. Her chest was going in and out and the hoe spit directly in my face.

"You damn right I had your Mom killed. I told you not to fuck with me before you even met her. I warned you through your Mom the first time in a letter, but you didn't believe me. Then you turn around and fuck a bitch from my job who I already hate!? Now you're flaunting that she's pregnant, and you're marrying her!? You've known her less than a year and you give her everything you've never gave me! I hate you, fuck you, her, and your fucking mother!" She had snot all in her mouth and spit flying from her lips.

I snatched the front part of her shirt, ripping it and using it to wipe my face. Then grabbed her throat while she was still against the wall.

"What pisses me off is how you know that you ain't shit. Since the first time you cheated, all the way to you fucking your boss for two years. You didn't kill my mother out of being hurt, you did it just to be a despiteful, evil, hoe ass bitch." I had my mouth tight and was close to her face when I talked. I wasn't choking her out because I wanted her to be alive and conscious.

I grabbed her jaw, making her mouth open and I took my sixteen-inch machete, placed it between her lips and started sawing back and forth. Like the *Joker* from all the *Batman* movies, I was putting a smile on that pretty face. Kamila was screeching loud and blood was spilling from her. The sound of her skin slicing open and then of her jaw cracking was everything. When I was done, her body dropped slowly on the floor. Her face was split wide open; looked like some horror movie type shit.

"Quest, you one twisted fuck." Cyrus said, shaking his head looking at Kamila's dead body. "I like it, though."

I chuckled at him as we walked out her house. After I got in the Comcast van, I changed my clothes while Cyrus drove. I laughed when he took his fake face off; it reminded me of Mrs. Doubtfire. He really looked like a Caucasian man with a thick mustache. As soon as I got dressed, my phone rang and it was Christian.

"Sugar tits—"

"My water broke, my Mama is driving me to the hospital since I was over her house. Where are you?!"

I was still stuck on her saying her water broke.

"Quest!?" She yelled my name snapping me out of it.

"I'm on my way to you bae, I'm coming." I hung up as we pulled to Cyrus' house. I knew he had to handle the Comcast van before its on the radar connected to Kamila. My ride was parked at his spot so as soon as I got out, I ran to my car, jumped in and took off to the hospital.

**

"I'm here bae, I'm right here."

"Where the fuck have you been!?" Christian looked like a possessed person. Sweating, her hair in that shower cap thing she sometime sleeps in and she look like she was in pain.

"I was speeding here...what the hell?!" I looked down where the doctor was at and all I saw was this black ball coming out her pussy. Her shit was stretched so wide a saw a little blood on the side.

"Bae, I think your pussy broke." I told her looking at her with my mouth open.

"She's fine dad, it's just the baby's head crowning," the doctor told me.

Christian grabbed my hand and yanked me close. "I need you to stand right here, let me squeeze your hand and shut the fuck up."

Man I swear her ass had more bass in her voice than I did. "Aight, anything you need." I told her, a little scared for my life right now.

"Ok Mom, give me a big push!" The doctor instructed Christian.

She closed her eyes, squeezed my hand tight as fuck then pushed. The process was repeated three times and then my son started crying. I have never known for childbirth to be the most disgusting—beautiful thing I have ever seen. Christian's Mama was in the room too and she was holding Christian's other hand.

"Bae, he got so much hair and his ass is chocolate like you." I told her smiling and kissing her face.

"That is so good." She said out of breath and snatching that shower cap off. My bae looked beyond tired and I had a newfound respect for her. Ain't no fucking way I would have went through that shit. I couldn't stop kissing her and telling her thank you.

"Here you go, Dad." The nurse said to me, handing me my son.

"Holy shit. Look at you, you're so damn perfect, just like your Mama. Chance Quade Foster, welcome to our family lil' man. Daddy loves you so much." I kissed his jaw and passed him to his Mama while I recorded them.

Chance was beautiful, a head full of hair, chocolate skin and a perfect size face. I couldn't believe I was a father. I let Christian and her mother bond with him, and I continued recording them. I zoomed in on Christian and Chance and a nigga got a little emotional. This was my family and I was beyond bless to have them.

Symba

"Christian you look beautiful, even with my Chancey-Chance on your boob." I teased her while she was breastfeeding.

Today was Mama's wedding and we were in the room with her, getting dressed. Her and Harvey's wedding was at this nice intimate chapel. The outside was my favorite because it was a nice water fall with a rose garden and a statue in the center. It was perfect for pictures and the weather was perfect as well. It was April and even though Mama wanted a March wedding she wanted to give Chance time to turn two months so he could be around people.

It was about sixty guests out there, including Harvey's kids. I met them yesterday at his house for dinner and they were pretty cool. We all got along which says a lot for me because I didn't like people that much. Mama wanted everything simple. Her colors were the traditional black and white which I thought was elegant.

Christian, myself and Nina were bridesmaids and my sister was her maid of honor. Harvey had his best friend as his best man, his sons were two groomsmen and his cousin was the third one. Helping Mama with her wedding was so easy because they were older and didn't want much. Like they weren't having a reception, they were going straight to the airport after they leave here to go to Paris.

"He is so greedy, and I want him sleep during the ceremony." She said while burping him.

"Don't be talking about my nephew," Nina said, putting on her earrings.

Our dresses were black, fitted with a slit on each side. Nina was five-months pregnant, so you could see her stomach rounding. Our hair was the same, wand curled to the side with black and white flower halos around our heads. Nina was feeling better since getting shot. I hugged her a little more than normal if I was around her. Christian did too; almost losing her scared the hell out of us, so we just showed her more love.

"Let me take him to Quest. I'll be right back." Christian said, putting Chance in his car seat. He was so handsome in his little black and white stripe sleeper with matching little scratch guard mittens on.

"Mama, your hair looks gorgeous." I told her looking at the stylist finish it then the make-up artist was done to.

Her hair was in this up-do with some pieces hanging around her face. She had a white robe on with her dress behind the curtain.

"Thank you, sweetie, I love it too." She looked in the mirror pleased and then got up to go put on her dress.

"Lanail asked if she could spend the night, again. It's

her last night in Nevada so I told her ok, she's moving with her aunt to Ohio." I told them while I put my heels on.

"Really, damn. I was hoping her Mama would have come around to letting her move back home." Nina said putting her shoes on too.

"I was as well, but her Mama isn't budging. She's hurt about Lanail pissing away her senior year." I felt bad for Lanail but then again, her decision making should have been better, Still, we had a good relationship. so I was letting her spend the night at my house. Dominick asked me to move in, so I was moving out anyway in the next week.

"That's crazy but maybe her being gone from the fast pace of Las Vegas will be good for her." Nina made sense.

Christian walked back in just as Mama was ready to show us her complete look. When she came out holding her bouquet of flowers, we all gasped.

"Mama, you look stunning." Lakota told her fighting back her tears.

"I agree, you look breathtaking." I told her too.

Her dress was a sleek cape-sleeve gown with a lace print, it was a soft cream.

Smiling at us she said, "Thank you all so much. Ok, let's do this." We all got up and headed out in perfect timing. Mama stayed back until it was her time to come out.

The double door opened as I put my arm through Harvey son's arm. The piano player was playing a beautiful piece as each pair walked down the aisle. Once we were positioned in place the preacher walked out. I looked in the crowd and saw Dominick sitting with Quest and Angel. He looked so handsome in his sky-blue button-up dress shirt. His hair was in that man bun I love, and his long brunette beard was freshly lined up.

Those eyes were in that sexy slant and I just wanted

to sit on his face. I didn't even feel me licking my lips, but I felt me get wet when he bit his bottom lip. Dominick always went crazy when I would lick my lips at him but sometimes, I couldn't help it. My heart skipped a beat when he got up and made his way towards me in front of everybody. I was praying he wasn't about to dick me down right here. It may sound crazy, but you never know with Dom. He walked behind me and whispered in my ear.

"I don't wanna have to postpone your Mom's wedding, so please stop licking them sexy ass lips at me before I fuck you in front of the father, the son and the holy ghost." He kissed my cheek and so smoothly walked back to his seat.

I was so turned on it was insane. All I could do was stand there and look stupid, trying to not show how horny I was.

Christian leaned to me and said, "I hope you know

God and the preacher heard everything you sinners just said." Leaning forward, her and Nina lowly cackled.

I played it off and looked behind me and sure enough, the preacher was shaking his head at me. I turned back frontwards and tried not to laugh. Thank goodness Harvey walked down the aisle after Lakota and his best man. Now it was time for Mama to enter as the doors reopened and the music started.

One look in your eyes and there I see

Just what you mean to me

Here in my heart I believe

Your love is all I'll ever need

Luther Vandross-Here and Now played, everyone was on their feet and she started walking. It was so beautiful but what made me cry was seeing Harvey's reaction. He was smiling so wide and looking only at her. He really loved her and I was all here for it, he grabbed her hand once she reached him and they stood face to face. I was so happy for Mama and prayed their marriage would last forever.

**

"Are you excited about Ohio?" I asked Lanail while I polished her nails. I had all the stuff the shops had to do gel nails, so I hooked her up. She spent the night last night and we had a lot of fun. We took a trip to Walmart, brought some movies and then I got her a few pair of pajamas and sports bras to take with her to Ohio.

"I am. I wanna start over, get a job and get my diploma. I still want to go to college and just get my life back on track. I feel like once I do that, then I can get my relationship back with my Mama. I wrote her a three-page letter in my journal, I think I'll mail it to her when I get to

Ohio."

"Is that what you were writing this morning?" I asked her while I finished her pinky nail.

"Yup, I get my feelings out better on paper." She held her hand out looking at the pretty orange she picked on in her nails.

"I think that's a smart plan, I can't see your Mama not forgiving you it will just take time." I told her while I cleaned up since I was done with her nails. Her aunt was picking her up in a few hours. I got up to put the nail stuff up and make us something to eat.

Dom Baby: *Please tell me you cooked, I'm hungry as hell and since you left me alone in that big ass palace I gotta come to you.*

I laughed reading Dominick's text; he was such a big baby but I let him know what I was making.

"Hey Symba, I need to ask a favor." Lanail peeked her head in my room.

"Sure, what's up?" I asked her.

"Remember my friend, the one who I told you was nineteen and she was into that mess too?"

"Yeah I remember." I told her, texting Dominick.

Me: *Lasagna, fried chicken and a salad.*

"Well, I told her I was leaving and she wants to come see me. She's not doing that stuff anymore. She said when I left, she did after. I just wanna tell her goodbye."

"That's fine by me." I gave her a light smile and walked to my kitchen so I can cook.

Dominick texted back.

Dom Baby: *I'm coming over and make this your last time sleeping away from me.*

"So spoiled." I said to myself, taking out the pot to boil my lasagna noodles. Lanail was in the living room watching TV. It was a little warm outside today, so I had the kitchen window open. My noodles were boiled, and I started layering my lasagna then I put it in the oven so I can start frying chicken.

"Symba, my friend is about to pull up." Lanail came in the kitchen and told me.

"Ok, I have enough food for her if she's hungry." I said to Lanail looking at what I was wearing to make sure I was covered. I had one some jeggings, a *Sailor Moon* tee-shirt and some purple Nike slides. Plugging up my air fryer I heard Lanail open the front door. After I put some wings inside the fryer, I washed my hands, picked up my phone and went to say hi to her friend.

"Hi—" I stopped in my tracks and dropped my phone when I saw Gunna holding Lanail by the back of her neck with a gun to her head. On the side of him must have been Lanail's friend. She didn't have a gun in her hand, but she was sitting on the couch flicking through the channels like what was happening was no big deal.

You see, Gunna didn't know where I lived. I met

him at the mall the day we went out. I lied to Dominick and told him he knew where I lived because I was mad he had that thot at his other house. He used Lanail's friend to get here. I felt so stupid. Dominick had been telling me to be careful with Lanail because she was associated with Gunna. I'm not saying this is her fault, I just should have been more careful.

"Gunna, what the hell are you doing?" I asked him while making sure I kept my hands in sight so he wouldn't think I was doing anything crazy and shoot her. He stood in front of my door, leaving it wide open like I didn't have neighbors.

"What I'm doing is getting you and that fuck face Dominick together. Them niggas came in my shit and took out all my people. Then Tina here tells me that Lanail is with you, so you two bitches are working with The Law to set me up." He was talking crazy as hell but looked even crazier.

Lanail was crying and terrified. I shook my head.

"You're wrong, we didn't set anything—"

"Bullshit, bitch! I had a hotel full of shot up clients that Lanial was supposed to fuck and then she comes up missing. You think you're untouchable because you fuck that white piece of shit!" His voice was loud and he pressed the gun harder in her head.

"Your beef is with me, let her go and take me." I pleaded with my hands up and my face looking so serious. I was so scared but not for me, for Lanail because she was helpless. Her friend used her.

Speaking of her friend, she started laughing and then looked at me. "You're just like this dumb bitch, you think he wants y—"

"Tina, shut the fuck up!" Gunna yelled at her. "You know what, you two would make me more money alive than dead. Let's roll."

"What?!" Tina jumped up and looked at Gunna. "You said you were killing these hoes and me and you were leaving for Philadelphia!" Her voice was so loud and high pitched, I was getting a headache.

Gunna seemed to be getting annoyed too because he shook his head fast, looking at Tina with frustration all over his face. "Bitch shut the fuck up!" While they shouted back and forth, I saw Dominick sneak up my porch steps. He put his index finger to his lips while he was holding his gun.

"No! You lied to me, you said you loved me and I was the only—"

POW!

Tina's body hit the floor with a hole in her head. My hands were still up, so Gunna knew it wasn't me. He turned around so quickly behind him and as soon as he did, Dominick shot him twice in the head. Lanail screamed and when his body hit the floor, she ran to me crying.

"It's ok, you're ok." I rubbed her back, soothing her. I was surprised I wasn't crying, and it was coming, but once I saw Dominick behind Gunna, I knew things were going to be fine.

"Y'all ok, he didn't hurt you, did he?" Dominick asked, stepping over the bodies like they were nothing.

"Yes, we're ok and no he didn't hurt me." I told him and Lanail went to the bathroom, so I hugged Dominick.

"I heard you offer to change places with Lanail. That was brave of you, Sym. But don't do that shit no more. I would have broken this whole world in half if something happens to you. I love you." He looked at me all loving then he kissed my lips. "Mine." That deep voice that was my drug said.

"Yours forever and I love you too."

Police sirens came down the street and we knew my neighbors called them. Dominick told me it was ok, just tell them what happened as far as Gunna and Tina breaking in to hurt me and Lanail and everything would be good. Lanail's aunt came and she couldn't wait to leave Las Vegas and start over. I hugged her tightly and we promised to keep in touch. She left me her journal and told me to give it to her Mama. Once she was gone, I left my house and didn't return until I moved all my stuff out. Now, I permanently live with Dominick and I wouldn't have it any other way.

Angel

"Thank you for dinner my Angel, everything was delicious." Nina's gorgeous ass told me after the waiter took our empty dessert plates away.

I had surprised her tonight with dinner at *Twist* by Pierre Gagnaire at the Waldorf Astoria. I had us get all dressed up, took out my Bugatti Chiron and made reservations at one of Las Vegas fine restaurants. We were on some heavy luxury shit tonight, I was so happy to celebrate my wife and our unborn child.

They both could have left me, and I would have been in this world lost as fuck. But they were fighters and strong, rather Nina was giving me a boy or girl, I was blessed to have both of them. Her belly was rounding out more every day; she had this taco and whole pickle cravings and I made sure to stay on it for her.

"You are more than welcome chicken nugget, I love making you smile." I told her, rubbing her hand.

"So, are you ready to open it?" She asked me smiling so wide. Today Nina had an ultra-sound telling us what the sex of the baby was. We had the lady write it down and put it in an envelope. We never knew when we wanted to open it, but I told her to bring it tonight and if we wanted to, then we would open it.

"I definitely am." I told her returning the smile.

Her pretty manicured hand picked up the envelope and I ain't gon' lie, my stomach was in knots.

"I can't, you do it." She gave me the envelope.

Laughing, I took it from her and ripped it open. It was a card that said boy or girl and the answer was written inside. I took the card out and we both took a deep breath.

"Before I open it, we both like Eli for a boy and

Nevaeh for a girl?" I asked her. We had picked those names out last month.

"For sure, I love those names." Nina said smiling.

I nodded my head and opened the card, but only I could see it. After reading the sex, I looked at Nina, smiling big.

"Oh my goodness, is it a boy? It's a girl? Oh shit is it twins!? Come on Angel!"

I cracked up because she was all over the place. I turned the card around. and she squealed loudly.

"A boy! Oh my goodness, I am having another boy!"

I pulled her chair close to mine so I could hug her. She was crying, but it was all happy tears. I know how extra emotional this was for Nina, considering her first child.

"Eli Nicholas McKay." I said to her, kissing the top of her head.

"Really, I thought we both agreed on Axel for the middle name?"

"We'll have more kids babe, I think the first one should have Nicholas as his middle name. When we have another boy, then he can have Axel, you cool with that?" I put some of her hair behind her ear.

"That sounds great." I kissed her, paid the bill and then we left to head to the suite I got us for the night.

**

"How do you know he's here?" I asked Cyrus when he gave me the address where Marlo possibly was.

"It's a guess; you said he was dealing with Nina's best friend brother so it would make sense that he would be there." He took the money from my hand.

"Naw he was dealing with Nina's best friend brother, his nasty ass was fucking him. Get that shit right."

I said and Cyrus laughed.

"Man I don't even like saying that out my mouth, you know I hate fag men." He told me as I walked off his porch.

"But yo' ass loves lesbians!" I laughed and opened the door to my car.

"Hell yeah, all my women gotta love pussy!"

That nigga was a fool but he was funny as hell. I put the address in my GPS and headed to it. I was praying Marlo was here because I was getting tired of looking for him. Although I would never stop, but it still was tiring. I wanted to focus on my wife, unborn child, my boys, our business and money. But Marlo would invade my thoughts and I knew it wouldn't go away until I kill him. Right now, Nina was out to lunch with my Pops.

I dug how close they were, and he was glad about having a grandson. This was perfect timing to handle this shit really quick and get back to my life. Whether Marlo was here or not, I owed Nina's best friend a bullet because she hurt my chicken nugget. I can give a fuck about a family code, that hoe could have told Nina about Marlo. I promised my wife I would kill all who made her stop smiling, and to me, this Talia bitch was one of those people.

"Perfect timing." I said out loud to myself when I saw a Toyota Corolla pull in the driveway. I hurried and went to the backyard next door so I could meet her before she went int the house. It was just my luck that she was going in the house through the side door. I had my gun on me but right now I was using Quest move with a sharp pocketknife in my hand. I opened it up the same time I rushed her using my other hand to cover her mouth.

"Calm down and answer every question I ask. If you fuck with me, I swear I will kill you right now. Nod if you understand." I told her in her ear, and she nodded yes.

"Are you Talia?" I asked her with my hand still over

her mouth. It was getting dark and the streets lights were coming on. I was ready to get this done and dip out while her block was quiet.

She nodded her head real fast.

"Good, now is Marlo inside?"

Her body trembled and she hesitated on answering but I pressed my hand harder on her mouth then she nodded yes quickly again.

"Where is he at in the house?" I asked her and this time I moved my hand a little so she could talk.

"H-He's in my brother's room; please don't kill me or him. I-I-I'm pregnant." She cried out and I looked at her from the side.

"You got pregnant by your best friend ex, and yo' brother's booty banger?" I didn't even give her nasty ass a chance to answer. I put my hand back over her mouth and told her to unlock the door and direct me to her brother's room.

We walked inside and up the four steps through her kitchen, then past the dining room was a hallway.

"Which door?" I asked her and she pointed to the one on the left.

I held my hand on her mouth tighter then lunged the knife in the side of her neck. When I hurried and pulled it out, her blood poured out like a fast faucet. I laid her gently on the floor, put the knife in my pocket and took out my gun before walking towards the door. I heard moaning and I swear I wasn't in the mood for some fag shit.

Opening the door, Marlo was laying in the bed with his eyes closed jacking off and holding his phone. I mean this punk ass hoe boy was so into it, he didn't even feel a full-grown person standing over him. I put my gun in my pocket and took out the syringe filled with a knockout drug. I used my mouth to take the top off and it made a pop noise. His eyes opened and before he could jump up, I used my hand to hold down his face and stuck the needle on the side of his neck.

"Well it's about time you woke up nigga, I was starting to feel neglected." I told Marlo when he finally came to.

I had him hanging by his wrists on a chain in our new complex. He was ass naked and beat the fuck up beyond words. I did this shit all alone because it's what I needed to feel better. It wasn't bringing back my brother or making Nina never had been shot, but it felt good to beat his ass. I put on my spike brass knuckles and punched him like a fucking boxing bag.

Then I burned him with my expensive Cuban cigars, twelve-grand a piece but this was a celebration. After I had my feel of that I took off the nigga's nails on his fingers and toes. Now he was yelling because when he woke up, he felt nothing but pain. But the basement was soundproof, and I had his mouth gagged. Grabbing his jaw,

I spoke.

"You took my baby brother from me and my family, then you tried to take Nina from me by shooting her. Aside from you being a down low fag, you's a fucking hoe ass disappointment to whoever the fuck your Pops is. But still, I'm not going to kill you." I stepped back smiling and folding my arms.

"I did what I wanted to do to you, so I fill fulfilled." I went over to my desk and pressed the intercom.

"Lori, send her down."

"Yes, sir." She responded and in seconds I heard the door opened.

I went to the bottom of the steps and met Nina.

"Hey babe, what was important that you needed me to come here?" She asked after I kissed her.

"I have something for you, something I promised you when I first met you." I told her walking her behind the steps and the brick wall.

Nina gasped when she saw Marlo hanging.

"Don't be scared, he can't get to you." I told her and when we got in front of him, Marlo's eyes bucked wide.

"I'm not scared." She said looking at him with her nose turned up. "I'm disgusted but relieved, I hated knowing he was still out there." She said loud enough so that he heard her.

I stood behind her and kissed her smooth neck then I rubbed her stomach. Marlo's eyes followed my hands and he started screaming, looking angry when he saw her big belly.

"Yeah nigga, I'm his wife, too." Nina said, holding up her hand wiggling her ring finger.

I smiled at how much of a boss ass my wife was talking.

"You never deserved me, and I was blinded to see it. But you made me better suited for someone beyond deserving. I hate you Marlo, and I wish you nothing but misery." She told him and I never seen her have so much hate in her eyes.

I wrapped my arms behind her waist, using my other arm to take my gun out and putting it in front of her. "Kill him." I told her and she took the gun out my hand pointing it to his head. I made sure to have my wife not scared of guns.

"You deserve this too, babe." She told me, so I stood back behind her and held the gun with her. I kissed her cheek and then we pulled the trigger. The bullet went between his eyes and that was the end of his rat-infested ass.

"That felt so good, is that a bad thing?" Nina asked me while I hugged her.

"Not at all chicken nugget, that nigga deserved to die. Trust me, this will be the only time I let you play in this world." I kissed her lips. "Come on gangsta, I'm ready to get your ass home." I squeezed her booty, making her giggle. I finally had everything I wanted, and I was keeping it safe with my life.

Epilogue
Nina

18 MONTHS LATER

Will you be my wifey?

(Yes I'll be your wifey)

We were in the middle of the dance floor, dancing our asses off to *Next-Wifey* song. All of us were dressed like we needed to be in a top-notch magazine. Quest and Angel had on a tailored Armani three-piece gold and burgundy suit with the suspenders attached to it. My man looked delicious. Dominick had on burgundy and gold too, but because he was the groom, he had a jacket with his but he had it off now that we were at him and Symba's reception.

Yup, my auntie was married like me and Christian. Her wedding was over the top big and beautiful, she didn't waste no expense. Her dream wedding was planned out to the T and she wasn't bitchy about it, either. Dominick had her so cocky as far as just knowing everything she wanted she was getting, all the way down to her custom Vera Wang halter beaded mermaid dress.

It fit her body like a glove with a beautiful train and a dip in the back. Me, Christian, Mama's, Grandma's and Lanail's dresses were designed by Vera Wang as well. Mama and Grandma had a two-piece pencil skirt and jacket, it was cream and gold. Me and Christian were her maid-of-honors, so we had a gold off the shoulder gown, painted on us with a high slit on the left side.

Lanail's dress was a gold spaghetti strap with her back out. We were so glad she was here with her aunt and Mom. Lanail graduated high school and was finishing up her first year in college. Dominick and Symba's wedding was at the Venetian Resort Hotel. It was so glamourous, like a dream in Paris or something; the lights she had all around, her burgundy velvet carpet she had for us to walk on, she had a grand piano and harp player and I don't know how, but they had *Avant and KeKe Wyatt* sing *Nothing In This World* while she walked down the aisle.

Those two together gave a sexy and mellow twist to it and it wasn't a dry eye seeing Symba walk down the aisle with her dad. Now, we're at this over size hall that was the perfect size for all of the people. They had just had their first dance and they called me, Angel, Christian and Quest on the dance floor and the D.J. played the *Next-Wifey* song.

Dominick sang along to the male part and it was so cute how he was dancing around Symba. When the girl part came, Symba sang along to it and Dominick held his ear like he was listening to her respond. He had Angel and

Quest doing it too.

Oh say you'll be my wifey girl

(Yeah, yeah, yeah, yeah, yeah, yeah, yeah, yeah)

Will you be my wifey?

(Yes I'll be your wifey)

Oh say you'll be my wifey girl

(Yeah, yeah, yeah, yeah, yeah, yeah, yeah, yeah)

"Yeahhh!" Dominick yelled dancing on beat. I promise, he was a light skin black guy. He took Symba's hand, holding it up while she danced on him to the beat while the song faded out.

Then the D.J. played *Jagged Edge-Let's Get Married Remix* and everyone got up then and danced. We made a soul train line, and everybody was getting down, even the damn mayor and her husband was getting it. Dominick and his parents went down it, Grandma and her husband, Burt and Mary went down the train and Mama went down the train with Eli, who was fourteen months.

My baby boy was so handsome and looked nothing like me; he looked like a spitting image of Angel and his brother Axel. Eli was so spoiled, but he was the happiest baby boy ever and he was so lovable. Christian and Quest's son, Chance, was about to be two-years old next month and he was about to be a big brother.

Hell yeah, her and Quest's rabbit humping asses were about to have a little girl; she was five months pregnant. I was so proud of my baby sister. Her and Quest started a husband and wife realty business and it took off so fast. They had a three-story office building and were gaining clients every day. After we were done with the soul train line, me, Symba and Christian went and stood to the side, watching all our family have fun.

"I think everybody in here is drunk." Christian laughed and said. She wore pregnancy so damn good.

"I know right, I've danced so much, I'm hungry again." I said looking at the buffet line.

Symba and Dominick had every soul food you can think of served and everyone was throwing down.

"Look, I knew he was going to make his way to her." Symba laughed pointing to Dominick picking their five-month daughter up. Nala Denise Reed was the prettiest baby girl ever. Her skin was caramel, she had some black tight curly hair and her eye color was that honey brown color from Dominick. They were in love and Symba was such an emotional mess when she was pregnant, but she loved it so much, she said she wanted to do it again by the time Nala was three.

Dominick's bike/guitar shop was doing good. He had all kinds of bike clubs who loved his business and his lounge was great for the food and the amateur nights. Symba took the leap and went into business with the dance school she worked at after she graduated. They added a new building that now taught general high school education. I was proud of them both.

"You know when you get pregnant again, you'll probably have a girl," I told her teasing.

Symba wanted another girl so badly. "Don't jinx me punk, you're having twins the next time you get pregnant."

I almost choked on my champagne. "Girl, bye! That's fertile Franny over there." I pointed to Christian, laughing.

She pouted and said, "Y'all got so many cracks."

Me and Symba laughed as the guys walked over to us.

"Aw shit, what's wrong with my wife?" Quest wrapped his arms around her kissing her.

"They're teasing me calling me fertile Franny."

We laughed harder when she pointed to me and Symba ratting us out.

"Y'all betta leave my sugar tits alone."

Every time he called her that, I cracked up. At their outside wedding, he said that in his vows. Everyone died laughing, including the preacher.

Dominick whispered something in Symba's ear and while he was doing it, this girl was licking her lips. Then he grabbed her hand and led her to the back of the hall.

"You muthafuckas are nasty!" Angel yelled to them laughing. He put his arms around my waist and kissed my neck.

I loved my sexy husband so much, aside from his business he does with Dominick and Quest. He opened a second club outside of Las Vegas and it was thriving. He made sure I was on my business to. I purchased an extremely wide amount of land so I could start the construction of my cheerleading camp.

We were all making moves and extremely blessed with how much our lives have changed. Pain, heartbreak, grief and fear had a hold of all of us in some way. I look in the mirror every day and can't believe my smile. I wake up with joy, my relationship with God was restored and I no longer thought he hated me. Even on days that are not so good, I still knew he loved me and my family.

"When we leave here, I wanna take you and Eli home. Get him in his pajamas, put him to bed and then get inside of you. I'm ready to work on his baby sister." Angel sucked on my neck after he said that.

I was giggling. "We can do that, for sure." I turned around and wrapped my arms around his neck.

"I love you my Angel, you have changed my life for the better." I told him honestly.

"I love you too chicken nugget, I still watch you in awe like the first day I met you." His smile made me melt and we kissed.

Eli called my name so loud laughing. Me and Angel

walked hand and hand to him. Angel lifted him in the air, tickling him and making him crack up.

Six people living in the same city had no idea that each person had something the other person needed. Ironic how life happens. I knew for a fact me, Symba and Christian loved our Las Vegas Outlaws with all our hearts.

The end! (Not Really)

I fell in love with these characters so I will be bringing them back in a spinoff very soon. Until then I hope you enjoy my next series and thank you all BESTYZ for making this series such a success.

---Londyn Lenz

Keep up with me:

My Facebook Reading Group: Londyn'z Bestyz

Facebook Author Page: Author Londyn Lenz

Please SUBSCRIBE to my YouTube channel: Londyn Lenz Besty Bratz Readers

Email: **Londyn_Lenz@yahoo.com**